# until then

*USA TODAY* BESTSELLING AUTHOR

# MICALEA SMELTZER

Cover Design: Emily Wittig Designs

Formatting: Micalea Smeltzer

Edits and Proofread: VB Edits

# prologue

### Izzy

CAMERAS FLASH NONSTOP, the paparazzi behind me yelling at every celebrity to "look this way" and "turn toward me," as if anyone can discern who *me* is in his mayhem.

I shuffle through the crowd, offering apologies when I bump into another person nearly every foot.

Desperately, I fight to get to my post where I'll be interviewing on the red carpet on behalf of The Tea—a celebrity gossip and news channel. This is the third year I've represented them here, and yet my nerves still rattle me.

"Am I sweating?" I ask. "I feel like I'm sweating."

Carla, an assistant from the show's production who's shadowing me today, pauses only long enough to give me a quick assessment before nudging me to keep moving. "You don't look sweaty. We're almost there."

1

She speaks into her Bluetooth headset, but I can't make out the words. It all sounds like gibberish in the chaos.

Years ago, when I started my vlog, I never dared to dream about these kinds of opportunities. It felt like too much to hope for. But as my vlog became more popular and my social media following grew, so did the offers I received.

"Here we are." Carla motions to where The Tea is set up on the carpet, camera and everything.

In a matter of seconds, I'm mic'd up and handed a separate microphone to pass to my interviewees.

Things go well as celebrities arrive. I even manage to interview one of my favorite actors, Samuel Owens, without peeing myself, so I count it as a win.

Not long after, Lux, the world's biggest popstar, makes her way over to me, practically swimming in a sea of glitter and wearing a shimmery silver dress that reflects the lights around us.

Carla takes the card from my hand and replaces it with a new one.

*Keep your cool, Izzy. She's just a person.*

Lux is one of my unicorns. A celebrity I've dreamed of meeting more than just about anyone else. At twenty-two, she's already reached uber stardom, surpassing many of the recent greats with chart-topping songs and albums and unmatched tickets sales.

Heart racing, I clear my throat. "Lux, thanks so much for chatting with The Tea tonight. You look wonderful. Who are you wearing?"

I loathe that question, but it's one I'm required to ask.

She looks down at the dress with a small smile, though there is a flash of annoyance in her eyes she can't hide. But with her head tipped, the camera likely missed it. "It's Gucci."

I paste on a smile. The last thing I want is for this interview to go south because of the questions The Tea wants me to ask. I glance down at the index card in my hand.

"What's your must-have makeup product on tour?"

Lux keeps the same small, almost bland smile as her fake silver lashes fan against her cheek. "I'm really into this rose-tinted lip oil right now. And no, I don't know the brand. It's one my makeup artist uses."

I bite my lip. "Um…" I clear my throat. God, this is already a disaster. Carla gives my elbow a squeeze, reminding me to keep going.

Hands shaking, because Lux is already edging away from us, I mindlessly read the question from the index card. "Is it true you're dating Cannon Rhodes from the band The Wild?"

Lux purses her lips, her eyes going almost as icy as her blond hair. "What kind of importance do my dress and makeup, or who I may or may not be screwing, carry?"

"I—"

"I've stated time and time again that certain topics are off-limits, and still you reporters push—"

I gape, my heart dropping. "I'm not a—"

"What's next on that little card of yours?" she asks with a sneer. I've never known Lux to behave this way. In every interview I've seen of her, she's been fun and bubbly.

"I…" I lower my head, read the next question, and close my eyes, doing my best not to cringe on camera. "There are reports of you leaving a hospital on tour. Is there any validity in the rumor that you had an abortion?"

"That's enough of this." She holds up a hand, effectively putting a wall between us.

Tears burn my eyes at the reprimand, though I understand her anger. I wouldn't want to constantly answer questions about what I'm wearing, who I'm dating, or what I may or may not have done with my body. It's pushy and invasive. The Tea has always leaned into these kinds of questions, but I've never been given questions as invasive as the one I just uttered.

Lux walks off then, saving me from having to ask the last question, which somehow feels worse than the one about abortion.

As she saunters away, I do my best to smile, despite the way nausea roils in my stomach. I have other people to interview, and I have to keep a brave face.

---

HOURS LATER, feet swollen from my heels and with cooling patches beneath my eyes, I sink into bed with Wonton, my beloved Maltese. And despite my better judgment—and knowing The Tea will probably have my head for it—I send a DM to Lux.

I type out, delete, and retype my response several times before settling on a message I think sounds okay.

**@izzy_james: Hi, Lux. I wanted to extend my sincerest apologies for tonight. The questions were uncalled for, and it's on me for not reading them ahead of time and vetoing them. As a woman who shares my life on social media, I understand what it's like to be asked invasive questions about your personal life. I'm terribly sorry I was a part of that for you. I'm a genuine fan of your music and all you do. I hope we can meet again under different circumstances.**

Once the message is sent, I force myself to turn my phone off. Otherwise, I'll be awake all night scrolling various social media apps in search of gossip about the disaster of an interview and anxious for a reply from Lux. The chances of her even seeing the message are slim, but I have to hope.

It's nearing eleven when I finally wake up. It's unusual for me to sleep this late, but I was out until the wee hours. Wonton, thankfully, had no problem sleeping in with me. He wiggles beside me, slowly rousing, and gives my nose a lick. Then he lets out a sharp bark—his demand to be let out.

I slip out of bed, and once I'm wrapped up in my robe, I open the sliding glass door to let him out back while I go to the bathroom myself. As I round my bed, I eye my phone where it sits on the nightstand, telling myself I need to wait at least five minutes before powering it on again.

After washing my hands, I step back into the bedroom and find Wonton pawing at the door, ready to be let back in. When I do, he runs straight out of the room to the kitchen for his breakfast. For such a tiny dog, he's extremely bossy. I snag my phone and stuff it in the pocket of the robe, holding strong. Once I've set his bowl of food down and started a pot of coffee, I finally give in to the temptation to check social media.

When the app loads and I navigate to the notifications, my heart drops.

**@luxonator3000: how cld u ask Lux those questions? So rude.**

**@brielle_luvs_lux: I can't believe you did that. I've loved your vlogs for years, but I'm unfollowing.**

**@izzyjamessucks: Don't come after our girl like that. Ur CANCELED.**

Comment after comment appears on my last few posts, all some variation of how much I suck. My following count has already dropped by three thousand. It's not a lot in the grand scheme of things, but it's enough for it to sting.

My DMs are filled with more of the same, though I do find

5

a message from Lux waiting. My heart beats rapidly and my hands shake when I click on it.

**@LUX: I appreciate your apology. I understand the questions didn't come directly from you, but next time I highly recommend you vet them beforehand. Best of luck,**

**Lux.**

Then, almost forty minutes later, there is another message from her.

**@LUX: Our interview is going viral. My team is on it, because frankly, I don't want it circulating any more than I'm sure you do. My fans are already going after you, so now it looks like I owe you an apology. I'm going to put out a statement and try to clean this up.**

I click onto her stories where a tired-looking Lux explains how the questions weren't mine but directly from The Tea. She pleads with her fans to understand that attacking me does more harm than good and that we've spoken privately.

My heart plummets. Regardless of her efforts, it won't be enough.

Not with her level of fame and the passion her fans have for her.

As my follower count continues to lower, I watch as everything I've worked so hard for slips through my fingers.

And anymore, without my vlog or my social media following, I don't know who I am.

# *one*

## Izzy

**May**
**Three months later**

BEING CANCELED over a celebrity interview was certainly not on my bingo card, but here we are.

I scroll through comment after comment, tag after tag. Each one reminds me of what a horrible person I am for the questions I asked of Lux. As if I'm the one who came up with them. And as if it happened yesterday. It's been *three* months, and even Lux herself jumped to my defense and begged her fans to stop harassing me. But the Luxonators don't mess around and I'm still enemy number one.

"Give it here." My best friend, Finneas, snatches my phone out of my hand and tucks it into his bag. "You have to stop looking at the comments. It's not healthy."

"I can't help it." My shoulders droop, along with my heart, as a sense of dejection I've become far too familiar with lately seeps into me. "It doesn't matter what I post or what I say, they're always ready to attack."

I built my social media platform from nothing, and now, at twenty-seven, I've amassed millions of followers across all platforms.

"You know what you need?" he asks, though he doesn't wait for me to respond before answering his own question. "A margarita. *And* to disable your comments."

"You know I can't do that." I swipe gloss on my lips and press them together. "It'll screw with the algorithm."

He waves the server down at our favorite downtown LA taco joint.

"Are you ready to order?" The dark-haired woman asks with a smile.

"Yes," Finneas says. "Two frozen margaritas, please. Chips and guac. And—" He pretends to scrutinize the menu as if we haven't been here a million times. As if we don't order the same thing each time. "Two orders of your al pastor tacos."

With a nod, she scribbles on her pad. Then she takes our menus and disappears.

Resting my elbows on the table, I cup my face in my hands. "I can't believe this happened." I'm hurt. Embarrassed. Angry. Still.

"It's not your fault, buttercup. It was bound to happen eventually."

My chest tightens with dread. "The entire internet hating me? *That* was bound to happen?"

"Maybe not the *entire* internet, but you know how it goes. When you reach a certain level of popularity, there will always be people who want to drag you down. The sad truth is there's no one people hate more in the world than a successful woman. Even other women. The interview was bullshit. I know that. You know that. Even Lux knows that. People will move on eventually."

I swallow back the emotion building like it does each time we discuss this. "I guess."

Normally, I pride myself on being positive. I like to see the bright side of things. In the days after the interview, I was sure that the controversy would blow over and be replaced by new juicy gossip within weeks. I underestimated the tenacity of the Luxonators.

When our server drops our drinks off, I snatch mine up and suck it down.

"Whoa, there." Finneas takes the glass from my hand and sets it on the coaster. "Let's slow it down."

"I need it." I reach for it, but he drags it to his side of the table, where I can't get to it.

"I didn't invite you here so you could get drunk, just a little buzzed."

Bottom lip stuck out, I huff. "I'll be good, promise."

Finneas stares me down, weighing the sincerity in my words, then slides my drink back over.

This time I take a smaller sip while maintaining eye contact with him.

I half expect him to pat me on my head and say, "That's my good girl."

"This will all blow over eventually. In a year's time we'll look back and laugh."

I'm not sure I'll *ever* laugh about it. I'm far too traumatized by the whole ordeal. People say the most unhinged things online. As if they've forgotten that the people they're talking to are *real* and have feelings. Or maybe they don't forget. Maybe they flat-out don't care.

"I hope so," I say, despite my doubts.

"Why don't you go visit your sister for a while? Get out of LA. You're not happy here right now, and I hate seeing you like this."

He has a point. I'd already planned to visit my sister in the next couple of months, and now that my invite to the brand trip I was slated to go on in a few weeks has been rescinded, I have more than enough time.

Trolls online and even people in the social media industry treat me as if I've committed murder, when in reality, all I did was read the questions I'd been given and instructed to ask. Even The Tea cut our contract short, as if they're not to blame for the entire debacle. Bunch of bitches.

Lips pressed together, I nod. "It would be good to get away for a few months."

"Months?" he asks, gaping. "I meant like a week. Two tops."

I shrug. "I like it there and I miss my sister. It's not like I have any obligations here. I'm not even filming videos right now, so I have the time."

Finneas frowns. "But I'll miss you."

"You can come visit."

Brows pulled low, he assesses me over the rim of his margarita glass. "In Maine?"

"It's not a foreign country. Even if it was, you have a passport."

His sigh is nothing short of dramatic. "But it's so far."

"Wow. And here I thought you loved me."

He sticks his tongue out. "I'll consider it."

By the time we leave dinner, I'm pleasantly buzzed, not drunk, and I feel a modicum better.

Still, I book my plane ticket before going to bed.

# Two

Izzy

THERE'S no place on earth that soothes my soul like Parkerville, Maine.

I can see why my sister chose it without even visiting. It screams *small coastal town* and *idyllic life by the sea*.

I turn the radio down as I navigate the RAV-4 I rented for my stay—a far cry from my BMW back home—toward town. The fabric seats smell faintly of cigarettes, despite the contract I signed that said no smoking in the rental.

When the town limits come into view, the smile that spreads across my lips is uncontrollable. Almost immediately I feel better than I have since the night of the interview.

I roll the window down and inhale the salty ocean air.

*Home.*

That's how I feel, like I'm returning to where I belong.

Once I turn onto Main Street, it only takes a minute before I'm parking beside my sister's store, Color Me Happy.

I grab the doggy backpack from the passenger seat and let Wonton out.

"Let's go potty," I croon to my beloved Maltese.

He makes quick work, hiking his leg up on the dumpster, and when he's done, I scoop him up and cover his head in kisses, his fluffy white fur tickling my nose.

"Let's go see Auntie Via."

The last time I visited, my sister gave me a key to her apartment above her art store, urging me to use it any time.

My chest goes tight. I really hope she meant that.

Her car isn't in the alley, so she's probably at her boyfriend's. He's eleven years younger than her, insanely hot, and absolutely perfect for her. She deserves someone who worships the ground she walks on after how things ended with her ex-husband.

When I unlock the door and push it in, all the air leaves my lungs.

"Oh my God." I slap a hand over my eyes—my poor innocent eyes.

I did not expect to walk in and find my sister pinned against the counter while Reid goes to town.

Nope.

With a shudder, I run back down the stairs, hugging Wonton to my chest, grateful I didn't lug my heavy suitcase along with me.

I quickly herd Wonton back into his bag, then start the car, ready to get the hell out of there. But before I can, Via's at my door.

"Izzy." She knocks on the glass, her face bright red with embarrassment. "I'm so sorry."

As I roll the window down, I do my best not to think about her boyfriend's butt. "It's okay. I didn't think you were home, so I was going to let myself in. You know, key and all." I hold up the key like I need it for evidence.

"When you texted that you were coming, I thought you meant next week or next month, not the next day. My car's at Reid's." Her words fall from her mouth quickly. "We came over in his to get some things and got ... distracted."

Movement in my periphery catches my attention, and when I find Reid standing in the open doorway of Via's apartment, shirtless, his jeans pulled up but still unbuttoned, I sigh.

"Hey, Izzy." With a smirk, he waves one hand.

I'm not sure it's possible to embarrass that guy.

"Hi, Reid." To Via, I say, "I'll stay at the inn for now."

"Wait." She purses her lips, her nose crinkling in confusion. "How long are you staying?"

"Through the summer." *Or forever, since I'm canceled.*

Her brows rise in surprise. "That long?"

"Mhm." I explained the debacle to her, but she's entirely inept at social media, so the whole thing went right over her head.

"Reid's leaving. Please, stay. It would be silly for you to stay at the inn."

From the look of things, it would be a terrible idea for me to stay here. I don't know why Via and Reid haven't moved in together yet, but I respect my sister for wanting to take it slow. She got married fairly young, and look how that turned out.

"Yeah." I nod at a shirtless Reid, who's still hovering by the door. "Sure looks like he's going to leave."

With a scowl, she shoos him inside. "I'll make him leave."

"It's fine." Disappointment flickers through me, but I keep

my expression light. "You weren't expecting me. I'll stay at the inn for now and figure something out."

The inn is cute, but it's not a great solution for the length of time I plan to be here. Being relegated to a single room would be torture.

"Izzy, I'm serious, please stay."

"Listen." I inhale and let it out slowly. "To be perfectly honest with you, after what I just saw, I'm not sure I'm capable of entering your apartment without throwing up."

Frowning, she mutters, "Fair enough."

I pat her hand where it rests on the open window frame. "I'm very happy for you, though."

Via laughs, eyes sparkling with amusement. "Thanks. You'll find someone special soon enough."

My heart pinches as the words hit. I'm not so sure about that. Guys in LA are incredibly vain. Disgustingly so. Most of the women are, too. Sure, I've had a smidge of Botox here and there and some lip filler myself, but most people who call the City of Angels their home go overboard. And more than that, I've yet to meet a single one who is capable of loving someone more than they love themself.

Forgive me for wanting to be someone's *everything*.

I've tried to find a man who had the potential, but each time I find one I think may be a genuinely good guy, lo and behold, the shine wears off and he ends of using me for some sort of connection.

In LA, I swear there isn't a single line that people believe isn't meant to be crossed.

"I'm going to go," I tell her. "I need to go see if they have a room."

"All right, but summers are busy here, so if they're booked, come back. Stay with me."

"I will."

*I won't.*

---

TWO HOURS later I find myself at my assistant's apartment. It was by pure happenstance that I hired Layla. Maybe it was even downright freaky, because she's from the same small town my sister now calls home. All the work I need an assistant for is virtual, so when I was looking, I didn't limit my search to LA. Layla has been a godsend, helping respond to emails, manage my schedule, and even edit the occasional video when I'm too busy.

"It's the lumpiest couch in existence." She cringes. "I'm sorry. Your back is going to scream at you in the morning."

When I set Wonton down, he immediately takes off to sniff the corner of said couch.

Layla's little girl is nowhere to be seen. Judging by the late hour, she is probably already in bed.

"A lumpy couch is better than the park bench I was contemplating."

I filled her in on the Reid and Via situation when I called, desperate for a place to stay. After much gagging on her end, since Reid is her little brother, she promised I could stay with her, just as long as I was okay with sleeping on the couch.

The inn is booked until what feels like the end of time—or through the summer, whichever comes first.

"Let me grab a pillow and blankets for you." With that, Layla disappears down the small, dark hallway.

My shoulders sag in relief. Her apartment is small, so accommodating me isn't ideal, but she didn't bat an eye.

Though this isn't a long-term solution. I can't stay here,

taking up space, for more than a night or two. I might have to go back to LA after all.

The thought makes my chest tight. It makes me want to scream.

When I moved to LA years ago, it was full of opportunities for my social media career, and many of the friends I had made as I built my business were living there, too. As much as I loved it back then, it hasn't held the same appeal over the last couple of years.

Layla returns with a stack of blankets and sets them on the edge of the couch before going back for pillows.

I'm surveying the room when Wonton growls at the kitchen cabinet, pulling my attention to him. Sometimes I wonder what's going on in his doggy mind. Why is the kitchen cabinet so threatening?

"All right, this is all I've got."

Heart easing, I take the pillows from a smiling Layla. "Thanks for letting me crash here. I'll try to make other arrangements tomorrow."

"Are you hungry?"

"I'm good." I give her a dismissive wave, but at the same time, my stomach rumbles, contradicting me.

With a laugh, Layla wanders to the fridge. The surface of it is covered with an array of magnets and family photos. "I have leftover Kraft mac 'n' cheese—princess-shaped, obviously. There's turkey and ham if you're okay with a sandwich."

My stomach rumbles again. "I'll take the mac 'n' cheese."

Layla heats it in the microwave while I fit the sheets and blankets onto the couch.

As I work, exhaustion from the day sets in. I travel often, and normally, it doesn't faze me, but after the Lux debacle I

17

find myself wearier than I ever remember feeling, no matter what I'm doing.

When my makeshift bed is made, Layla sets the warm bowl on the counter, along with a fork. "You can use my shower, too."

"Bless you." I sidle up to the cabinets and rest a forearm on the Formica.

Smiling, she perches on the edge of the counter, watching me devour the macaroni. "How are you doing? And be honest with me."

Layla knows better than anyone what I've been dealing with, since she fields my emails and messages.

My stomach twists, and I grimace. "Why do you think I'm here?"

Her lips turn down in sympathy. "You can talk to me. I'm happy to listen."

"I know." I inhale another bite of food. "But you already know most of the details. The follower count, the brand deals I've lost. I used to love making YouTube videos, and anymore, that isn't even fun."

The things I used to find joy in leave me feeling anxious and stressed.

She gives me a sad smile. "It'll blow over eventually."

That's what I thought, too, but I figured it would have happened by now. Instead, internet trolls continue to edit new videos with clips from the interview, keeping the fuel of hatred going.

In record time, I've finished my princess-shaped meal. I quickly rinse the bowl and load it into the dishwasher. "If you don't mind," I say with a sigh, "I'm going to shower and go to bed. Or … couch."

The sympathy in her eyes as she watches me make my way

to the bathroom only makes what's become a permanent ache in my chest more acute.

When I get out of the shower, Layla has already gone to bed, and Wonton is asleep on my pillow. With a sigh, I scoot him over and lie down.

She's right. The couch sucks. But I find myself drifting off to sleep within minutes.

# three

Izzy

*POKE.*

   *Poke.*

   *Poke.*

I crack one eye open, finding a grinning Lilibet with her index finger extended, ready to shove it into my cheek again.

"Hi, Lili." With a groan, I heave myself up to sitting and wipe the drool from my mouth.

The little girl tilts her head and frowns up at me, thoughtful. "Why are you sleeping on our couch?"

"Lili," Layla admonishes from the hallway, her hands on her hips. "I told you to let her sleep."

Lili's brows shoot up as she whips her head around and faces her mom. "She was already awake."

Head dropped back, Layla huffs. "Sure she was."

Wonton, finally roused by the commotion, yips, launching his tiny body at Lili and showering her with kisses.

While the two love on one another, I rub at my eyes, willing my body to perk up. Sadly, it's not working. Only an espresso shot—or five—will be capable of that.

Layla, dressed for the day, shuffles into the kitchen. "Bacon and eggs sound good to you, Izzy?"

With a grateful smile, I nod. "Sounds delicious."

I change into fresh clothes and take Wonton out to potty. He spends an awful long time sniffing a light post before finally hiking his leg and peeing. Boys.

When he's finished, he makes sure to kick the grass with his back feet.

While he searches for a spot to finish his business, I turn my phone on and check my messages. There is a string of texts from Finneas. Unsurprising. As well as a few from my sister. Even one from Reid that pulls a bark of laughter from me.

**Sorry you saw my ass**, it says. **Best one you've seen, right?**

With a shake of my head, I respond with a middle finger emoji. Almost immediately, he sends a crying-laughing one back. At least one of us isn't traumatized by the situation.

I reply to Finneas next, apologizing for not checking in. I also fill him in on the accommodation situation and warn him that I might be back sooner than I expected.

Who knew the little town of Parkerville, Maine, was such a destination in the summer months? I've only been out here in the fall or winter, maybe the very start of spring, since I tend to travel more for brand trips or destinations I want to vlog in the summer.

Via's texts are the last ones I read.

She feels terrible, of course, promising that if she'd known, she would've picked me up at the airport and we would've had a girl's night. It's not her fault. In my haste to get the hell out of LA, I didn't make it clear that I was coming right *now*.

**I'm fine.** I tell her. **I stayed the night with Layla.**

> Via: You couldn't get a room at the inn?

> Me: It's booked until the end of time.

Rather than respond via text, my sister calls.

"Come back over here. We'll figure something out."

"No." I pinch the bridge of my nose. "It's okay."

She and Reid go back and forth between their apartments. It doesn't feel right to take over her space, now that I've really had time to think about it.

"I feel terrible," she says, her voice wobbly.

"Via," I say her name slowly, hoping she can hear the sincerity in my voice. "I'm a big girl. I'm all good here. Promise. I'm out with Wonton, but I'm heading in for breakfast now. Love you, bye."

Before she can protest again, I end the call.

Now that Wonton has finished his business, he's hovering at my feet. So I scoop him up under my arm and carefully climb the steps to Layla's apartment. It's not a bad place, but the stairs have definitely seen better days, so better safe than sorry.

Back upstairs, I hang Wonton's leash on the hook by the door, alongside Lili's purple raincoat.

"Just in time." Layla slides a plate down the counter and peers at me over her shoulder.

Relief washes over me. The macaroni and cheese I scarfed down last night was barely enough to satiate my appetite. Since the tiny table in the corner only has two chairs, I take my plate to the couch and curl my legs under me while I eat my breakfast.

Wonton jumps up beside me, knowing I'll share my bacon and eggs with him.

"I was thinking," Layla begins. "If you're okay with it, you could stay with my dad."

Confusion curls through me at the suggestion.

Her dad?

Derrick Crawford?

The man I set my sister up on a date with, not knowing yet that she'd had a one-night stand with his son? The son she's currently dating?

A pit forms in my stomach. I don't think Derrick is capable of hating anyone, but his feelings for me probably hover somewhere close.

"Uh." I swallow thickly. "That's okay."

"No, I'm serious," she goes on, brushing a piece of hair behind her ear. "He's all alone in that house now, and he has plenty of space. He wouldn't mind the company."

Go back to LA, go back to being miserable and hating every second of my life? Or tough it out with Derrick for a bit?

Living with him, temporarily, obviously, probably wouldn't be difficult. He doesn't seem like the kind of man that would give a woman trouble. But there's a good chance he hates me. I'd spend the whole time stressed about it, and the worst part is the major crush I've been harboring for the guy.

I would never in a million years admit to Layla that I have a crush on her *dad*.

But I *do* need a place to stay.

My stomach twists, making my breakfast feel like a lead ball.

"Fine," I say with a sigh. "As long as he's okay with it."

"He will be," she promises with a smile.

---

DERRICK'S HOUSE is a cute bungalow on an idyllic suburban street full of shaded yards thanks to all the large trees.

Layla gave me her key and assured me it was okay to head over and get settled. So after a stop at the grocery store so I could pick up a few staples as well as stuff to make dinner tonight to thank Derrick for letting me stay here, I'm standing in the middle of the living room.

I let Wonton down, and he takes off with a yip to check out the house.

"Don't pee on anything," I warn him.

The house is homey. Straight out of a Nancy Meyers movie. It's warm. Lived in. Nothing like the white-on-white-on-white spaces in LA. This is the kind of home I've always dreamed of having.

In the kitchen, I put the grocery bags on the counter and get to work unpacking them. Wonton sits dutifully at my feet, hoping I'll take mercy on him and give him some sort of treat.

Once everything is put away, I return to the living room and take my suitcase upstairs to the room Layla told me would be mine. Since I'm planning to be here for a few months, I put my clothes in the dresser that sits beneath a small, mounted TV.

Wonton pads down the hall and pokes his fluffy white head inside, tail wagging victoriously when he finds me.

I got Wonton shortly after I moved to LA. He belonged to a neighbor—a puppy she'd brought home for her spoiled kids, only to find out they had no interest in taking care of a dog. She was planning to take him to a shelter when I bumped into her, and the second I saw his sad, little puppy face, I knew he was mine.

From what Layla mentioned, I should have a few hours before Derrick gets home. Owning his own construction company keeps him busy. That's how we met—he was renovating my sister's art store and apartment.

Speaking of my sister, I've ignored her last few texts.

Not because I'm upset with her, but because I'm not ready to talk. She's bound to ask more questions. She'll want to know the truth behind why I'm here. And no matter how I explain it, she won't understand. Not for lack of trying, but because she can't relate to what I do.

MacBook in hand, I settle on the bed. Almost immediately, Wonton curls into a ball beside me and begins snoring like an old man, even though he's six.

I browse Amazon, adding things to my cart that I forgot in my haste to get away. Then I order shampoo and conditioner from Ulta. There isn't a physical location anywhere close, but I'm picky about what I use on my hair. Or maybe it's that my hair is picky. If I don't use a certain kind of shampoo and conditioner, it'll be greasy within hours.

As I shop, trepidation still plagues me. Is Derrick really okay with having me around? And does he really want to share the house with another person? It's only been about a year since Layla moved out with Lili.

He's probably enjoying the bachelor life, and here I am, throwing a wrench in his plans.

# *four*

## Derrick

THERE'S an unfamiliar car parked on the street in front of my house, but I don't think much of it since the driveway next door is full. Steven and his wife have six kids. Between them, their spouses, and their children, it feels like they've got an entire city congregating over there sometimes.

Across the street, Mindy steps outside with her Pomeranian under her arm. The instant the dog sees me, it growls. Annoyance flares inside me in response. I still haven't forgiven the thing for biting my ankle a few weeks ago when I was mowing and Mindy, who was out for a walk, stopped by to chat.

With a hand in the air in greeting, I continue to my front door. I'm exhausted and the last thing I want to do is get caught up in conversation. Mindy is nice, but she's chatty.

When I step into the house, I immediately know something

is wrong. If it weren't for the smell of sautéed peppers cooking, the white dog running straight for me would have tipped me off.

"What the fuck?"

A clattering sound in the kitchen makes me cringe.

Because I know exactly who I'm about to be confronted with.

Izzy James rounds the corner wearing a sheepish smile. "Um, hi. I'm making dinner. Hope that's okay."

Stunned, I stare at her, at a loss for why she'd be in my house. Why she'd be making *dinner*.

The smile melts off her face. "Oh no. Layla didn't ask you if I could stay here, did she? I'm so sorry." She wrings her hands, chin lowered. "Let me finish this, then I'll pack my stuff. I'll be out of your hair in no time."

I set my lunchbox down and dig my phone out of my pocket. "She called, but I was working, so I figured I'd call her after I got home and showered."

Izzy shuffles awkwardly from side to side. "She gave me her key and told me to take the spare bedroom."

With a hand held up between us, I dial Layla.

"Hey, Dad," she answers. "How was work?"

Despite my annoyance, my chest warms like it does every time I hear my daughter's voice. Even so, I keep my tone neutral and get to the point. "Good. Were you calling me for something?"

"Yeah," she ways, a long breath leaving her. "Izzy needs a place to stay. She has a lot going on and she can't stay with Via because ... well, you know how she and Reid are."

I grunt at this. I don't like thinking about my son's sex life.

Layla continues, her words coming fast. "The inn is

27

completely booked. I know I should have okayed it with you first, but I went ahead and sent her over there."

"I'm aware."

She curses under her breath. "You're home?"

"I'm home."

She huffs, making the line crackle between us. "I'm sorry, Dad."

"It's fine. We'll talk later." I swallow back my frustration. It'll keep.

"Be nice to her. She's had a lot to deal with lately."

I roll my eyes up to the ceiling. "I'm always nice."

"Mhm," she hums. "Love you, bye!" She hangs up before I can respond.

Once the screen goes dark, I drop my phone to my side and survey Izzy.

She doesn't cower beneath my gaze. I have to give her credit there.

"Seriously. I thought you knew."

With a *humph*, I cross my arms over my chest and do my best to ignore how good it smells in here. "So you said. How long are you in town for?"

She grimaces. "A few months."

"A few months?" I balk.

In the time I've known Izzy, I've never seen her embarrassed—not truly. But this time, her cheeks turn bright red, and finally, she averts her gaze.

"That was my original plan," she says, back to wringing her hands, "but I think maybe I'll head back sooner. Don't want to be in anyone's hair."

Squinting, I really study her. The way her nose wrinkled when she mentioned going home, the defeated slump in her shoulders, her dull eyes. "Did something happen?"

"Happen? When?" She snaps her head up and scans the space, blinking uncomfortably.

"Something must have happened if you're here and you're planning to stay so long."

She waves a dismissive hand, but the pain in her next words belies the casual move. "Just work stuff."

*Just work stuff*, my ass. It's much more than that, judging by this interaction, but if she doesn't want to talk about it, then I won't push her.

"Listen," she shuffles her feet, "we can talk more about this later, I don't want to invade your space or anything, but dinner is going to be ruined if I don't get back to it."

"You're not invading my space. You're fine to stay here as long as you want."

Kicking her out would feel like leaving a wounded stray on my front porch and not helping.

"Are you sure?" She bites her lip, fingers wringing together nervously.

"I'm sure." I doubt she can get into too much trouble in one summer.

My mouth waters when I'm once again hit with the delicious smell. "What are you making?"

"Enchiladas."

I purse my lips, keeping my expression bland. "Interesting."

Groaning, she throws her hands up in the air. "Don't tell me you're one of those guys who only eats meat and potatoes."

I shove my phone into my pocket and smirk. "What's wrong with a good steak? Or a burger? I do like pasta, too."

She puts a hand to her forehead. "You like beef. Is that

29

what you're telling me? These *do* have beef. You know, buried in the tortilla and spices."

"I'm sure it'll be great." I'm not going to complain about a hot meal, especially one I don't have to make. "If you don't mind, I'm going to shower first."

"No problem. I'll get it plated up."

With a nod, I bend down to take off my boots, and I swear I hear her mumble something like: *"And try not to think about you naked."*

But when I look up, she's gone. So I step out of my boots and set them by the front door. Even though it's been over a year since Layla and Lili moved out, it still feels weird not seeing a pile of Lili's tiny pink shoes on the mat. My kids thought I'd be thrilled to finally have the house to myself, but that couldn't be further from the truth.

My kids, and my granddaughter, are my life. It was inevitable, the day they'd move out and start their own lives, but the longer Layla stayed, the easier it was to convince myself it would always be that way.

The house is eerily quiet these days, like the life has been drained from it. A home is meant to be lived in and with the hours I work, my time here is limited.

Upstairs, I turn the shower on and take off my sweaty clothes. The house is small, so even from up here, I can hear Izzy singing along to some pop song.

For a minute, I let myself imagine that my wife is the one downstairs. It's rare I let myself think about her anymore, as horrible as it sounds, because even after all these years, it still hurts. I moved out of the house we shared not long after she passed away because the memories there threatened to drown me.

But once in a while, it's impossible to bury thoughts of

what life would be like if she were still here, if we were doing the things we always talked about.

With a shake of my head, I banish the thoughts and step into the shower. I wash thoroughly but quickly so I don't hold up dinner, and once I'm clean and wearing fresh clothes, I feel a million times more human.

Outside my bathroom door, Izzy's fluffy white dog greets me with an excited bark. I study him, then eye the door. I'm sure I closed it behind me, but it's cracked open now.

"Did you sneak in?"

He wags his tail in answer, pink tongue hanging halfway out of his mouth, too damn cute for his own good. I pick him up, and he instantly cuddles into my chest.

*Should I get a dog?*

Immediately, I dismiss the idea. While it would certainly help with my loneliness, I'm not home enough to give a pet the attention it needs. Sure, I could scale back my hours, it's my business after all, but I built it from the ground up, and I *like* it. I don't just want to manage my guys. I want to be on site working beside them.

"You're just in time," Izzy says when I pad into the kitchen. She sets two plates of food on the table.

Setting Wonton on the tile floor, I appraise the food. "It looks … good."

She throws her head back with a laugh that would be infectious if I didn't know it was at my expense.

"I don't know whether you're trying to convince yourself or me. What matters, though, is how it tastes." She appraises the table with a satisfied smile. "What do you want to drink?"

I cock my head, giving her a look that says *seriously?*

She clears her throat. "Right, your house. You can get your own drink."

31

I do just that, opting for a can of Coke. I don't drink much alcohol. Neither do my kids. Not after the role it played in my wife's death.

Izzy watches me expectantly, like she's eager to see my reaction to her enchiladas.

Suddenly itchy from the scrutiny, I roll my shoulders and arch a brow at her. "Izzy?"

"Yes?" she drawls, rubbing her finger over the top of her water glass.

"Are you going to watch me eat this?"

"Absolutely." Wearing a wide smile, she nods so vigorously I worry her head will snap off. "You might lie and say you hate it, or lie and say you love it, but the eyes always tell the truth."

With a sigh, I pick up the fork and use the side of it to cut off a sizable bite.

"Make sure there's a good amount of sauce on it."

Every inch of the enchilada is drenched in sauce, so I'm not sure what she's worried about.

She taps the fingers of her left hand against the table, her teeth pressed into her plump bottom lip, as she watches me bring the fork up to my mouth.

The moment the taste registers, an *mmm* bursts out of me without my permission.

Her smile is so bright, my instinct is to put up a hand to block the shine. A happy Izzy is pure sunshine, chasing away all the shadows.

I chew and swallow, then give her a nod. "It's good."

She wiggles in her chair, clearly satisfied with this development. "See? It doesn't hurt to try new things."

"Let's not get carried away." I go in for a second bite and

discover it's just as good, if not better, now that I know what to expect.

Chuckling, she picks up her fork. "I can't believe you've never had enchiladas."

"I've had tacos. Does that count?"

She stares me down, eyes round with horror.

"I take it that means no?"

"Absolutely not."

Neither of us says anything while we continue to eat. Periodically, I steal a glance at her, half expecting her to disappear, but every time I look, she's still there.

"You know," she begins, the soft sound of her voice wrapping around me like a gentle embrace, "I was looking in your refrigerator and couldn't help but notice a distinct lack of green things."

"My fridge is fine," I bite out, that warm sensation disappearing in a cloud of irritation.

More because of myself than her, I suppose. Because she's not wrong. I was much better at fruits and vegetables and healthy snacks in the house when Layla and Lili were here. Now, I've become an all too frequent flier of the frozen food section of the grocery store. If it's quick and easy, it's probably in my refrigerator.

Izzy rests her elbow on the table, giving me a wry smirk. "Did all the men in the universe get together and collectively decide that their favorite word is *fine*?"

"Would you prefer I use *okay*? Or perhaps *acceptable* would be better?"

A derisive laugh escapes her. "I'd prefer more than a one-word response, but thanks for trying."

With a gulp of my Coke, I rack my brain for an acceptable topic. For reasonable questions that may segue into a real conversation. "Back to our conversation earlier," I say, though in the back of my mind, I realize that this probably falls more into the touchy category than the acceptable one. "What sent you running all the way across the country?"

Deflating before my eyes, she stabs at a piece of enchilada. "You wouldn't understand."

Three words have never made me feel so old. So I respond with three of my own. "You can try."

She inhales a deep breath and pushes the food around her plate. "I was interviewing a celebrity on the red carpet a few months ago. It didn't go well, and her fans canceled me. Now..." She shrugs, twisting her lips to the side. "Now, I'm here."

It hits me then, how much I really *don't* understand. "You interview celebrities?"

"Sometimes." With a sigh, she drops her fork to her plate with a clatter and leans back in her chair. I can't help but survey the space behind her. Take in the simplicity. It's no doubt worlds different from what she's used to in LA. "For the record, I'm *not* running away."

Brow arched, I tilt my head. "Sure looks like it."

She puffs out her cheeks. "Has anyone ever told you that you're kind of rude?"

I sip my Coke, assessing her over the can, then set it down gently. "Only you."

Something about Izzy brings out my combative side. Whether it's her or my insane attraction to her, I can't be sure. But the attraction is absolutely an issue. She's the same age as my daughter. Lusting after her is wrong.

And now she's living in my house for who knows how long.

"I'll go back to the grocery store tomorrow," she announces, picking up her fork again, the defeat rolling off her all but gone.

I'm too tired to understand her meaning. "Huh?"

"To pick up veggies and stuff. You can't live off protein shakes, frozen pizzas, and those gross prepackaged meals in the freezer." She sticks her tongue out, shuddering in horror.

"Don't knock them until you try them."

They're barely palatable, but I suddenly feel the need to defend my food choices.

"Sure," she drawls, eyes twinkling with amusement like she knows I'm full of shit.

"You've never even eaten gas station food, have you?"

"Ew, no." She shudders violently, the force of it making the table tremble between us. "Not a chance."

A niggle of mirth works its way through me. This woman is something. So, teasing, I ask, "You mean to tell me you've never had a gas station slushie?"

Straightening, she shakes her head. "Nope," she says, popping her lips to emphasize the *p* sound.

There's no stopping the scoff that escapes me. "We're getting one."

"What?" She blinks at me, her eyes swimming with confusion.

"After we clean up, I'm taking you to get a slushie."

Brows knitted, she frowns. "Am I going to keel over from a sugar rush?"

I tilt my head and hum, feigning deep thought. "It's possible, but I think you'll survive."

As we finish dinner, Izzy never loses her worried expression. Once the dishes are washed and put away—my dishwasher has been broken for months and I haven't gotten around to fixing it—I pick up my keys and twirl them around my finger.

"Let's go."

As if I've sentenced her to prison, Izzy skulks after me, shoulders rolled in and feet dragging, with Wonton toddling behind her. At the door, she crouches down to kiss his head.

"We'll be right back. You can't go to the gas station."

I flick the front porch light switch on, though it's not quite dark yet—the beauty of summer. Izzy follows me to the truck and hops into the passenger side with ease.

The nearest station is within walking distance, but if Izzy is really as unused to sugary drinks as she let on and does pass out from a sugar rush, I'd rather not have to carry her home.

The radio blares, a country song about a pickup truck and dirt roads.

In my periphery, Izzy shakes her head, and when I turn, her lips are quirked in amusement.

When I lower the volume, she says, "A country boy? Should've known."

"What did you expect?" I ask, putting the truck in reverse.

Deadpan, she says, "Whale noises."

A guffaw so violent flies out of my mouth that my back presses into the seat behind me. "Whale noises," I mutter.

"They're very soothing. Very Maine."

I turn right at the stop sign. "Have you gone whale watching here?"

Beside me, she peers out her window, watching the scenery pass by. "Not yet. I want to, though."

With a thorough look around me, I take a second to study her before focusing on the road again. Damn, the sad droop of her mouth is like a punch to the gut. I'm sure it has more to do with what's going on in her life and less to do with whales. Even so, I find myself volunteering, hoping to cheer her up. "I'll take you sometime."

Slowly, she turns my way, her lips tipping up. "Derrick Crawford, do you own a *boat*? If so, why is this the first I'm hearing of it?"

I shift in my seat, rolling my shoulders to dislodge the discomfort soaking into me. "Yes, I have a boat. But I work a lot, so I don't take it out often."

"Well, now you're obligated." She holds out her pinky to me. "Swear on it."

I loop my pinky through hers like I've done with Lili a thousand times and pull into the lot of the station.

Quickly, I hop out and round the hood so I can get her door, then I hustle past her to hold the one to the store, too.

"A gentleman," she croons. "I like it."

In the back of the store, I introduce her to the slushie machine. It doesn't get past me that these were a staple when I was a kid. And when I was a kid, Izzy wasn't even close to being a thought in her parents' minds yet.

"You've got cherry, blue raspberry, Coke, and watermelon. They rotate the watermelon flavor in every so often. Sometimes it's lemonade or strawberry instead."

She eyes the cups stacked to the side. "What do you normally get?"

"Coke."

"I should've known." She laughs softly and chooses one of the smallest cups.

"Which one are you going for?" I ask, grabbing a cup for myself.

With a hum, she studies each one, watches the way the frozen mixtures swirl in the plastic windows. "Can I mix them?"

"Yeah," I say, popping a plastic dome onto my cup. I get in position, then pull on the handle and fill it with frozen Coke. "That's what my kids always did."

Eyes suddenly round, she points at where I've just released my hold. "I'm not sure I'm capable of working the handle without making a mess."

Biting back a chuckle, I hand her my cup and take her empty one. Then I pop a plastic dome lid on it. "Which ones do you want?"

"Blue raspberry and cherry."

I mix the flavors, creating several layers, and when the cup is full, I pass it back. Then, with two red plastic straws in hand, I nod for her to follow me to the checkout.

"Hey, Derrick." Greg, the same guy who's worked here for the past ten years, greets me. "Good day?"

"Can't complain."

Before he's finished ringing up the slushies, I'm holding out cash while I steadfastly ignore Izzy, who's standing at my side and pulling out her wallet.

"You didn't have to do that," she says, ducking under my arm when I hold the door open. The warm evening breeze stirs her hair. It's a long, thick curtain hanging past her breasts. A part of her anatomy I shouldn't be thinking about. "I could've gotten my own."

I lift a shoulder and let it fall. "Slushies were my idea."

"Hmm. I guess you have a point there." She flashes me a sly smile.

Once we're both seated in the truck again, I start it up and adjust the AC, but I don't pull away yet. I want her to try the slushie first.

Straw held out, I wave it in front of her. "Go on. Try it."

Carefully, she removes the wrapper, that simple move holding my attention. Her nails are long and painted pink. For a moment I wonder if I should've taken it off for her, but she pulls the straw out with ease.

She gives me one last skeptical glance before she wraps her lips around the red straw and takes a sip.

Her eyes widen in pleasant surprise, and a small hum of satisfaction rumbles in her throat. "Oh my God, that is *good*."

I chuckle. I'm equal parts amused and pleased by her reaction. "See?"

She nods quickly, exaggeratedly, in an impression of a bobblehead. "How have I gone my entire life without having one of these? This is like *the* perfect summer drink. This gas station better get used to seeing me. I'm about to be here every day."

My chest flutters with a mix of excitement and pride because I was the one to introduce her to something she's never had before.

"I'm glad you like it."

"It's fantastic." Her cheeks hollow around the straw. "The combination of flavors is perfect, but I think I like blue raspberry the best." She eyes me then, long lashes fanning against her tanned cheeks. Freckles dot the bridge of her nose.

The innocence of her joy reminds me of a simpler time in my life, before reality came crashing down.

"We can go back." She puts her cup in the holder and snaps her seat belt in place, at the same time snapping me out of my reverie. "Don't feel like you have to sit here until I finish."

"Maybe I want to sit here." I finally open my own straw

and take a sip of my slushie. Then, for reasons I don't understand, I hold it out to her. "Want to try."

I expect her to take the cup from me, but I should know better. This is Izzy. She never does what I think she will. Rather than reaching for the drink, she leans in close. And as her hair falls like a curtain around her face, brushing my fingers, she wraps her lips around my straw.

Though I know it's a terrible idea, I can't help but study her mouth. The plump, pink lips and how they purse as she sucks.

*Look away.*

It's what I should do.

But I don't.

I can't.

And for a moment, the world stands still.

It only starts spinning again when she licks her lips and pulls away. "Not as good as mine."

With a shake of my head, I take a sip, hoping to hide my embarrassment and cool the heat in my cheeks. "You just don't want to admit mine is better."

"Or maybe," she takes another sip of her own slushie like she's chasing away the taste of mine, "you have bad taste, and this is an entirely different discussion all together."

I let out a low breath. "Touché."

We stay there, parked in the gas station parking lot, until we've finished our slushies. When we're done, I get out and toss them into the trash can near the entrance of the building.

"Thank you," Izzy says when I get back in the truck.

Confused by the genuine awe in her tone, I frown. "It's just a slushie. You don't have to keep thanking me."

With that, I roll my window down partway and put the truck into reverse.

She's focused on something outside the passenger window,

her voice so soft I almost miss it, when she says, "It's more than that." Then she clears her throat and, voice louder, adds, "This is the first time I've been genuinely happy in months."

I don't reply, because my heart is aching for her, and frankly, I don't know what to say. I just crank the volume up on the radio and navigate toward home.

# *five*

## Izzy

I'VE BEEN WORKING nonstop for more than a decade. I was a literal teenager when I started my YouTube channel. After I graduated from high school and focused on social media full time, I would film a handful of videos each week—more, if inspiration struck—so that I'd have drafts ready to post every couple of days.

Initially, after the Lux incident, I continued posting like normal. After the third week, though, it became obvious that I needed to step away. I'd also stopped filming videos in bulk to have on hand since I was feeling so low.

My camera sits like a heavy brick weight in my tote bag, taunting me to pull it out and film as I stroll down Main Street.

It's a beautiful, warm day. The sun is bright and the air is salty from the ocean. Wonton walks ahead of me, a bounce to his step. He's clearly happy to be out and about after being holed up for the past few days. I've only been out to stock up on veggies, since Derrick is apparently allergic to the color green.

Until now, I didn't realize what a tourist town Parkerville becomes in the spring and summer months. Far more people mill around than I've ever seen here before. Even on the day Via opened her studio. They stroll leisurely down the sidewalks, checking out one pop-up shop after another that are set up like a flea market. I wander over to one, eyeing the silver jewelry.

"Sit," I tell Wonton.

Dutifully, he obeys, his tongue hanging halfway out of his mouth while he smiles up at me.

"He's cute," the woman at the booth says. "Maltese?"

"He is."

"Do you mind if I pet him?"

Holding a bracelet made with sea glass beads, I smile at her. "Go for it. He loves the attention."

She doesn't have to be told twice. Without another word, she rounds her table and drops to her knees to give Wonton scratches.

"Do you make these?" I ask, holding another bracelet up to the light.

She tilts her head back and inspects the jewelry with a fond look on her face. "Yeah. I do it in my spare time. If I don't keep my hands busy, I feel like I'm going crazy."

With a small laugh, I clutch the bracelet and move down her booth to the selection of necklaces. "I know how that is."

Having so little to do for the past few months has made me all but certifiably insane. The good news is that I'm finally putting a dent in the giant to-be-read list I started several years ago.

But it's difficult, this place I'm in. Because I don't quite know who I am if I'm not filming. It sounds pathetic, even in my own mind, but it's really all I know, and I've always loved it.

Though this time away from filming has spurred questions in my mind about the future. About what comes next. Because even if I hadn't been canceled on the internet, I can't vlog and post fashion and travel videos forever.

I end up purchasing the bracelet and a few rings before I continue on my way. There's a coffee shop on Main Street that I've always loved working in, so I head there. Only I don't have anything *to* work on.

Scooping Wonton under my arm, I go in to order.

The woman behind the register smiles in greeting. "Izzy, it's been a while. Your usual?"

This is the thing I've come to love about Parkerville—everyone knows everyone and everything. Sure, nosy people can be a pain, but so far, I've found that most of the townsfolk here are genuinely caring, and that's something special.

"That would be great," I say. "And whatever Via's usual is, too. It's good to see you, Cindy."

She clicks a few keys on the register, then looks up at me, brows lifted. "Any pastries today? I know how much you love our oatmeal cookies. They should be out of the oven in about five minutes."

I slam a hand over my heart. "You're speaking my love language. One, please—actually," I correct, "make it two."

I have no idea whether Derrick likes oatmeal cookies. Most people seem to find them bland, but I'm their chief advocate. Now oatmeal *raisin* cookies? That's a different story. Those belong solely in the trash.

Still, despite not knowing his cookie preference, I want to

bring him one. To share a treat I love with him like he did when he took me for a slushie.

I tap my card to pay and add a few dollar bills to the tip jar.

"Thank you, dear." Cindy passes me the receipt.

With Wonton still curled under my arm, I step off to the side. While I wait, I scan the coffee shop. It's quiet this morning.

Inside, it's a mix of reclaimed wood from a variety of buildings in the area and new bright-blue subway tiles that serve to bring the ocean across the street closer.

The mix of the old and new is comforting, charming.

In LA, everything is shiny and sterile. Modern and minimalist. There's such little personality there. Not in the places, nor in most of the people.

To me, the things that have been around for a while hold the real appeal.

*Yeah,* my conscience taunts me, *like Derrick.*

"Your order's ready, Izzy."

I startle, my heart lurching. The way she's watching me, head tilted in concern, tells me Cindy's already said that more than once.

"Sorry," I rush out, scurrying to the counter. "Thank you."

I put the cookies in my tote and precariously balance both cups until I get outside, where I set them on a table and put Wonton down. He wags his tail and turns in a circle, his sweet little face full of so much excitement.

"We're going to see Auntie Via, just like I promised." While I get the cups situated again, I take a moment to appreciate the flowers growing along the outside of the building.

Wonton gives an annoyed yip, telling me to get my ass going.

Via's store is about another mile down the long stretch of road along the coastline.

By the time we make it there, I'm sweating, and the ice in her drink is melting. Oh well.

"Hey." She brightens when she sees me and steps around the front desk to throw her arms around me.

I've heard horror stories from my friends about how fucked up sibling relationships can be, but despite our age difference, we've always been close. Via's my best friend.

"For you." I pass her the iced coffee, then let Wonton off his leash to run around.

"Thanks." She takes a hearty sip, her eyes dancing as she surveys me. "I can't believe you're staying with Reid's dad."

I shrug. "What choice do I have if I'm going to stay in town?"

"You could come back and stay with me." She bumps my shoulder.

"In your little fuck pad? I think not. I'm not dumb enough to turn down a good clean bed for your couch. There's no telling what it's endured."

Laughing, she squats to pet Wonton, who's stopped in front of her. "I guess I get it."

"I can't believe you're still in your honeymoon phase."

The words come out a little sharper than I mean for them to. I really am happy for my sister. Even so, I can't help but wish I could find love like that, too. I've yet to find the kind of guy who's ready to settle down and live out a fairy tale with me.

"I think when you meet the right person, it's always like that. We disagree and fight at times. But we love each other too much to stay mad for long."

My sister has stars in her eyes every time she talks about

Reid. I wouldn't be surprised one bit if he's planning a proposal soon. He's just as head over heels for her.

"I promise I'm okay at Derrick's," I say when her expression morphs back into one of concern. "You don't need to worry about me, promise."

I might not be in the best headspace, but I am okay. That has to count for something.

"As long as you're sure." She presses her lips together, studying me like she's looking for a sign that I'm not.

"We're doing okay. He works a lot, so I barely see him."

Though when he's home, I'm usually trying to shove something green down his throat. He turned his nose up at the green smoothie I had for breakfast this morning and that was before I could offer to make one for him.

"So, what's your plan while you're here?"

Shrugging, I wander over to the section of her store where she keeps a wide selection of pottery for painting. "Right now, I'm taking a break and seeing where life takes me."

"Are you going to vlog?"

I'm studying a pig with wings when the question registers, and my body involuntarily stiffens. I set it back down beside a unicorn horn. I'm sure both trinkets are popular with the kids. "I might, but I'm not going to force myself."

As I say it, I swear the camera in my tote bag gets ten pounds heavier.

"And today, I'm going to paint one of these, then take a walk through town." I look back over my shoulder at my sister, hating the worry swimming in her eyes.

I'm *fine*. Maybe not *good*, but I am okay. That has to count for something.

"All right." She crosses her arms over her chest, still

wearing that concerned expression. "Why don't we go get lunch? I can close down the store and—"

"You don't need to do that."

Her face falls. Dammit.

Quickly, I say, "But I'd love to have lunch with you. Only if you want to, though. I don't want my presence in town to negatively impact your business."

"It couldn't possibly. We'll go after you finish your project. Pick a piece." She flicks her fingers at the wall of pottery and heads back to the front.

I end up choosing a plate. Yeah, it's a boring choice, but I've gotten it into my head that I want to make a collection of dinnerware full of pieces painted by me or by someone I love. An eclectic mix of pure happiness.

I pick out my colors, then squirt dollops of each onto the palette. I might not be an artist like my sister, but I still love the creative break.

When I'm settled on a stool, Wonton skedaddles over to lie at my feet.

I spend the next two hours meticulously painting little flowers around the edge of the plate. Layering the paint so that it will show up once it's fired in the kiln takes forever, but it's relaxing. Cleansing. And when I'm finished, I'm impressed with what I've created. For a first attempt, it's damn good.

"Please tell me you're almost done." Via wanders over to my side, wrapping her cardigan around her body. It might be hot outside, but it's downright frigid in here. "I'm starving. Do you hear my stomach?"

She points at her belly, and, as if on cue, it rumbles.

"I'm done." I angle back from the table. "What do you think?"

Leaning in, she studies it with a soft smile. "It's beautiful, Izzy."

"I'm going to do a whole set—plates and bowls. Maybe even cups."

"That'll be cute." She cautiously picks up the plate and sets it on a table with the other items that need to be fired. "I'd be more enthusiastic if I wasn't so hungry."

"All right, all right." I stand, then head for the sink in the corner to wash my hands. "Let me get some food in you before you get hangry."

"It might be too late," she warns, hanging a sign that says *Closed for lunch* on the door.

We walk down the street, then cross over onto the pier, where the restaurants and shops are only open in the warm months. Via chooses a restaurant I haven't been to yet, and we're quickly seated at a table outside that overlooks the water.

The people at the table next to us get their food as we're perusing the menus, the scents floating in the air making my stomach rumble like my sister's. I guess I was so focused on painting that I didn't notice how my hunger was setting in.

"What's good here?"

Via peers at me over the top of her menu, brow arched. "It's fresh seafood, therefore everything."

"Good point." I study the menu, struggling to make a decision because every choice sounds incredible.

When our server arrives to take our order, I'm forced to choose, so I go with the fish sandwich with sweet potato fries and a side salad.

Once the server leaves, I look out over the railing to the water beyond. With the ocean breeze stirring my hair, causing it to tickle my shoulders, I close my eyes and inhale the salty scent, allowing it to center me.

I don't go to the beaches around LA. Too loud. Too busy. Too ... everything.

But here? It's perfect. Calm and crisp. Filled with families. Kids laughing, dogs barking. It's simple in the best way. Even the tourists are different here. Moving more slowly, enjoying the moment.

"I've missed you," Via says, bringing my attention back her way. "It really is nice to have you here."

"Thanks." I pull an elastic off my wrist and twist my hair into a knot. I miss a few strands when I secure it, so some still blow around my face.

"I know I struggle to understand your job and your life, but you can talk to me about anything."

My sister watches me, lips pressed together, half her face hidden behind oversized sunglasses. Even so, I can sense her sincerity.

I *have* tried to explain what I do, but she doesn't get it. I can't fault her for it, either. Unless a person has lived it, it's difficult for them to see what I do as real and meaningful. Social media isn't real life, that's what most believe, and to an extent, that's true. But it is my life. So logging off and refusing to let the comments bother me isn't as simple as it sounds. If only it were, my life would be far easier.

Rather than tell her that, I take a sip of my water. Then I plaster on a smile, and respond with "I know."

She frowns at my half-hearted response, but she doesn't ask more, and I leave it at that. I don't want to keep rehashing my problems with someone who doesn't understand.

Conversation, thankfully, moves away from me. Instead, we talk about her shop and Reid and her rocky relationship with our parents. They've always been hard on her in a way they aren't with me, but I didn't truly understand the depths of that until a few years ago. As the youngest child—and because, frankly, I was less inclined to care about their wishes since I did what I wanted anyway—I had it easier.

"You should come to book club this week," Via says as the server appears with our food. She gives her a grateful smile, and then it's just the two of us again.

I unravel my napkin and pull out my silverware. "You mean the book club where you never read said book and instead gossip nonstop?"

She grins, her eyes twinkling. "That's the one. Though we do actually read the books now that we've all given up the pretense of enjoying anything other than romance."

"So, does that mean I should read the book before coming?"

She shakes her head. "Nah, we still don't really talk about the books. Just bring a snack or drinks."

"I don't know," I hedge, forking a bite of my salad.

"If you're going to stay for a while, you might as well incorporate yourself into the core of our town. Book club is the best way to do that."

My chest tightens with apprehension, but I take a deep breath and will the sensation to dissipate. "Fine, I'll come. Send me the information."

With a victorious smile, she types the details into her phone. My cell dings a moment later.

"Now you have no excuse."

I unlock the device and scan the text she sent: The address, along with a list of foods *not* to bring—staunchly vetoed by Glenda. Good ole Glenda. I've missed that crazy lady.

On instinct, I open Instagram and take a photo of my meal

for my story—excluding the salad I already dug into. Before I post the image, though, I hesitate. It's been a while since I've posted anything, and despite my newfound haters, I do try to upload photos and stories periodically so the people who follow me and actually care know I'm still around. So with a deep breath, I post it to my story—making sure not to tag my location or the restaurant.

Then, before the messages can roll in, I put my phone away.

"Do you have to pay Derrick rent or anything?"

"Huh?" I say stupidly. The question catches me off guard. I haven't even considered it. *Shit. I should have offered.* "No. I mean, he didn't mention anything about it."

"He's a nice guy," she continues. "He probably doesn't want you to anyway. I was just curious."

Suddenly anxious and frustrated with myself, I nibble on the end of a fry and change the subject. I'll come back to it later. When I'm alone. "How are things with him and the whole you and Reid situation? Still awkward?"

Via twists her lips. "It's fine, I suppose. But I'll probably always feel a little awkward about it."

She gives me a pointed look. The same one she always gives me when she wants to silently remind me that I'm partly at fault in the situation. But how was I supposed to know that Derrick was the father of the guy she'd hooked up with?

After lunch, Via heads back to her store, and I continue on wandering through town. I stop off at the bookshop where Via's friend Ella works and pick up a stack of romance novels. For decades, Ella's grandpa owned and ran the store. When she took over, her grandfather was adamant that they not sell romance, so she hid her inventory in a closet and made secret sales. After the older man passed away, Ella transformed the store, and now every shelf is bursting with romantic literature.

When I get back to my rental car, I pull out the collapsible water bowl I carry with me and let Wonton drink. Then I strap him in his carrier and buckle him in.

Already, it's after three, so it's time to head back to Derrick's house and start dinner.

*Is Derrick a fan of salmon? I hope so.*

When I pull in, Derrick's truck is in the driveway, which is surprising. The guy works all the time, from what I hear. I ease my car in beside his, already thinking about how I'll get all my things into the house without making more than a trip or two. I step out of the car, but before I can grab even a single bag, I freeze.

Derrick is mowing the yard.

Shirtless.

He's pushing the lawnmower toward me, oblivious to my presence. A pair of big headphones sits over his ears, and his lips move along with the music he's listening to. His chest is bare, skin glistening with a sheen of sweat.

All the air leaves my lungs.

I'm not oblivious to Derrick's good looks. I'm human, after all. But the sight of him sweaty and half naked like this has me squeezing my thighs together.

It's been an embarrassingly long time since I last had sex.

That's got to be why I'm reacting like this.

Right?

I quickly avert my gaze, then whip around to get Wonton from his carrier before he catches me drooling over him. Without bothering with my books or other goodies, I take Wonton inside.

I've come back out and loaded my arms with my

purchases, and I've almost made it back to the front door, when he shuts the lawnmower off and yanks his headphones off.

"Hey," he says, that deep timbre only encouraging whatever is going on between my legs. "I was thinking we could order pizza for dinner. How does that sound?"

"Uh…" I swallow, searching for words. "I-I was going to make salmon."

He wrinkles his nose in disgust. "Pizza. There's a magnet on the fridge with the name and website. Look up their menu and see what you like, and I'll order when I'm done."

Under normal circumstances, I would argue with him, remind him that salmon is the healthier choice and tell him he can forget about his pizza. But his shirtless state has rendered me mute.

So I simply nod and scurry inside like a little mouse. One who peeks out the window, watching the way the muscles in his torso and arms flex when he restarts the mower.

I squish my eyes closed.

There's no doubt about it—I have a date with my vibrator tonight.

### Derrick

"WHAT IS THIS?" I glare at the plate Izzy slides in front of me with my so-called breakfast on it.

"Avocado toast and a boiled egg. It's good for you. Healthy."

I glower at my new tenant. "I'm not going to fall over dead because of a couple of slices of bacon."

"Maybe not yet." She sits across from me, the disgusting contents on her plate matching mine. "But in the future ... you never know. You should be thanking me. I'm looking out for your arteries."

"Thank *you*," I mutter.

She smiles beatifically, swishing her dark waterfall of hair over her shoulder. "You're welcome."

"This is that LA gut-healthy bullshit, isn't it?"

With a roll of her eyes, she takes a bite of her toast and

swallows it before responding. "People all over love avocado toast. It's not solely an LA thing."

Grimacing, I pick it up and sniff it. "I'm going to be hungry five seconds after I eat this."

"No, you're not," she argues. "It's filled with good fats and protein. You'll be surprised. Trust me."

Trust Izzy? Not a chance.

Because I'm starving, and because, though I'm much larger than Izzy, I have a feeling she'd take me out if I even thought about getting bacon out of the fridge, I take a hesitant bite.

It takes a moment for the flavors to register, and when they do, shockingly, it's not terrible. With another careful bite, I continue my assessment.

It's not the greatest thing I've ever eaten. It's a little slimy, the texture not quite to my liking, but it's edible.

Izzy smiles knowingly. "Not bad, huh?"

"I'm not saying I love it," I warn her with a pointed finger. "But it's better than it looks."

She does a little shimmy, basking in her win.

With the toast held out in her direction, I say, "I guess I can expect more of this shit in my future, huh?"

Wearing a smile so big she's squinting, she nods vigorously. "Oh, yeah."

For the next several minutes, we eat in silence. It's not uncomfortable, but I still find myself racking my brain for a subject to talk about. Because strangely enough, I *want* to chat with her.

"I was thinking," I say, pulling her attention from her plate, "we could take the boat out this weekend if you want."

The way her whole face lights up makes me want to fist-pump the air in victory. She's been morose in a way that, until now, I thought was impossible for someone as bubbly as she is.

It's only been a few days, but I figured she'd have perked up by now.

"Really?" She grins, bringing her toast to her lips. "That would be fun."

I only got the boat out once last summer, after Lili begged for a solid week. I'm a sucker for whatever my granddaughter wants.

"Saturday good with you?"

She wipes her mouth on a paper napkin I don't recognize. I tend to use paper towels. What's the point of buying two products that have virtually the same purpose?

"In case you hadn't noticed"—she waves a hand a little wildly—"my calendar is free."

I give a gruff chuckle. Her sass probably shouldn't entertain me as much as it does. "You can invite your sister if you want."

She arches a brow. "And your son?"

Lips pursed, I nod. "I can extend the invitation if you prefer?"

She bites her bottom lip, an innocent gesture I shouldn't find seductive.

"Actually"—she flips her hair over her shoulders and drops her focus to her plate—"if it's okay with you I'd prefer to keep it just us. My sister ... she's worried about me, and I'm fine, really. Or I will be." Licking her lips, she peers up at me through her lashes. "But I'd like to relax and look for whales without having her hovering over me like a mother hen. I might throw her overboard."

I choke back a snort at the visual.

I can't say I'm not relieved that she doesn't want them to come. I've moved on from my disastrous dating experience with Via, but the awkwardness between us remains.

Izzy hops up from the table with her empty plate, snatching mine as she goes. It's only then I realize I've eaten the whole thing.

"I made lunch for you," she says as she sets the plates in the sink.

I really do need to fix that dishwasher now that she's living here, too.

Frowning, I tilt my head and assess her. "Lunch?"

"Yeah," she says over her shoulder, wearing a bright smile. "You know, the meal people typically eat in the middle of the day."

I join her at the sink and take one soapy plate from her hands. "I don't normally bother with lunch." After a quick rinse, I dry the plate with a dish towel, then start the process over with the second one.

With a brow raised, she gives me an unimpressed look. One that says she could complete the task on her own. But she's already doing a lot around here. I don't mind helping, and I'd feel guilty watching her work while I sat at the table.

"If you don't want it, it's no biggie. Just take it with you. Maybe someone else will eat it."

I choke back a growl that comes out of nowhere. What the hell? The visceral reaction is unexpected, but the idea of giving one of my guys the lunch she made for *me* doesn't sit right.

"I'll eat it." I might regret this declaration once I take my first bite, but when she smiles from ear to ear, I find myself smiling back.

"Good, I think you'll like it."

That means I'll hate it.

Turning away, I open the cabinet door. "I gotta get going."

Izzy whirls around, nearly smacking me across the face with her too-long hair, and scurries to the fridge. When she pulls out an actual lunchbox, like the kind I used to send to school with my kids, I stare down at it in disbelief.

"*Spiderman?*"

"I know," she sighs dramatically, shoulders drooping, as I take it from her. "You're more of a Grumpy Cat kind of guy, but I couldn't find that kind of merch anywhere but eBay, and I was not paying fifty bucks for it, so Spiderman it is." With a pat to my chest, she saunters away, then she bounds up the stairs. Wonton lets out a yip and runs after her.

For a moment, I'm still, staring at the space she just occupied, soaking in the heat left behind by her touch.

It takes me a moment to gather my bearings, but when I do, I grab my keys and I'm gone.

DESK WORK IS my least favorite part of the job, but I have to spend at least one day a week in the office.

Jessica, my assistant, gets up from her desk with a groan. Hand on her large stomach, she makes her way over. Her shadow looms above me, begging me to look up, though she doesn't speak.

With a sigh, I tip my head back. "Yes?"

She places a hand over her heart. "I know you love me, but you really need to take a look at those applications I emailed to you and hire a temporary assistant. I'll be on maternity leave in a matter of weeks."

I pinch the bridge of my nose. Jessica has been working for me for years. She knows how I like paperwork organized, and she can handle most calls or problems without my help. She'll only be gone for a few months, but the idea of having to work with someone new annoys me.

"I'll look at them today."

She stares me down, lips tugged into a doubtful frown. "I'm serious, Derrick. Especially if you want me to train them before I go. We're down to the wire." She taps her finger against my desk. "Pick someone."

"Okay." I give her a solemn nod. "I'll have a name for you by the end of the week."

With a harrumph, she says, "Sooner." And then she strides back over to her desk, hand to her back. "Whether you like it or not, I could go into labor any time, and then you'll be left with no one."

She's right, but it doesn't change how badly I don't want to deal with this.

"I could handle the paperwork while you're gone."

She snorts, spinning her chair to face me. "You *hate* paperwork."

I prefer to be out there with my guys, but it's only a couple of months. How bad could it be? "I know, but it's not forever."

With a grunt, she tips to one side and reaches for her bottle of water. "It's long enough. There are a few good candidates on the list. Stop being a big baby and pick someone."

Easier said than done, but I'll have to try.

# seven

## Izzy

FOR REASONS UNKNOWN, I'm on edge as I head to book club. It's ridiculous, really. I know all these ladies, and even if I didn't, I never get flustered when I meet people.

Once I've parked on the street in front of the house, I climb out, then open the back door and grab the plate of crostinis I made along with the twice-baked potato poppers. I considered filming the process, but in the end, I left my camera where it's been, in my bag, since I arrived in Parkerville.

The sight of Via's car in the driveway relieves a fraction of my anxiety. At least my sister is already here.

*Get it together. There's nothing to be nervous about.*

Except Glenda. She's a loose cannon.

Heart beating and hands shaking, I juggle the dishes of food and use my elbow to knock.

It opens, and then I'm blinded by Ella's excited smile.

"Izzy!" She takes the food from me and ushers me inside. "Come in, come in. We're waiting on a few more people."

While Ella heads for the kitchen with the dishes, where I'm sure there is enough food for twenty more people than will be in attendance tonight, my sister waves me over to the couch where she's chatting with a few other familiar faces.

"Not much longer now, right?" Via asks the heavily pregnant woman at her side.

For a moment, dread washes over me, but it's tempered when I note the genuine smile on my sister's face. She battled infertility for years before her divorce, and often, it can be hard for her to be around pregnant women or babies. But lately it seems like she's in a better place.

I've offered to be her surrogate, and I meant it. We've talked about it here and there, but she says she's at peace with how her life has played out, and she's certain that when she's ready for kids, she'll look into other options like adoption.

And when it finally happens, she'll be the best mom ever.

The pregnant woman rubs at her stomach, excitement shining in her eyes. "Six more weeks, maybe less."

Across the room, Glenda calls out, "Six weeks gives us plenty of time to throw you a baby shower."

The woman sighs. "I've told you, that's not necessary. Just being here with you all is enough for me. Even if I can't have the wine."

"We *want* to," another woman chimes in.

My head is on a swivel as the women volley back and forth. Their familiarity has already eased my trepidation about being here tonight. It's comforting, this closeness they share.

I have friends in LA, but none of the relationships I have are like this. Most are, unfortunately, superficial and mutually beneficial. In fact, if I walked away from LA and my social media, chances are Finneas is the only one who would keep in touch.

Small towns often get ragged on, but in my mind, having such close relationships with other members of the community is special.

"Oh," my sister says, turning to me. "Izzy, this is Jessica."

The pregnant woman beside her waves.

"Cassandra." Via points out the woman who joined in with Glenda about wanting to throw a baby shower. "Susan, Anna, Mindy, Tammy, and Lucy."

With a wave, I give the group a nod. I've met most of them before, but only in passing, so I didn't have names to put with faces.

"I heard you're livin' with Reid's daddy." Glenda's drawl is unique. It's not quite southern but not northern either.

"Where'd you hear that?" I ask, wishing I had grabbed a drink before I joined Via on the couch, if only to have something to do with my hands.

"Around. I talk to people besides this lot." She points to the gathered women, brow arched expectantly. "Well, are you?"

I mimic her expression, though mine feels a bit more exasperated. "I didn't realize it was a question."

Smiling so big I'm surprised her face doesn't crack in half, Glenda wags a finger at me. "I like you."

Via gives my knee a light swat. "My apartment is small, and the inn was full, so Derrick generously offered her a place to stay."

Technically, he was forced into it, but I have no interest in getting into that debacle.

"That's kind of him," Glenda says, eyeing me. "He's a good man. Good looking, too. And single."

Via drops her head back and howls with laughter. "Glenda,

I beg you, *please* don't try to set my sister up with my boyfriend's dad."

My stomach knots. What would my sister think if she knew I check Derrick out on a near constant basis when he's at home? Maybe it's wrong, but it's damn near impossible not to. Daddy Crawford is *hot*.

"Why not? They'd be a great fit."

The way Via shudders in horror stings. Not so much with hurt, I guess, but with disappointment. Though I don't understand why. I'm not looking to date Derrick, and I'm pretty sure he's sworn off the idea of dating altogether after how disastrously things went with my sister.

For the next hour, the group yammers on about how great it would be for Derrick to find a girlfriend. They move on from considering me as an option to naming every decent woman in a fifty-mile radius.

I stuff my face with food to keep myself occupied and to avoid uttering anything incriminating. As much as I'd like a glass of wine, I stay away from the alcohol so I can drive back to Derrick's house. I don't want my sister or anyone else volunteering to give me a ride home.

At the end of the night, I say my goodbyes to the ladies and hurry out to the car, but before I can make my getaway, my sister appears beside my window, forcing me to roll it down.

"Don't let them scare you away. They're a fun bunch, I promise."

"They're great. I'm just…"

I don't know how to explain that I'm floundering. I've had my life figured out since I was a teenager, but now it's spiraling out of my control. Then, to top it all off, I'm attracted to my pseudo-landlord. I've only been in Parkerville for a week, and I'm already making a mess of things.

I settle on "tired," which isn't exactly a lie.

I haven't slept well in months.

Via's lips tug down and her eyes shine in sympathy. "Is there anything I can do?"

With a smirk, I cock my head to the side. "Yes, Via, why don't you get some sleep for me?"

She rolls her eyes. "Your sarcasm is not appreciated, but at least you're feeling well enough to joke."

"Don't worry about me," I insist, starting my car. "I'm going to go home and shower, put on a face mask, and vegetate on the couch."

She arches a brow, her face lighting with interest. "Home, huh?"

"It's a figure of speech," I sputter, even as my face heats.

Laughing, she steps away and lifts a hand. "Go relax and try to sleep tonight."

I hum and shift my car into drive. "Yep, I'll try."

As if I haven't been trying for months. I've tried every herbal remedy under the sun and all kinds of yoga positions before bed. Despite my absurd attachment to my phone, I even left it in another room at night for weeks. Still, my quality of sleep didn't improve.

I'm afraid I might be a lost cause.

"I love you. See you soon." Via waves, taking another step back.

I give a soft "I love you too" before I roll up the window.

I shoot Derrick a text, warning him that I don't plan to make dinner tonight since I gorged myself at book club. That way he can pick up his go-to artery clogging fast food. Whatever floats his boat.

His response is a simple thumbs-up emoji.

He's not home when I arrive, which I expected. After

letting Wonton out, I head straight for the shower, where I turn the temperature up so high I practically scald myself.

The bathroom is practically a sauna when I get out and wrap a towel around my torso. As I go through my after-shower routine, I quietly sing along to the music playing from my phone, swaying my hips to the beat. I spray leave-in conditioner into my hair and gently work through my long strands with a comb. My hair is past my breasts now, a feat I've accomplished without extensions, despite what rumors online might claim. I love my long hair, but there's no denying it's a lot of work.

When I've worked through all the tangles, I wash my hands and push my hair back with a headband so I can apply a face mask. The mask smells strongly of eucalyptus, and the charcoal color wants to adhere to my fingers. Once I'm finished, I scrub around my nail beds until they're thoroughly clean, then I set the alarm on my phone so that I remember to wash it off.

I learned my lesson after I fell asleep while wearing a mask years ago. I broke out so badly that it took almost six months to get my skin sorted out.

When Wonton sniffs, I scowl down at him. "Listen, I know I need a pedicure, but it's going to have to wait."

He sneezes in response.

I finish up in the bathroom and change into my comfiest pair of pj's—the kind of pj's that are almost transparent and falling apart, yet feel so good I can't bear to throw them away.

Downstairs, I find the house empty still. So far this week, Derrick has been home by this time. I tell myself not to worry. He's probably working late or stopped for food or...

Or he's on a date.

It's an absurd thought.

Not because Derrick isn't dateable. He's the opposite, in fact. Fuckable, too. But he *doesn't* date. My sister was the exception, and look where that got him.

Still, jealousy rises up inside me, rushing forward like a hot, uncomfortable wave.

My attraction to Derrick needs to take a hike. He's not interested in me.

I'm probably feeling this way because it's been so long since I've had sex. I'm just craving some touch. That has to be it. Right?

I settle on the couch with a bowl of popcorn—my favorite snack—and turn the TV on. Wonton jumps up and curls up next to me with his head on my leg. Nothing on TV captures my interest, so I end up scrolling through Netflix before eventually settling on one of my all-time favorite shows.

My love for *Gilmore Girls* has never wavered, despite how many times I've watched the series from beginning to end. Rory drives me nuts half the time, but my love for the small town and the mother/daughter antics keep me coming back.

Maybe that's why I like Parkerville so much.

It's like Stars Hollow in a way. Small and quaint, with unique people and town customs. Only it's coastal and has more stoplights.

I'm halfway through the first episode when the front door opens. Derrick holds a bag from the local diner in his left hand, while he fights to get his key out with the other.

"Long day?"

The scream that escapes the grown man is so high-pitched, I wince. The keys finally come free of the lock and go flying over his head before landing in the bush outside.

He grabs at his chest like he's clutching his pearls. "What the fuck is on your face?"

"Uh." I tap my cheek where the face mask has hardened. "A face mask?"

"That shit is scary." He points at me, wearing an accusing glare.

"Scary?" I repeat while he searches for his keys just outside the door.

He finds them quickly and locks up behind him.

I fight a grin at his exasperated expression when he faces me again. "What's scary?"

"It's all gray and white and zombie-like."

"Careful," I warn, teasing, "or I'll put one on you."

His eyes widen comically. "Not a chance."

"Don't be such a baby," I call after him as he heads into the kitchen with his food.

He doesn't respond, but I do hear him shuffling around in there, opening and closing cabinets and then the fridge.

I focus on the show again, and I'm surprised when he returns a few minutes later and sits in the leather club chair in the corner.

The living room is the definition of cozy. The TV is mounted above a fireplace and is flanked by bookshelves filled with a variety of books and other knickknacks, including pictures of Reid and Layla over the years. There are several of Lili, too. It's clear Derrick loves his family.

"What's this?" He points at the TV.

"You've never seen *Gilmore Girls*?"

It makes sense, I suppose, since he's a guy, but I love the show so much I find this news downright blasphemous.

He shakes his head and takes a bite of his burger. Through a mouthful, he says, "Nope. Can't say I have."

Dramatically, I drop my head back against the couch and

sigh. "Welcome to the best show ever. This is the first ever episode. I'll start it over."

He straightens. "No, you—"

"Too late," I say with a smile.

He glances at the stairs like he's tempted to run away. Instead, he settles back, grumbling a little, and before long, he's sucked into the show like I knew he would be. We watch three full episodes, only pausing for bathroom breaks and so I can take off my face mask.

"We can watch more tomorrow," I tell him after I've turned the TV off and am folding up the blanket I pulled off the back of the couch halfway through the first episode.

"I don't watch much TV," he admits. "At least not shows, and certainly not in order. I'm usually too tired after work, so I only turn it on for background noise."

He follows me up the stairs, and we pause in the hallway in the space between the master bedroom and the guest room.

"The bookshelves," I blurt out when it looks like he's about to take off again and disappear into his room. Suddenly I'm not ready to part ways. "Around the fireplace. Did you make those?"

His brows furrow, like he can't figure out where I'm going with the question. "Yeah, I did."

"I love them. The dark green paint works well in the space."

He nods silently, the simple move effectively cutting off the conversation I'd tried to start and leaving us standing together awkwardly.

It's like the confidence that has always come easy to me is sucked into a vortex when he's around.

Wonton nips at my toes, startling me. "I better go to bed," I blurt out, throwing my thumb over my shoulder toward the guest room.

He nods, stuffing his hands into the jeans he didn't change out of when he came home. "Good night, Izzy."

Once we've gone our separate ways, I dive into bed and burrow under the covers. On the other side of the quilt, Wonton scratches at the fabric before he circles and plops himself down.

After I've composed myself a bit, I respond to a text from Finneas, then plug my phone in to charge.

That's when the master bathroom shower kicks on.

Eyes squeezed shut, I curse myself silently.

This might be the worst thing imaginable. Derrick, a few feet away. Naked. Wet.

With a shaky hand, I snatch my phone off the nightstand, navigate to the white noise app, and tap on the whale sounds.

Calm. Soothing. Nature.

But also water.

Water like Derrick's currently standing under.

I clutch the pillow from the other side of the bed and cover my face. Then I scream into it.

# *eight*

## Derrick

WITH A SIGH, I honk for a third time.

I'm a patient man, but after twenty minutes, that patience is slipping. Izzy swore she'd be right out, so I loaded up. Yet here I sit, still waiting.

The front door opens, but before I can exhale in relief, she's sticking her hand out and waggling one finger in the air.

I cover my face with my hands to stifle my annoyance.

I thought I was doing a good thing when I offered to take her out on the boat, but if she can't even make it out the door on time, I can't imagine the day will go well.

Finally, the door opens again, and she descends the front steps with a tote bag so big slung over her shoulder that I have to wonder if she's hiding a toddler in there.

I can't help but survey her, taking in the teeny tiny jean

shorts and the loose sweater falling off her shoulder that reveals a pair of thin straps tied around the back of her neck.

Bright yellow flip-flops slap against the brick walkway as she makes her way to the truck.

She hops in wearing a cheery smile, like she hasn't made me wait out here for nearly half an hour.

I arch a brow as she puts the tote bag between her feet. "Do you have everything?"

She twists her lips in thought. "ChapStick, sunscreen"—she ticks the two items off while reaching for the seat belt—"a book, iPad, cell phone, magazine, snacks." With a click of the buckle, she nods once. "Yep, that's everything. What about you? You look…" She takes me in, then shifts in her seat and peers into the back seat. "Unprepared."

"All I need is my hat." I hook my thumb over my shoulder to the fishing hat on the bench seat.

Lips lifting in amusement, Izzy shakes her head. "Such a simple man. Just a hat. Would you like a round of applause for your lack of needs?"

"Your sarcasm is unappreciated," I gripe as I put the truck in reverse.

Izzy laughs, the sound bright, airy. But quickly, she sobers and asks, "Do you mind if I roll down the window?"

"Go for it."

Eagerly, she presses the button that lowers the window, and when her dark hair whips around her face, her expression softens into one of contentment. It might be the most relaxed she's been since she arrived.

Some of my anger dissipates as she melts into the seat and lets out a small sigh. I don't know what drove her from LA, what's plaguing her this way. But if the simplicity of an open window and wind in her hair can make her feel better, then who am I to rain on that parade?

Angling forward, she turns the volume on the radio up. "Your country music is beginning to grow on me."

"Is it now?" Fighting a smile, I rub my hand over my mouth.

One side of her lips is turned up sardonically. "It's not so bad. I'm open-minded."

"Are you?"

She scoffs. "I *am*. My mom always emphasized the importance of giving new things a chance. She was mostly referring to vegetables, and I still hate brussels sprouts, but the sentiment applies to many things."

We're quiet for the rest of the short drive, letting the music fill the silence. It's surprising just how comfortable I've become in her presence.

I'm almost to my friend's house, where I park my boat during the warm months, when she says, "Sorry for making you wait. I didn't want to forget anything."

Still gripping the wheel one-handed, I lift a shoulder. "It's fine."

She straightens, turns my way, and stares me down, practically boring a hole in the side of my head. "You honked the horn three times. I know you were pissed. Don't even try to deny it."

I chuckle, amused. "I thought maybe you fell asleep."

"Mhm," she hums. "Sure."

I turn down the street, and as I approach the driveway, I slow the truck.

"Uh, Derrick," Izzy says, scanning our surroundings, "I hate to break it to you, but we're at someone's house. Not a dock."

"Dock's in the back," I explain, pushing the button to roll up her window.

Lips pursed, she looks around again. "I thought you had your own boat."

As I park the truck off to the side, I give her a slow nod. "I do, but my buddy Brooks doesn't, so he lets me store it here. He takes it out on occasion. Someone might as well use it, since I don't get it out often."

She gathers her hair behind her head and secures it with a light blue elastic from around her wrist. "I'm glad we're getting out today. You should get to enjoy it."

I hop out of my truck and snag my hat from the back. Izzy follows suit, then trails me to the backyard and down to the dock.

Before we board, I check the exterior of the boat for damage. When I find nothing, I step on, then hold a hand out to Izzy to help her aboard. Once I'm sure everything is in working order, I crank the engine. In the seat beside me, Izzy turns my way, hair blowing in the breeze, and grins.

In response, my stomach makes a weird cartwheeling, somersault-type motion.

A sensation I haven't felt since I was a teenager.

The sun reflects off her dark hair, making the freckles sprinkled across her nose stand out even more.

*I'm attracted to her because she's a beautiful woman, that's all. It ends there.*

If I tell myself this enough, maybe I'll eventually believe it.

As I guide the boat through the inlet and out to the ocean, I find myself constantly looking over at Izzy. Her joy is infectious. Her ponytail whips behind her, and little wisps of hair float around her face. Big, bug-eyed sunglasses hide part of her face. On anyone else, they'd look ridiculous, but it's hard to deny that they suit her.

I drive around for a while before I lower the anchor and come to a stop in a calm part of the water. I took my shirt off a bit ago, the heat getting to me, and when I turn around and face Izzy fully, her brows lift above the frame of her glasses, and she takes a long, slow look.

*Fuck.*

I might be out of practice, but I *know* what that look means.

I avert my gaze, pretending not to notice the way she's checking me out.

I can't say the same thing for my dick, though. That's one body part that thoroughly appreciates the attention. With a sharp breath in, I snatch my shirt off the floor and quickly sit down with it in my lap, feeling like a horny teenager, having to hide my boner.

Ridiculous.

Thankfully, Izzy is too busy rifling through the toddler-sized bag to notice.

With an "aha," she yanks out a tube of sunscreen, then begins slathering it on her body. "I put some on before I left the house, but I better reapply." At my speculative expression, she adds, "I have a friend who got skin cancer, and it's made me a wee bit paranoid."

"A wee bit?" I mimic as she works the creamy white lotion into her skin.

"Okay, more than that, but sunscreen is important. Do you have any on?"

"No."

Her eyes widen in horror, and her jaw goes slack. "Derrick," she scolds.

75

Dammit. The way she says my name does nothing to help my dick settle down. I frown down at my lap in annoyance.

"When I'm done, you can use this." She holds the bottle up.

"I'm good."

Eyes narrowed, she huffs at me. "No, you're not."

I sigh. There's no arguing with this woman.

She finishes with her legs, then stands and takes her over-sized sweater off.

*Fuck me.*

The tight, tiny hot pink bikini top hugs her perfect tits, and the jean shorts sit low on her hips. As I take her in, it's impossible not to imagine what it would feel like to put my hands there. How soft and warm the skin above her waistline would be against my rough fingers.

Clearing my throat, I look away, my face heating.

Her laughter floats over to me. "It's just a little skin, Derrick. No need to be embarrassed."

With a scoff, I roll my eyes. "I'm not embarrassed."

"Sure you're not," she drawls, holding the tube of sunscreen out to me. "Can I trust you to apply it yourself, or do I need to put it on you?"

Heart jumping at the idea, I snatch it from her, making her giggle, the sound light enough to float on the breeze.

I only put the sunscreen on because that threat wasn't an empty one. Izzy will certainly do it herself if I don't cooperate.

She turns her back to me, and for a moment, I think maybe I'll be safe, at least for a bit. But clearly, the universe hates me, because before I can look away and continue with my task, she wiggles out of her shorts, revealing cheeky bikini bottoms in the same bright pink as her top.

"I can feel you staring at my ass."

My stomach plummets, and I drop my eyes and the sunscreen bottle.

"Fuck," I curse, scooping it up.

Izzy laughs again, this time more heartily. I want to be annoyed with her, but it's impossible when I like the sound this much.

I focus my attention on the sunscreen again while she goes back to messing with her tote. This time she pulls out a book from her bag of wonders, the cover bright purple and illustrated.

"That a kids' book or what?"

Brows jumping, she shakes her head and lets out a sigh. "Definitely not. I guess that makes it above your reading level. Sorry about that."

"Touché." Lowering my head, I get back to applying sunscreen on my chest, but it doesn't soak in the way it should. "What kind of stuff is this? It won't go away."

She stretches out on the built-in bench and bends her knees so she can prop her book against her thighs. "It's the *good* kind of sunscreen. Don't be such a baby."

Lip curled in annoyance, I survey the white layer coating my skin, holding my greasy hands out at my sides.

With a sigh, she sets her book down. Then she hauls herself up and comes over to me. "Want some help?" she asks as she shuffles closer.

"Uh—"

Without waiting for my response, she grasps my bicep where I've missed a massive spot and goes to work, using her thumbs to massage the sunscreen into my skin.

"Fuck," I bite out, my eyes threatening to shut. "That feels good."

"You work too hard. Your muscles are probably due for a good massage."

I grunt in response, noncommittal. As much as I don't need her hands on me right now—thanks to my dick that still hasn't settled down—I can't find the words to tell her to stop.

In fact, words fail me entirely when she comes around in front of me and crouches, hands on my chest to work it into my skin.

Her proximity makes my brain short circuit. Her eyes are a unique shade of green with gray and specks of gold. I've never seen anything like them.

"Your eyes are pretty," I blurt like a teenage boy who doesn't think before he speaks.

Her hands still on my chest, and she meets my gaze. "Thanks."

I clear my throat, hands on my knees in a death grip. "You're welcome."

What the hell is wrong with me? I'm forty-four years old and I'm getting tongue tied over a twenty-seven-year-old. She's the same age as my daughter. Yes, I was only eighteen when I became a parent, but that doesn't make it okay to lust over a woman so young.

I stand abruptly, causing her to wobble and nearly fall back on her ass. Before she can tumble, though, she catches herself with a squeak.

"Sorry, thought I heard my phone," I lie.

"It's okay," she says, popping up and capping the sunscreen, shaking her head and wearing a wry smile. When she looks up, she scans my face, then moves lower until …

In my haste to get away, I'd forgotten why I was sitting and covering myself.

Izzy breaks out in a wide smile. "Aw, at least some part of you is happy to see me. Hi."

And then she waves. At my dick.

Head dropped back, I groan. "Can you not?"

"He's waving at me. Why shouldn't I return the greeting?"

I press the pads of my fingers into my eyes, wishing I could disappear. Instead, all the move does is make my eyes burn. Because of course they're still covered in a layer of sunscreen.

"Fuck, fuck, fuck," I curse. "That burns."

"Hold on." Izzy's hands are cool on my heated skin as she guides me to sit back down. "I'm going to pour water in your eyes. It'll be cold, but it'll help."

I appreciate the warning, because it's *frigid*. There's no stopping the way I jolt when my senses register the temperature.

"It was in the freezer," she explains when goosebumps pimple my skin. "It's all I have, sorry."

On the plus side, the ice-cold water does wonders for calming my boner.

When she's done with the water, she fetches a towel from her bag of wonders and dabs carefully at my eyes, then urges me to open them slowly.

"They're a little red," she explains, biting her lip as she assesses me in concern. "But I think you'll survive."

"Thanks," I mumble, saying a silent prayer that she never brings up this incident again.

She moves away, blessedly giving me space. Not that there's much of it. It isn't like my boat is huge.

Once she's settled on the bench again, she repositions her book. But a moment after she plucks her bookmark out, she slides it back in and closes it. "What are the odds of seeing any whales today?"

My instinct is to rub at my eyes again, because the amount of skin on display is driving me mad, but I resist the urge. "Your odds are about the same any day, but we'll come out again if we don't see any."

Her eyes light up in a way that has my stomach twisting. "Really?"

"Yeah. You've gotta see your whales, right?"

Her answering smile feels like a kick to the gut. It's bright and pure and genuine.

"Right."

---

HOURS LATER, I'm tired and my stomach is growling in protest. Izzy offered to share her snacks with me, but I can't in good conscience eat her food.

Once we dock and the boat is secured, we head back up to the driveway. We've just reached the truck when Brooks pulls in.

"Hey, man," I call out as he hauls himself out of his truck.

Brooks owns the local plumbing company, and he's one of my go-to subcontractors, so we work together often.

"Hey. Took the boat out? How was it?"

"Yeah." I thumb over my shoulder at Izzy, who's getting settled in the passenger seat. "Izzy was hoping to see whales. No luck today."

Brooks arches a brow and peers around me. "Izzy? You got a girlfriend I haven't heard about?"

With a bark of laughter, I shake my head. "No, she's my daughter's friend. Kind of her boss, I guess. She needed a place to stay while she's in town." I open the vehicle door and step to one side. "Izzy, this is Brooks."

She's frowning at her phone, but when she looks up, she forces a pleasant smile. "Hi," she says. "Nice to meet you."

He dips his chin and waves, and after I've closed the door again, he lets out a whistle. "She's pretty."

"And young," I growl.

He smirks, his chest shaking with barely contained laughter. "Oh, Derrick."

"What's that supposed to mean?"

"Nothing."

For years my friends have been urging me to move on. To date. Fall in love. Get married again.

But it's easier said than done. I lost the person I loved once. What's to say it won't happen again?

Not wanting to get into it with him, I open the back door and toss my hat in, then grasp the handle of the driver's door and throw an "I'll see you soon" over my shoulder.

"Mhm," he says, his tone far too smug for my liking. "Bye."

By the time I'm buckled in and the engine is running, Izzy has tucked her phone away. The happiness she emanated earlier has vanished, and there's a heaviness to her posture.

I hesitate to ask, but I can't just ignore the sadness rolling off her. "What's wrong?"

With a shake of her head, she looks out the window. She doesn't ask to roll it down, nor does she make any move to do it herself. I lower it for her anyway, earning myself the tiniest tip of her lips. The move is almost imperceptible, but I feel like I've won something. I'm not sure what exactly, but it feels good. "You can talk to me, you know," I tell her as I pull out onto the road.

With a sigh, she faces me. "I posted a photo from today on my story and … I don't know what I thought, but I didn't expect to get so many nasty messages."

"What's a story?"

She exhales loudly. "You don't do any social media, do you?"

I shake my head. "Nah, sorry."

"It's a post that's only available for a limited time, like twenty-four hours. Typically, you post something you want to share but that you don't necessarily want to remain out there for the world to see forever."

"Okay?" I ask. "I feel like I'm missing something."

She taps the button on her door to roll up the window, quieting the truck cab so it'll be easier to hear each other. "I don't know how to explain this in a way you'll understand, but long story short, a lot of people on social media hate me right now. It's why I'm here, to get away from it all."

"Hold on." I ease the truck to a stop at a red light. "So that miserable look on your face when I got in the truck was there because people who exist in that stupid box"—I point at her phone—"hurt your feelings?"

"I…" She slumps further. "When you put it that way, it sounds pathetic."

"Those people aren't even *real*. Not to you, anyway. You don't know them. They don't know you. Anything they say is bullshit. You realize that, right?"

Absentmindedly, she rubs at her chin. "Logically, I know you're right, but mean words are still mean words."

"Explain what they're pissed about," I say, and when she grimaces, I add, "If you want." I don't want to make her rehash the issue if it bothers her that much.

"I interviewed Lux a few months back." At my blank expression, she sighs. "She's a pop singer—*the* it girl of the moment. Anyway, I was working for The Tea. They'd given me a list of questions to ask, but they were pretty invasive and…" She trails off with a shrug. "Here we are."

I lower my head and give it a firm shake. When I look back up at her, I have to bite back a smirk. "Do you realize how dumb all of this sounds?"

She regards me with misty eyes, rubbing beneath her nose. "That's usually how it goes when an influencer gets canceled. Sometimes it's legit, but more often than not, it's silly. And no one ever *really* gets canceled. People get bored and move on eventually, but since Lux is so huge, the animosity is hanging over me longer than it should."

"Maybe there's a reason for that," I suggest as I turn onto my street.

"Huh?" In my periphery, her face falls. "You think I deserve this?"

My stomach twists. Shit. "No. I just mean that maybe you were meant to slow down. Live life a little *without* a camera in your face. The last time you were here, I saw you at the coffee shop. Did you know that?"

Brow furrowed, she shakes her head.

"You didn't even notice me because you were too busy talking to a screen."

"I…" Her cheeks redden. "I didn't?"

"I was going to say hi, but you were pretty engrossed. So I figured whatever you were doing must be important."

I put the truck into park in the driveway and cut the engine.

Izzy gapes at me. "I'll always say hi to you, Derrick. I'm sorry I didn't see you."

Shrugging, I pull the keys from the ignition. "Your work is important."

With her lip caught between her teeth, she turns from me and surveys the yard out the window. "It *was*. Now, I'm not so sure." With that, she hops out and tosses that gigantic bag over her shoulder like it weighs nothing. Then she heads for the door without looking back.

After a moment to gather my wits, I follow.

# nine

## Izzy

NOTHING BEATS the feeling of a shower after a day in the sun. The turkey wrap I make for dinner after is a close second, though.

It continues to plague me, what Derrick said about seeing me in the coffee shop. Until that moment, I thought I'd always been hyper aware of him. Sure, I tried to set him up with my sister, even after I discovered my attraction to him, but that was because I don't live here. It was clear the moment I met him that he's not the type for a fling, so it wouldn't have made sense for me to pursue him.

Once I'm settled in bed, I open up my laptop and scour my vlogs from the last time I was here. I spent a lot of time at the coffee shop during that visit, so there's probably a clip from there in almost every video. But I search through each one without luck. I don't see him in any clip.

I should let it go. What's the point, anyway? But it's become this nagging thing, like a hangnail I can't help but pick at.

Next, I search my unused footage—I save stuff for at least six months before I dump it to make space—and that's where I finally come across the video.

I'm sitting at a table with my back to the counter. He comes in and glances my way. The smile that takes over is almost instantaneous. His eyes crinkle at the corners, and his mouth moves in a way that looks like he's saying my name. But I'm oblivious. If I had been wearing headphones, I could understand. But there was no good reason for me to have missed his greeting.

His shoulders fall slightly, and he turns back to the counter and orders. While he waits for his coffee, he peers over at me every now and then. And when he has his drink in hand, he starts toward me. Halfway to me, though, his face hardens, and he shakes his head. He changes course then and heads out of frame and presumably out the door.

A lead ball forms in my stomach.

I didn't notice him. How could I not have sensed him?

I watch the clip again and again and again.

Guilt creeps through me as I cut the clip and save it separately so it's easier to find. It's not the end of the world, of course. I was in the zone, doing my thing. Even so, it still bothers me. And Derrick was right. More often than not, I'm so focused on what's going on inside my phone or through the lens of my camera that I'm missing out on life.

My social media presence has created many opportunities for which I'm grateful for, but I want more. I want a husband and kids. Real, lasting friendships. And social media can't give me that.

I close the laptop and set it on the nightstand. Then I flop back onto the mountain of pillows. Wonton curls up beside me, resting his head on my knee.

Despite the anxiety curling inside me over my social media presence and my future, I manage to fall asleep quickly.

———

IT'S the middle of the afternoon on Monday when Derrick comes bursting through the door, a string of expletives flying from his lips.

With my heart in my throat, I sit up from my reclined position on the couch, setting my book on the coffee table. "Derrick?" I call out.

He doesn't respond. I'm not sure he even realizes I'm here. So I slip off the couch and follow him into the kitchen, where I find him at the sink, fingers laced behind his head, his chest heaving.

"Hey." I place a gentle hand on his back. "What's going on?"

His eyes, full of frustration and maybe even fear, drop to mine. "I should've listened to Jessica."

Frowning, I tilt my head. "Huh? I'm missing something here, big guy."

With a huff, he drops his hands to his sides. "Jessica has been telling me for weeks, months really that I need—"

I shake my head and hold up a finger, urging him to slow down. "Hold on, who's Jessica?"

"She's my receptionist—no, that doesn't sound right. She's more like an assistant. She handles my calls and scheduling. Anything else I need."

"Gotcha." I cross my arms over my chest and lean against the counter. "Go on."

"She's been telling me for months that I need to hire someone to help me while she's on maternity leave." His fingers tremble with agitation when he shoves them through his hair. "I thought I had time. But she went into labor today. It's too early. They were able to stop it, but she's on bed rest, and I don't have the help I need. I told her I could do it myself, but really—"

"I'll do it."

He inhales sharply and zeroes in on me, his eyes wide. "What?"

"I can handle it."

"Izzy." That single word is laced with a heavy dose of doubt. I should probably feel offended, but if anything, it makes me more eager to help, because now I want to prove him wrong. "How?"

"I'm a quick learner. She uses a lot of the same stuff I do for scheduling, so that part should be easy. I'm smarter than I look, you know." I tack on the last bit a tad defensively. The assumption that because I work in social media, I don't know how to function in the physical world irks me.

He rubs his jaw, brows furrowing, and turns away. After a moment, he stiffens and turns back. "Is the dishwasher running?"

"Yeah," I say slowly, dropping my arms to my sides and smirking. "I fixed it."

Confused, he frowns. "You … you fixed the dishwasher?"

My smile grows. "I did."

"How?"

"I watched a YouTube tutorial and figured it out."

He eyes the running dishwasher, then assesses me. I have

no idea how long it hasn't worked, and I wasn't sure I *could* fix it, but I figured it wouldn't hurt to try.

With a sigh, he says, "You're hired."

Giddiness surges through me. I hold my hand out to shake on it. "Thanks, boss man."

"Don't call me that," he grumbles, slipping his hand into mine.

I salute him. "Aye, aye, Captain."

He walks away with a muttered, "What have I gotten myself into?"

---

I RIDE with Derrick the following morning, since he's working in the office for the day rather than on site. I'm fairly certain he's only working in the office to get me settled in and to make sure I don't screw things up.

Until now, I hadn't realized that he owned a store front. Or something close to a storefront, I guess. The main space is filled with samples—floors, counters, tile, and more—and there is a small office space in the back.

"It's rare for anyone to come in," he says, flicking the lights on. "But customers will pop in here and there to look at samples. Typically, I've scheduled it with them, so I'll let you know ahead of time. They can take samples with them, but they should return them within seven days. Just take their name and number before they leave."

Once he's given me the rundown, I set Wonton down and let him check the place out. I didn't exactly ask for permission to bring him, but when I scooped him up and carried him out to the truck, Derrick didn't balk, so I think it's safe to assume he's okay with it.

I settle into a pink chair at the desk that must be Jessica's and take in the items scattered across the surface. Among the stacks of paperwork, there's a *World's Best Mom* mug filled with pens and a dog-eared paperback next to the computer monitor. In a small town like this, it's hard not to wonder if the woman who works for Derrick is the Jessica from book club.

So I shoot off a text to Via. She'll know.

*Yes*, she replies almost instantly.

I turn on Jessica's computer, and when a small screen pops up, notifying me that it needs an update, I sigh. If she's anything like me, she's been putting it off. While it does its thing, I scour the desk and various Post-its full of information. I organize things in a way that makes sense to me, deciding I'll write important information in my own notebook. That should help me keep up with all the things I'll need to learn.

I can feel Derrick watching me while I organize Jessica's desk into a state in which I can function.

When I'm wiping off the surface I've uncovered, he says, "That's the cleanest I've seen this desk since Jessica started."

I pull out my notebook and a pink pen. "Some people thrive in chaos. I'm not one of them." When he continues to watch me, I say, "I don't need a babysitter. If you need to go do something, you can."

"I'm fine right here."

"All right." Refusing to let his scrutiny bother me, I rifle through my purse and pull out my blue light glasses.

A few years ago, I was steadfastly against using them, but I spend hours in front of a screen editing videos and planning other social content, so eventually, I realized the benefit, and they became a must. Now, I don't like to use the computer without them.

"I didn't know you wore glasses."

UNTIL THEN

I type in the password Jessica forwarded to Derrick and familiarize myself with the home screen. "Only when I'm on a screen, which, admittedly, is a lot."

He lets out a gruff sound in reply.

A few hours later, the computer files are organized in a way more suited for me, and I'm moving on to alphabetizing his customer list when Derrick stands and stretches. The groan he lets out has me squeezing my thighs together, and the strip of skin the move exposes above his worn jeans doesn't help me at all.

I hate to admit it, but I've used my vibrator more since moving in with him than I have in the last year combined.

"I'm going to get coffee. You want anything?"

"Ugh, yes." Caffeine is exactly what I need right now.

"Do you want to go with me, take a break, or do you want me to bring something back for you?"

Shooting to my feet, I snatch my purse off the edge of the desk. "I'll go with you. Come on, Wonton." I pat the side of my leg.

Obediently, my little white dog pops up from where he's been snoozing under the desk and scurries over for me so I can put his leash on.

Outside, the sky is a worrisome gray color, but Derrick strolls with his hands in his pockets like nothing is amiss.

"Should we lock up? Bring an umbrella?"

He turns and walks backward, one brow cocked. "It's Parkerville, we don't worry about locking shit up, and so what if it rains? It's not far."

I reply with a hum. I guess he has a point.

Wonton follows after him, his tail wagging eagerly. I can't blame him. If I had a tail, it'd no doubt do the same.

As we approach the coffee shop, I give Derrick my order so

I can walk Wonton a bit more. He's giving me the signals that he needs to go potty, and the last thing I need is for him to have an accident in the office.

Derrick is still in the shop and Wonton has finished his business, so I sit at a table outside to wait. When the wind stirs the hair around my shoulders, I eye the darkening sky with trepidation, hoping we can make it back before the skies open up. Getting rained on won't be the end of the world, but I'd rather not spend the rest of the day hanging out with a wet smelly dog.

The coffee shop door opens, and Derrick steps out with the bottom of both drinks cupped in one massive hand.

I can't help but gape. There's something so hot about that— that his hands are so large and capable that he can handle both cups so easily.

"Hey," he says, in that deep, gruff voice of his.

My heart tugs, and for a minute I let myself pretend he's mine. It's been a while since I dated, and I miss it. My last serious relationship ended after we realized we just weren't a great fit, but for a while there, I hoped we were headed toward marriage and babies.

"Thanks." I take the cup from him and stand.

"I got something for you, too." He plucks a pup cup off the top of his where he's been balancing it and crouches in front of Wonton.

With an eager tail wag, my pup accepts the gift.

Derrick's smile is warm as he watches my little dog lap up the treat. It only takes a minute for Wonton to finish the dollop of whipped cream, and when it's gone, Derrick tosses it into the trash can and we start back to the shop.

Thunder rumbles in the distance, sending skitters of goose bumps along my skin and making me jump.

Derrick curls warm, gentle fingers around my elbow. "It's just thunder."

"I don't like thunderstorms," I confess on a whimper, eyeing the darkening sky.

He assesses me, his thick brows drawing into a nearly straight line and his mouth turned down. "What happened to make you hate them?"

I purse my lips and twist them to one side, hesitant to tell him. It's silly, I suppose, my fear. But I take a steadying breath and go for it. "When I was seven, my dad forgot to pick me up from school after a field trip. The chaperones must have thought I was gone, because they all left. And a storm came through and..." I shrug and lower my focus to our feet. I can feel his sympathetic gaze on me, and I hate the pity there. "I was really scared that day, and that feeling never went away."

"I'm sorry," he says softly, his fingers grazing mine as we walk.

A shiver works its way up my spine, half fear and half excitement from the touch. Attention still fixed on my feet, noting that they are in desperate need of a pedicure, I shrug. "It's dumb."

"No, it's not. Your feelings are valid."

The statement is simple, but it goes a long way in making me feel better. With those simple words, I feel lighter, more understood.

I'm almost smiling, in fact, when we make it back to the store ahead of the rain.

Wonton, hyped up from his pup cup, runs in circles around us, making me laugh in the way only he can. Dogs have a unique ability to cheer a person up without even knowing it.

Derrick scratches at his beard, though one side of his mouth is lifted. "Should I have skipped the pup cup?"

I dismiss his words with a wave of my hand. "He'll calm down soon enough."

At the computer once more, I get to work making calls to check on orders for floor and tile that Jessica has recently placed, hoping for further details so I can update the transaction ledger.

Derrick watches me from his desk, like maybe this is some sort of silent test.

Have I passed? Or does he still think so little of my abilities? I might have an unconventional job, but I'm not totally inept. Not even close to it, really.

What I lack in formal education, I make up for in life experience.

At the end of the day, we shut everything down and flick off the lights. Then, with Wonton tucked under an arm, I make a mad dash for Derrick's truck in an effort to avoid getting soaked to the bone.

He hops in with a grunt and cranks the engine. The temperature has dropped significantly thanks to the summer storm, so he turns off the AC. When I continue to shiver, he taps the button to turn the heat on.

"You okay?" he asks when lightning sparks in the distance.

"I'm okay." I bury my face in Wonton's neck and inhale, calmed by his familiar clean doggy scent.

"I could stop at the diner and—"

"Not a chance, boss man. I'm cooking dinner."

He gives me a sheepish, crooked grin. "You can't blame me for trying." He pulls onto the street, heading toward home, and after a few minutes of quiet, says, "You did good today."

Pride weaves its way through me, and I fail epically at hiding my smile. "Did I pass?"

He rolls his eyes, that grin turning into a smirk. "If you

plan on hanging around for a few months, then yeah, the job is yours if you want it."

"I do. I … I don't plan on going back to LA any time soon." *Or ever.* That part is new, but each day I'm away only gets easier. I don't miss it at all.

"Is it really that bad? This thing with the singer and her fans?"

I twist my lips. "It could be better," I finally answer. "But in the grand scheme of things, no. I've been feeling unsettled for a while, though. I think this was the nudge I needed to get out."

He dips his chin, his attention remaining on the road. "It's okay to outgrow a place. People, too. It happens."

"I know," I whisper, digging my fingers into Wonton's fur. He gives the side of my hand a lick. "But I don't know who I am outside of that life."

He glances over at me as he pulls into the driveway. After he's come to a stop, he puts the truck in park, but he makes no move to get out. "Easy, you're just you—whoever you are now."

I meet his eyes, my chest tightening at the honesty in his expression. "I guess."

"You'll figure it out."

*I hope so.*

As I'm stepping onto the driveway, a giant clap of thunder sounds, startling me. Wonton lets out a scared squeak and leaps from my arms.

"Wonton!" I scream as he darts away from me. "Wonton!" I chase after him, all my own fears of storms melting away.

Derrick curses behind me, his steps loud on the pavement.

At the edge of the driveway, he clutches my elbow and spins me around. I'm already soaked, with my hair plastered to my forehead. He's just as drenched, his shirt sticking to his wide chest and water running down his face.

"What happened?"

"He got scared and jumped out of my arms!" I spin out of his hold, cupping my hands around my mouth. "Wonton!" I call, searching for him. His white fur shouldn't be too hard to spot in the gloom.

As water streams off Derrick's nose, he shoves his long fingers through his wet hair and stares me down, no doubt seeing every bit of the fear that overwhelms me. As much as the storm terrifies me, losing Wonton is so much worse.

"Go into the house—"

"What?" I round on him, my heart pinching. "No!"

"Go into the house," he repeats, pointing a forceful finger. "Stay there in case Wonton comes back. I'll look outside."

"Are you sure?" I ask, my bottom lip trembling, despite the way I try to stop it. "I can—"

"Inside, Izzy."

With a deep exhale, I obey, calling for Wonton as I go. My chest is collapsing in on itself, and my heart has cracked in two. He took off so quickly, and he's not familiar with the area. There's no telling what direction he went. He's wet and scared and—

My thoughts fall away, my brain shutting down into protection mode.

Once I'm inside, I sink to the floor in front of the glass storm door and shiver while I wait.

# ten

### Derrick

I CAN'T FUCKING BELIEVE I'm crawling on the muddy ground under a bush to rescue a fluffy white dog. Not so fluffy now, I suppose, since he's wet. And not quite as pristine white, if he's covered in mud like this. Izzy's mournful cries were like a kick to my gut. Despite her fear of storms, she'd be out here all night looking for him if she had to.

"Come here, bud." I inch closer to him. I'm soaked through, and it'll take a lot of work to get all the mud out of my jeans, but it's worth it if it means I can take this little guy home to his momma.

With a whimper, he cowers, his little body trembling.

I hold my hand out so he can smell my fingers, hoping it reminds him that I'm safe.

Wonton crawls forward an inch, giving me a tiny sniff.

"It's me, bud." I curl my fingers, urging him forward, but instead of coming closer, he backs off.

Another crack of thunder echoes in the sky, quickly followed by a strike of lightning so close it illuminates everything around us.

Wonton takes off again, letting out a yelp.

Cursing, I crawl out from under the bush and scan the yard in search of a flash of white. But visibility is becoming nonexistent in the deluge, making it impossible to see more than a couple of feet in front of me.

"Fuck," I curse, running in the direction I think Wonton went.

I scour the area for another twenty minutes before my boots are so wet, my feet squelch inside them each time I take a step and I'm so chilled I can't stop shivering. Hating to give up but having no other option, I head home. The last thing I want is to see the devastation on Izzy's face when I return empty-handed, but searching on foot like this will do me no good, and I'll be lucky if I don't end up sick.

I call and whistle as I make the trek back to the house, determined to shower and change and head back out in my truck if he hasn't shown up by the time I'm done.

When I pull the storm door open and step inside, I find Izzy curled on the floor in front of me.

Shit. I felt bad before, but this is so much worse.

"Izzy," I whisper.

Her head snaps up, eyes red and puffy from crying. "Did you find him?" She scrambles to her knees, her face falling when she takes in my empty hands.

Despite being soaking wet, I kneel on the floor and take her into my arms.

"C'mere."

She wraps her arms around my neck and holds on, sobbing into the crook of my neck. I'm still so cold my extremities are mostly numb, but I'm not about to let her go.

"He's my best friend." Another sob escapes her, followed by another so strong it racks her body and mine. "And now he's out there all alone and scared."

I cup the back of her head and rock from side to side. "I saw him."

She pulls away from me so abruptly she nearly bonks me on the nose. "You did?"

A heavy sigh escapes me, and my shoulders droop. "I climbed under a bush. I almost had him there, but he got spooked and ran off again. Once I'm showered and changed, I'll take the truck out to look."

It's only then that she fully takes in my current state.

Soaking wet.

Covered in mud.

I sneeze, turning my head just in time to keep from hitting her with the force of it.

"Fuck." Her hands flutter around my body like butterflies, but neither lands on me. "You need to get out of these clothes."

I fucking hate that my brain immediately thinks about *her* taking my clothes off. Fuck. I'm an asshole.

Clearing my throat, I gently slide her off my lap and stand. Then I hold a hand out and help her up.

"Maybe by the time I'm cleaned up, the storm will have let up."

Her bottom lip trembles, and I can't resist putting my thumb there.

"Hey," I soothe. "We're going to find him."

I'll stay out all night long if I have to. There's no way I'll stop until the little guy is home.

She nods woodenly, full of uncertainty. I can't blame her.

I hesitate for a second longer before letting my thumb drop from her mouth. Then I take the stairs two at a time to get away from her before I do something stupid.

I'm still shivering violently as I kick my boots off and head for the sanctuary of my shower. I redid the bathrooms about three years ago, and since then, I've kicked myself for not doing it sooner. I live for the rainfall shower and multiple sprayers at the end of a long workday.

Unfortunately, luxuriating in here will have to wait. Eager to get back outside to look for Wonton, I take a shower so quick, it reminds me of the days my kids were babies and time to myself was nonexistent.

Outside the window, the rain is still coming down, but it's eased up significantly.

Still, I pull on a pair of jeans and a sweatshirt, then dig out my raincoat.

Downstairs, Izzy is curled up on the couch, her eyes redder than before.

"Come on." I jerk my head at the door. "Let's go."

Without hesitation, she scoops her own rain jacket off the cushion beside her. Then she slips her feet into a pair of boots.

"He has to be so scared," she says in a soft whimper as we're creeping down the road.

"Or maybe he's having the greatest adventure of his life," I counter, though I'm pretty sure the small dog is terrified out of his mind.

She rolls down the window and calls his name, then turns back to me, her lip caught between her teeth. "How far do you think he could've gotten?"

With a deep inhale, I tap my fingers against the steering

wheel. "Even scared, I don't think he would've gone far. He's probably hunkered down—"

"Wonton!" she screams as she throws the door open and undoes her seat belt.

I manage to slam on the brakes before she leaps from the car.

"Wonton!" she cries, running for the sopping wet dog who's crouched by the front steps of a house a few streets over from mine.

He wags his tail, but he makes no move to get up.

Worried that he's injured, I hop out of the truck and jog through the rain that's lightened up dramatically. Near the house, Izzy drops to her knees and scoops the dog against her chest.

She buries her face in his neck, shoulders shaking with heavy sobs. "I'm so happy you're okay." Her voice cracks on the last word.

She stands carefully and turns back to the truck, only to halt when she sees me.

"Thank you." She crosses the distance between us and tips her head back, not the least bit fazed by the rain running down her face. "Thank you for looking for him in the rain and for coming back out now. Just … thank you."

She stands on her tiptoes and brushes a gentle kiss to my cheek. My skin burns from the touch.

"I guess we can get dinner from the diner after all," she says with a pat to my chest before she heads back to the truck. "I certainly don't feel like cooking now."

Her flippant tone after the chaos of the past two hours or so has me throwing my head back and laughing.

IZZY IS CURLED up on the couch with her food while Wonton runs around in circles, then scoots along the carpet, drying himself off from the bath she just gave him.

Biting into her BLT, she watches her dog, her eyes twinkling.

"God, I'm so glad he's okay."

Plate in hand, I sit beside her on the couch. "I am, too."

She bumps my arm lightly with her elbow. "He's grown on you, hasn't he?"

"He's impossible to resist," I admit, watching him spread himself out on the floor and push off with his back feet.

Her smile is wide, pleased. When she turns back to her dog, she affects the dog baby voice that should annoy me but only endears me to her further. "That's right, because who's a good boy? You're a good boy. No one can resist your charms. Not even Mr. Grumpy Pants."

"Grumpy Pants," I huff. "The nerve. Insulting me after I was out in the pouring rain crawling through mud after *your* dog."

"You're right. I'm sorry." She leans over, and at the same time, I shift in my seat, unaware that she was planning to plant a kiss on my cheek. The move causes her lips to land on the corner of my mouth instead. It's not a real kiss, but fuck is it close.

We both freeze, breaths held and eyes wide.

She moves away first, face flaming red. "Sorry," she mumbles, looking down at the to-go box in her lap. "That was ... sorry. I didn't mean to."

"S'okay," I mutter. I reach for my Coke, though I watch her out of the corner of my eye.

She's fucking cute. Her long, dark hair is pulled up into a

high ponytail, and she's dressed in a white tank top, gray shorts, and a pair of white fuzzy socks.

I quickly avert my attention to my drink before she can catch me checking her out.

Wonton, adorable menace that he is, hops up on the couch between us and shakes his damp body.

"Wonton," Izzy laughs, breaking the tension between us. "That's not nice." With her next breath, she's distraught, her eyes filling with tears. "Buddy, I don't know what I would've done if we didn't find you." She peers up at me, sniffling. "That was the worst couple of hours of my life. I'm not exaggerating."

"All that matters is he's here and he's safe."

She slips a piece of bacon from her sandwich and holds it out to the dog. "Should I put *Gilmore Girls* on again?"

I'd appreciate the distraction. It'll help me to avoid thoughts of the not-really-a-kiss and the fact that my dick didn't get the memo.

"Sure."

With a hum, she cues up the show, then settles her back against the couch.

Though focusing on the TV helps, I can't stop myself from stealing glances at her every now and again. If she notices, she doesn't show it.

I spend the next hour or so trying to focus on the storyline while getting lost in thoughts about Izzy. I can't help thinking about how she's only been here a short time and dreading what it'll be like when I'm alone again.

# eleven

## Izzy

THE BOAT ROCKS from side to side lazily, the rhythm soothing in a way I've never experienced before. I didn't quite believe Derrick when he said he'd bring me out on the boat, knowing how infrequently he uses it, so it was a pleasant surprise when he suggested we spend the day on the water again.

I rest my knees on the cushioned seat, arms crossed on the fiberglass edge of the boat, and scan the waters for any sign of whales. How disappointing it must be for people who pay for whale-watching trips while on vacation, only to come across none.

Derrick shuffles items around in the cooler he dragged along. "Water?"

I shift to face him. "Sure."

He tosses an ice-cold bottle to me, and I nearly drop it.

"You put sunscreen on, right?" I joke as I shake the bottle to remove the excess water on the outside of it.

With a muttered curse, he pinches the bridge of his nose. "Yes, Izzy. I don't need your ... assistance in that department this time."

Giggling, I twist the cap off my water and peer at him over my shoulder. Perhaps it's wrong to be this attracted to a man almost twice my age—my assistant's dad, at that—but I can't help it. His energy draws me in. He's magnetic in an accidental way.

He slides his sunglasses on and looks out at the water.

"Think we'll see any today?" I ask him.

With a shrug, he tugs his shirt away from his skin. "You never know."

I watch for another few minutes, then decide I'll settle down with my book.

"I didn't expect you to be such a reader."

Slipping my bookmark out, I peek at Derrick over the top of the page. "I feel like I should be insulted."

He grimaces. "I didn't mean it in a bad way. I just figured you were too busy for that." He wiggles the fingers of his right hand at my book when he says *that*.

I can't help but shoot him a smirk. "I'm full of surprises."

The breath that gusts out of him is half exhausted, half amused. "That you are."

---

"WE BETTER HEAD IN," he says about two hours later.

I set my book down and stifle a yawn. "I didn't realize it was getting so late."

He lifts his hat off his head and uses an arm to swipe at his forehead. "I'm sorry you didn't see any whales today."

Straightening, I tuck my book back into my bag. "It'll happen." I feel certain of it. "Good things come to those who wait, right?"

"I don't know about that." His shoulders droop a little, and his smile is self-deprecating in a way that makes me want to backtrack. "If that were true ... well, suffice it to say I've been waiting a long time."

"What is it you're waiting for?" I dare to ask, angling forward to study him.

He drops his head, his forearms resting on his knees. "It's selfish."

With a quiet snort, I tuck a piece of hair behind my ear. "I doubt that."

Derrick might be the least selfish person I know.

His cheeks hollow, and for a minute he's quiet. Eventually, he blows out a long breath and focuses on me. "I loved my wife very much, and moving on hasn't been easy, but I still ... want that. A partner, a lover, a best friend."

My heart clenches at the longing in his tone and the sadness etched in the lines on his face. "You can have that."

He surveys the ocean, squinting against the light despite his sunglasses. "I'm not so sure."

"Why is that?" I press, even though I probably shouldn't.

"I haven't dated much, but in my limited experience, I haven't found anything even close to a meaningful connection. I'm not sure there's another right person out there for me. Maybe I need to find a way to be okay with that. Maybe it's better if I'm alone. I wouldn't have to worry about being hurt again. For a long time..." He swallows audibly, clears his throat. "I thought I'd never feel normal again. Honestly, if I hadn't had to go on for my kids, I'm not sure I would've survived it."

It's a stab in the gut, knowing he feels as though he can't have love again. If there's anyone in this world who deserves to find it, it's Derrick.

For an instant, I lose my mind and am tempted to tell him that *I'm* standing right here. But I bite my tongue. I can't stand the thought of his rejection.

Instead, I plaster on a smile. "Let me make a dating profile for you."

He blinks at me, confused. "A dating profile?"

My chest tightens, but I push the sensation away. This will be good for him. "Yeah, you know, on an app."

"Fuck no," he sputters. "No thanks." He swishes his arms through the air in an X motion like he can banish the thought from existence.

"Come on." I elbow his side in a playful attempt to deflect from how this topic has me wanting to hurl over the side of the boat. "They're not so terrible."

*I'm such a liar. Dating apps are the literal worst.*

He *harrumphs*. "I'm too old for that shit."

"I'll take the photos for you."

*Shit. Why am I so determined to get him to agree? It doesn't bode well for me and my stupid crush if he gives in.*

He gives me a thorough once-over, lips pursed. "No."

Relief washes over me. I clench my jaw tight and sit on my hands in an effort to keep myself from saying or doing something I shouldn't, and he doesn't broach the subject again.

A short time later, we dock, finding Brooks and his family grilling hotdogs and burgers in the backyard.

"You two hungry?" Brooks asks, waving us over. "We have plenty of food."

Derrick looks to me, gauging my interest, so I give him a shrug. I'm fine with sticking around for a bit.

When we reach the group, Brooks shakes my hand. "It's good to see you again, Izzy. This is my wife, Maura." He points to a middle-aged woman sitting at the picnic table with a glass of wine. "My daughter Amanda and her girlfriend Felicity." A nod toward the couple cozied up on an outdoor love seat.

They can't be older than sixteen, and it's obvious they're in that sickeningly sweet state of puppy love that makes me smile.

"And last but certainly not least, is Jackson. Our wild child." He points to a little boy running in circles with a golden retriever. "Take a seat and help yourself to snacks."

With a grateful nod, I leave Derrick with Brooks and join Maura at the picnic table. Once I'm settled, I put a handful of chips on a plate, then add a dollop of dip.

"It's nice to meet you," I say to Maura.

She sets her phone aside. "Nice to meet you, too. It's good to see Derrick *actually* using the boat and doing something other than work."

I look over my shoulder at him. He and Brooks are chatting, having migrated to the dock, both with beers in hand. As I'm watching, Jackson barrels into him, looping his arms around Derrick's legs.

"How old is Jackson?" I ask, turning my attention back to Maura.

"Six," she answers with a wistful smile. "Total surprise. A wanted one, but a surprise, nonetheless. We struggled with infertility after we had Amanda and had given up on more children. Then Jackson happened." She wraps her fingers around the wine bottle and gives it a wiggle. "Want any?"

"I'll never say no to wine."

She grabs a red plastic cup from a small stack at the end of the table and fills it with a serving.

I thank her and take a sip, appreciating the crisp flavor, even if drinking wine out of a plastic cup is far less appealing than from a wineglass.

"Brooks said you're staying with Derrick for the summer?"

I turn my attention from the cup to Maura. Her dark curls are cut to her chin, the style so gorgeous it has me pulling at the ends of my hair, wondering if I should do a chop.

"Yeah, my sister is Via. She's dating—"

"Reid," she finishes for me with a nod. "He's a good guy."

"He is." I take a sip of wine and leave it at that, because I don't have the first clue where she's going with that comment.

"So is Derrick."

Stomach dipping, I meet her eye, unable to ignore the tiny smile fluttering at the edge of her lips like it's desperate to break free.

I don't know what has the words flying out of my mouth, but I ask, "Are you suggesting I date him?"

She shrugs, and the smile breaks free. "You're quite a bit younger than he is, but I wouldn't judge. He deserves to find someone who cares about him. Age shouldn't stop that." She wrinkles her nose. "Unless it's illegal, but you don't look *that* young."

A bark of a laugh escapes me. "I don't know whether to say thank you or be offended."

With a laugh, she shakes her head in a way that makes her curls bounce. "Sorry. I may have already had a bit too much to drink. I don't drink much, so I'm a lightweight."

"It's okay." I'm not offended in the least. It takes a lot to ruffle my feathers. Like an entire army of Luxonators coming after me.

"I want him to be happy," she goes on, undeterred. "He's made comments about dating here and there over the years, but then..." She swirls the wine in her glass. "Nothing comes of it."

Before I can stop myself, I blurt out, "I offered to set up a profile for him on a dating app."

Maura's eyes light up, and she straightens. "Now, *that* is a great idea."

"Izzy, you want a hot dog or a burger?" Derrick asks, suddenly much closer than I realized.

Cheeks heating—because, shit, I hope he didn't hear us talking about him—I say, "Always a burger."

With a nod, he saunters back to the grill, where Brooks is removing the hot dogs.

Maura snaps her fingers, the action bringing my attention back to her. "Wait, are you the woman Layla works for?"

I lift my cup in the air and give her a wry smile. "That'd be me."

"Amanda looked you up. Said you're pretty famous."

My heart lurches a little, and I swallow back my nerves. "I don't know about *that*. I'm not a celebrity. I just post videos." I stare down at my cup. In LA, it's easier to feel confident about what I do and the following I've built. Here, though, where life feels so *normal*, I feel uncomfortable talking about that part of my life.

"Regardless of how you want to frame it, it sounds like you're very successful."

Lips pressed together, I dip my chin in acceptance, grateful for her perspective and kindness. When I look up again,

Derrick is waving me over to the grill. So I give Maura a small smile, then I stand and head over to his side.

"What's up?"

He holds up a plate. "What do you want on your burger?"

"Oh." I contemplate the spread of condiments set up on the foldable table beside the grill. "I can do that." Stepping closer, I reach for the plate, but he holds it out of my reach.

"I got it."

"Um, all right." I bite my lip. "Cheddar cheese." I point and he adds it to my bun. "Onion, pickles, mayo, and mustard."

He adds the toppings and assembles my burger. "Here you go."

"Thanks," I say, taking the plate.

Our fingers brush as he releases it, causing a shiver to skate up my spine.

He frowns in confusion, his head tilted. "Are you cold?"

"No." With that, I scurry away, head lowered.

*Twenty-seven. You are twenty-seven years old. You're on the cusp of thirty. Why are you acting like a nervous, flighty teenager?*

I want to crawl into a hole and hide away.

Instead, I force myself to return to my seat. Maura raises a brow at my plate as I get settled, then looks at Derrick, shaking her head in amusement. "He might not realize it yet, but he's into you."

I take a bite so large there's no chance that I can respond. I stick with a shake of my head instead.

Maura gives me a knowing look. "We'll see."

# twelve

### Derrick

IZZY SPINS away from the computer, shoving her glasses into her hair as she goes.

"You know"—she drawls, crossing her legs, which makes her skirt inch higher up her thigh—"it was my understanding that you spent most of your time out in the field, yet since I started, you've been sitting at that desk day in and day out."

"I ... well..."

She bites her lip, but her grin is too big to hide. "It's like you don't trust me to handle this job. It's been almost two weeks. Have I not proven myself competent yet?"

She certainly has. She might even be better than Jessica—not that I'd ever tell either one of them that.

"I've got things to handle here right now," I lie, brushing my fingers over my lips. "It has nothing to do with you."

"Mhm," she hums, that dangerous smile still large. She spins the chair again in a circle and stops when she's facing me. "We should go on a field trip."

"A field trip?" Confusion drips from my words.

"Yeah, to one of your projects. Let me put on a hard hat and some work boots and get dirty." She winks, the gesture pure sass.

I'd like to get her dirty in a different way. Maybe by shoving her over the desk and yanking up her skirt. I'd slide her underwear to the side, see if she was wet and—

My stomach drops. *What the fuck are you doing thinking about her like that?*

It's a terrible idea, but I still find myself saying, "You really want to see a jobsite?"

"Absolutely." She nods, her smile less calculating and more genuine. "I'd love to know what all these phone calls and emails result in."

Doing my best to shove my previous thoughts away, I shut off my computer and stand. "All right, come on."

Her eyes go round like saucers. "Really? It was that easy?"

"Don't make me change my mind," I growl, heading for the door. "I'll meet you at the truck. I'm going for coffee."

When I return five minutes later, she's in the truck with Wonton sitting on the center console, his tongue hanging out.

I hop in, passing her a matcha.

"Thank you." She accepts the cup and takes a generous sip. "Perfection, as always. I can't believe I didn't know your storefront was here. Every time I've visited, I've spent at least a few hours working at that coffee shop."

I put the truck in reverse and lift a shoulder. "It's not like I have a big sign out front."

"Yeah." She eyes the front of the building as I pull away. "About that … I think you should add one."

I don't need to even think before I respond. "No."

An exaggerated puff of air escapes her. "Why not?"

"I get plenty of business without it. Word of mouth is all I need."

"You're so…" She struggles to find words as she sets her cup in the holder between us.

"Old?" I suggest, my chest pinching in frustration.

Frowning, she picks at the frayed edge of her shorts.

I jerk my gaze away, focusing back on the road, and take a cleansing breath in.

"I was going to say set in your ways, but if that's how you want to frame it, then I guess … yeah."

I have no response. Either way, I suppose she's right. We're silent for the rest of the drive, the atmosphere awkward thanks to me.

I pull up outside what used to be a bank a few towns over. My team has been refurbishing the place with the goal of turning it into a party venue.

Handing Izzy a spare hard hat from the back seat, I say, "Wonton can't go in. I'll leave the truck running."

She nods, then presses a kiss to the top of her dog's head. I've never met another person who loves their dog the way Izzy loves hers.

Massive stone columns flank the double set of doors of the main entrance. They're heavy and old, but intricately carved. Originally, our customer requested we remove them, but I convinced him to let them stay, encouraging him to preserve some of the history here. I can't help but smile every time I see them. While much of what I do requires me to update older structures, I love to maintain original work if it's sound and can be worked into the design.

Izzy follows me inside, head swiveling, taking it all in. All that's left here are a few finishing touches, but sometimes those small details take the longest.

"This place is gorgeous," she says, her voice echoing off the blank walls and tall ceiling. "Wow." She spins in front of me. "This is spectacular, Derrick. Truly."

Her praise shouldn't mean any more to me than the average person's, but fuck if it doesn't mean *everything*.

"You like it?"

"I love it."

Above, on a set of scaffolding, Larry says, "Hey, boss. How's it going?"

Izzy's eyes shine. "Boss man," she mouths.

"Good," I call back. "Looks like you guys will be wrapping up soon."

"That's the hope. Haven't seen you around much lately."

With a sigh, I shove my hands into the pockets of my shorts. "Been busy."

Larry smirks, his attention shifting to Izzy, who's walked away from me to take in the back area where we've kept a wall of safe-deposit boxes.

"I can tell."

Glowering up at him, I walk away, gritting my teeth and ignoring the way he chuckles.

As I approach, Izzy turns, her face lit up. "Do you have before pictures? I'd love to see how it started."

"Sure, back at the store."

The way her eyes are glowing when she looks at me shouldn't make me feel this way. Like she's the whole world and I haven't been living until now. It's *wrong*. I had a wife, and I loved her very much. I still love her, even after all these years. To make matters worse, Izzy is *young*. Twenty-seven. Layla's age. She has her whole life ahead of her, and I—well, I don't have one foot in the grave, but it feels wrong to rob her of the things she should experience if she were involved with someone her own age.

Clearing my throat, I step away and let her take the rest of the place in. Though by the way her eyes keep darting back to me, it's clear she's confused by my sudden distance.

How can I explain that I'm simultaneously drawn to her like a moth to a flame and terrified of the fire?

We don't hang around for long, and the moment we're back in the car and Izzy has removed the hard hat and smoothed down her hair, she says, "Can I see more?"

I know it shouldn't matter, but my heart expands with pride at her excitement. At the knowledge that she wants to see more, that she so obviously cares about something I'm passionate about. It's been a long time since someone truly cared about my interests the way she does. She *genuinely* wants to be a part of this.

Several hours later, several *projects* later, we return to the shop to work for another hour before heading home.

Izzy put her hair up a while ago, but now she lets it down. I have to fight the urge to run my fingers through the dark wavy strands that fall halfway down her back to see if it's as soft as it looks.

"That was so much fun." She drops into her chair, making it spin slightly. "I understand why you love this." Clutching the edge of her desk, she rights her chair and straightens, then wiggles her mouse to wake up her computer. "Taking something and tearing it down to the bare studs only to create something new? Incredible." She lets out a wistful sigh. "Do you have any projects starting soon? Would you let me film one from start to finish for my channel?"

I cock my head and take her in: the slightly mussed hair, the bright eyes, the pink cheeks. "Projects can take months."

"I-I know," she stutters.

"Do you plan to be in town that long?"

Ducking, she tucks a piece of hair behind her ear. "I ... yeah, I think so. If I get to be too much, though, let me know. I'll look for an apartment."

"An apartment?" I raise a brow. "That *is* long-term thinking." I hesitate before saying it, but ultimately decide to blurt it out. "You're not going back to LA, are you?"

For a moment, she watches me, trepidation taking over her excitement. Then she gives a slow, subtle shake of her head. "I don't plan on it. I don't know when I first realized it, but I'm so much happier here. The idea of going back feels ... suffocating." She bites her lip and slowly meets my eye like a tentative, wounded animal.

My gut clenches at the uncertainty swimming in those green depths. *Does she think I'm going to kick her out of my house? Tell her it's a horrible idea?*

"You should do what makes you happy."

Her responding smile is small, nervous. "I'm still not sure what that means for me, but regardless of all the *drama*"—she sticks her tongue out in disgust—"it was the wake-up call I needed. I've always loved what I do, and I don't want to stop, but it's time for me to pivot."

"Well"—I lean my chair back, going for a casualness I don't feel—"you're welcome to stay with me for as long as you need."

"I appreciate it." The smile she gives me this time seems happier, more genuine.

When she turns back to the computer, she even sits taller, like she's been carrying a weight around. Like my simple offer of support has lightened that load.

Like maybe I've given her a renewed sense of purpose.

# thirteen

## Izzy

"I CAN'T BELIEVE I'm doing this," Derrick grumbles, though he makes no move to pull away from me.

"It's face mask night," I say, spreading a charcoal mask over his forehead and cheeks. "You *have* to join in."

He makes a huffing noise, but that's the extent of his argument. I take it as a win, since he remains steady and doesn't fight me as I continue my work. His attention stays fixed on me as I spread a thick layer over his skin, making it hard to ignore how close our bodies are in this tiny hall bathroom. He's propped up against the sink, and there are only a few inches between his chest and mine. I have no doubt my nipples are hard, since our proximity is all I can think about. Dammit, why didn't I put a bra on after my shower?

As if he heard me cursing myself, he lowers his gaze to my

119

chest before quickly looking away. His Adam's apple bobs when he clears his throat.

It's on the tip of my tongue to tell him it's okay to look. That I *want* him to look, but the fear of rejection keeps the words at bay. I can handle it when a guy isn't into me, but I'm not sure I could handle it if *this* guy wasn't into me.

When I'm finished with the mask, I step to my left and wash my hands. The move, unfortunately, brings us elbow to elbow and hip to hip. Unless he moves, there's no way around it. "All done," I whisper softly.

Finally, he straightens and moves past me, but not until after he gives my hip a soft pinch. "My face better be as smooth as a baby's butt after this."

Laughing, I dry my hands on the towel that hangs from the ring on the wall. "I'm not sure about that, but your pores will look *fantastic*."

"That'll have to be enough, I guess." He smiles, his eyes crinkling at the corners.

As I turn, I find him standing in the doorway, blocking my exit, and my stupid, treacherous mind wonders what it would be like if he leaned down and kissed me. Backed me up against the sink and lifted me onto the counter. His mouth on mine. His hands on my skin. His scent invading my nose.

I have to bite my lip to keep a moan from escaping.

I desperately need my vibrator, but that will have to wait.

Finally, after an awkward moment of silence, he moves away from the door, taking my fantasy with him and down the stairs.

I count to thirty before I follow.

"Popcorn?" I ask, already pulling a box out of the pantry.

"Sure." He picks up a piece of homemade pizza we haven't cleaned up yet and takes a bite. He insisted he wasn't going to like the feta and apple flatbread pizza, but then devoured his in its entirety.

"That's *my* piece," I scold him, but there's no malice in my tone. Only pure amusement. The man still doubts me in the kitchen, but with any luck, he'll change his mind soon. Except for the tofu tacos last week, he's enjoyed all the meals I've made.

He smiles and takes another bite. "Do you ever film cooking videos on your channel?"

"No." I stick the popcorn bag into the microwave and push the button, then turn back to him. With my elbows propped on the island, I rest my chin in my hands. "Cooking is for me. I don't want to make it feel like a job. Setting up a camera and talking through every step, then editing and blah, blah, blah? That's like work, and I don't want to risk ruining something I love."

Brows lowered, he lets out a thoughtful hum. "I never thought about that—how whatever you film, even if it's something you've always loved, becomes a job."

"I keep certain things to myself," I admit, tapping my nails against my cheek. "I cherish them more because they're only for me. I was thinking…" I wet my lips, working up the nerve to broach this subject. "If you're cool with me filming a project for my channel—you never gave me an answer when I asked—would you also be willing to let me help with design choices?"

He gives a gruff laugh, pulling out a kitchen chair. He plops into it and crosses his arms. The light above the table bathes him in an orange glow. "I'm not HGTV, Izzy."

"I know. But I…"

He doesn't let me flounder for words long. "Film, help, do whatever you want."

Hope blooms in my chest. For the first time in months, genuine excitement consumes me.

It's tempered a fraction when the microwave chimes. So I pull it out, tear the bag open, and dump the contents into the large bowl.

"Want any other snacks?" Derrick asks. "I made brownies."

I freeze, bowl clutched to my chest, breath catching. "Brownies? When?"

"While you were taking a nap."

"And you're just now telling me?" I chastise teasingly. "Blasphemous."

A tiny grin spreads his lips. "I'll grab them."

While he does that, I scurry into the family room with the popcorn and get comfortable. My couch in LA is for show rather than comfort. It never bothered me before now. I've played into that lifestyle for so long that I never considered choosing furniture with different priorities in mind. But that's just one of many things about my life that have left me unsatisfied. I don't regret my career or my move to LA. It was the right move for me at the time, and the location was the right place to be for my goals. But I've outgrown it.

Derrick settles beside me with a tray full of brownies. His added weight causes me to dip closer to him. He doesn't say a word when he leans forward to set the brownies on the table and my toes bump his leg.

I cue up the show, and we settle into companionable silence. We keep the popcorn between us, both sneaking pieces to Wonton periodically. I'm still not over the night he got spooked and ran away. Losing my furry best friend is a devastation I don't want to contemplate.

"Is this supposed to feel crunchy?" Derrick asks, wiggling his nose in a way that makes the mask crack.

"It hardens as it dries." I try not to laugh at the way he grimaces.

He huffs lightly. "The things you women do for beauty."

"It's worth it. You'll see."

It's totally possible he won't agree, but I love how soft my skin is after I rinse it off.

When the episode of *Gilmore Girls* is over, we head upstairs to wash off our masks. I've just rinsed the last bit off my face when Derrick calls out to me from his bathroom. "It won't come off! Help me!"

I dry my face on a fluffy towel, chuckling, then pad into his room.

I've never crossed this threshold before. Bedrooms are sacred spaces. One must be invited in like a vampire before entering. A large, warm-colored rug covers the majority of the hardwood floor, and his king-size bed is set between two windows. The headboard is made of a dark fabric that's both masculine and stylish, adding to the aesthetic of the whole cozy room.

"Did you decorate your room yourself?" I ask when I join him in the bathroom.

He looks up with his hands still on his face and the mask smeared all over him and into his facial hair. "Yeah. Why?"

I glance back over my shoulder. There's a bookcase beside his dresser, filled with books and other memorabilia. And … oh, wow. An old record player and a neat stack of vinyls on the floor.

"It's beautiful," I finally answer after a prolonged staring session. "You really like records, huh? I have a small collection back in LA. There's a record store attached to a coffee shop down the street from my apartment. It's one of my favorite places to go."

He arches a brow, top lip twitching with amusement at my word vomit. "Nothing beats vinyl."

"That's where Reid gets his love for it, huh?"

He doesn't answer me, but his eyes get heavy, and the air thickens with tension. Our bodies seem to draw into one another.

*Kiss me. He's going to kiss me.*

I'm ready for it.

Prepared.

*Craving.*

Wonton barks downstairs, dissolving the moment. It goes up like a cloud of smoke as we both startle back.

Derrick turns back to the mirror. "I tried to get it off, and it just..." He shrugs in a helpless way. "It keeps getting everywhere."

"Dampen your face again."

He leans over the sink and does as I've said and then I carefully wipe at the remaining mask with a cloth.

"Add more water."

We work together until there isn't even a speck of mask left in his beard.

Once I've rinsed the washcloth and he's patted his face dry, we hesitate, watching each other in the mirror. But he doesn't let it linger. With a thick swallow, he turns the light off and leads the way back downstairs.

We settle on the couch, pretending nothing at all happened upstairs. All the while, my body aches with want from the kiss that never was.

"Brownie?" Derrick asks.

I want to say no. I'm not in the mood for one now, but it'll keep my mouth occupied and hopefully distract me from my thoughts. So I say, "Sure."

When he holds the plate out to me, I thank him and take a square, the texture perfectly chewy. And when I take a bite? It takes all my strength not to moan.

Yep, perfection.

Can he do nothing wrong? It would go a long way in calming my raging hormones if he had at least a flaw or two. His love for bacon and processed foods drives me a wee bit crazy, but it's not enough to keep my libido in check.

As I finish my brownie, Wonton sniffs the blanket, searching for crumbs, and because I'm a paranoid dog mom, I give him a gentle shove away and make sure there are none.

With a sigh, I lie on my side and prop my head on a throw pillow. Onscreen, Lorelei and Rory get up to all their antics.

"Who's your favorite character so far?" I ask Derrick.

He purses his lips, giving my question some serious thought, which I appreciate. Anything *Gilmore Girls* related is serious business.

"I like the mom."

"Lorelei?"

He shakes his head. "No, her mom."

I blink at him, flabbergasted. "You're an Emily fan? I'm horrified." Even though I love Emily *now*, I'd hardly expect her to be a first-time watcher's favorite character.

He shrugs. "I think she's misunderstood. She doesn't always go about things in the right way. But it's clear she's been hurt in the past—probably her own upbringing—so healthy communication isn't her strong suit. It's obvious she loves Lorelei, though, even if she doesn't say it."

I'm quiet for a moment. "That isn't at all who I thought you'd pick."

He chuckles and pulls my feet onto his lap, eliciting a squeak of surprise from me. "Who'd you think I'd pick?"

Ignoring the way my heart rate has increased, I clear my throat. "Luke."

Derrick lifts one shoulder and lets it fall. "I like Luke, but my favorite is definitely Emily."

"I truly don't know what to do with this shocking piece of information." I grin.

In response, Derrick digs his thumb into the arch of my foot.

Eyes rolling back, I groan with pleasure. "That feels good."

He does it again, and before I know it, he's massaging my feet.

With his hands on my body like this, it's next to impossible to avoid thinking about the almost-kiss.

*I'm not crazy, right? He wanted to kiss me.*

Doubts settle into my mind. Could I have imagined the whole thing?

My mind spirals, and when I can't take it anymore, I pull my feet from his grasp and pause the show. "I'm tired. I need to go to bed," I blurt out in a gasping breath.

More like I need to go to my room so I can pull out my vibrator and pretend it's not Derrick I'm thinking about.

Face scrunched with confusion, he stutters, "I ... okay."

Wonton happily follows me up the stairs to bed, where I close the door and lean my back against it.

I need to get over this ridiculous crush.

It's not good for me or my sanity.

# fourteen

## Derrick

AFTER LAYLA and Lili moved out, time felt sluggish. But since Izzy's arrival in May, the hours and days move by at a rapid pace, one that makes me want to hold on with both hands and beg it to slow down. To give me time to think, to catch my breath, to just *be*.

The Fourth of July has been a low-key affair for the past couple of years. I haven't bothered to take the boat out since my kids typically prefer spending it with their friends.

I can't blame them for not wanting to hang out with their dad, even if it stings. That's one of the hard parts of being a parent—for years, life revolves around those precious beings. Days are spent caring for them, parents are attuned to their needs and their wants. Then the kids grow up, and suddenly they have their own lives.

When Izzy mentioned taking the boat out for the Fourth, I

was quick to say yes. Until then, it hadn't hit me how badly I need to have something to do, something to look forward to.

"Maybe this will be the day I see whales."

Beside me, she carries a small yellow and white cooler. I've never seen it before, so it must be a new purchase. It was unnecessary. If she'd mentioned needing a cooler, I would have pulled out one of the three I've got stored in the garage. Her tiny hot pink bikini top is missing today. It's been replaced by a white one dotted with cherries. Fucking cherries. Her usual jean shorts sit low on her hips, the barest hint of her matching bikini bottoms poking out. Her bright yellow plastic flip-flops match the yellow towel slung over her shoulder, and her dark hair is pulled up in a high ponytail—one I can't seem to stop myself from tugging on like an obnoxious boy on the playground.

Side-eyeing me, she says, "Reid and Via should be here shortly, and Layla said she's already—"

"Grandpa!"

Lili barrels through the yard toward me, her legs carrying her as fast as they can go.

She's growing up way too fast.

"Hey, pumpkin." When she launches herself at me, I scoop her up and kiss her cheek. "Are you excited about taking the boat out today?"

"*So* excited," she says as I set her back on her feet. "Am I old enough to go tubing yet?" She clasps her hands beneath her chin. "Please, oh, please say I am!"

I thought that as I got older, as my kids got older, they'd stress me out less. What I didn't account for was grandchildren. Somehow, I think most of my gray hairs are from Lili.

"We'll talk to your mom about it."

I send up a silent prayer that Layla will shoot down the idea so I don't have to be the bad guy.

"Yay!" Lili throws her arms in the air and takes off toward her mom, who's just now making her way around the house.

Beside me, Izzy's lips twitch in amusement.

"What?" The word is a gruff exhale.

"Oh, nothing," she singsongs.

"Spit it out."

Her tote slips down her shoulder, and I mindlessly slide it back up.

"You deflected Lili's question like a pro. Now the ball is in Layla's court, and you're banking on her telling Lili she can't. That way, you don't have to be the bad guy."

I narrow my eyes on her, and her grin gets bigger.

"You don't have to tell me I'm right," she says flippantly. "I know I am."

"Give me that," I gripe, grasping the handle of the cooler.

"I've got it," she insists, just like she did when we got out of the car.

Once we reach the dock, she waits for Layla and Lili to catch up, and I get the boat ready.

Ten minutes later, we're loaded up, and Lili is strapped into a life vest that I put on her myself so I could make sure the straps were secure. But Reid and Via still haven't arrived.

Hands on my hips, I turn to Layla. "Where's your brother?" Then I pivot to Izzy and add, "And your sister?"

Izzy looks at her freshly painted red nails. How do I know they're freshly painted? Because she sat at the kitchen table last night doing them herself. "Sorry," she says without looking up. "I don't have a tracker on my sister."

"I'll call him." Layla pulls her phone out of her tote bag.

I wave her off. "It's fine, but if they're not here in ten minutes, we're heading out without them. Got it?"

With her lips pressed together in concentration, Layla types out a text to her brother anyway.

She's just put her phone away when the two people in question crest the hill coming from Brooks's driveway.

"Hey!" Reid calls out with a wave, then cups his hands around his mouth. "We're coming! Sorry!"

I take it back. My grandchild is not the cause of most of my gray hairs. My son has earned that distinction.

When they reach the boat, Reid hops on with ease, then offers his hand to help Via.

"Hey," Via says to me with a shy, soft smile. "Thanks for inviting us."

I give her a nod, wishing things weren't so awkward and wondering if our interactions will always be like this. We went on a single date. That's it. The age gap between her and my son is large, but it's not … well, it's not the gap Izzy and I would have. Not that anything is ever going to happen between us.

It can't.

Now that we're all here, we head out onto the water. Izzy moves over to Lili's side and whispers something I can't hear above the sound of the motor and the waves.

The sun is high in the sky, and the day is hot. I applied sunscreen before we left the house, only because Izzy stared me down and watched me do it.

Thankfully, Layla agrees that Lili isn't quite old enough to go tubing. It's possible we're both being overprotective, but I'm okay with that.

Once we've found a calm spot, away from the other boaters, I lower the anchor.

Reid and Via are quick to jump into the water to swim, laughing and splashing and so overwhelmingly in love that I can't help but feel a pang of longing.

I assumed that, eventually, being single would get easier. Instead, that longing, the desire for a connection, continues to grow. Anymore, it's so acute that I'm not sure it'll ever be quelled.

My eyes drift in the direction of Izzy like they have no choice.

She's on the bench, next to Layla, head tossed back in laughter.

*Look away*, I tell myself.

But I can't.

I take her in, my attention gliding down the smooth column of her throat, to the perfect breasts threatening to spill out of that too tiny top, down her stomach to her hips and her crossed legs. Her skin looks warm from the sun—golden and shining with some sort of oil.

"Grandpa?" The sound of Lili's voice snaps me out of my trance. Thankfully, Izzy is deeply absorbed in her conversation and hasn't noticed the way I've been drooling over her.

"Yeah, princess?"

"Did you bring your fishing stuff? Can we fish?"

Thankful for the distraction from the too-beautiful woman on the boat, I nod. "I do. Let me get it set up."

Lili chats my ear off about her friends, the day camp she's been attending, and basically anything and everything else she can think of. All the while, I force myself to keep my focus from veering back to Izzy.

It's been way too long since I got laid. That's got to be the problem. I might not date much, if at all, but I've had the occasional hookup. I'm only human, after all. But it's been over a year since my last, so I just ... need to go out and find someone. Once I do, all this will go away.

It *has* to. I don't want to think about the alternative if it doesn't.

---

NOTHING BEATS WATCHING the fireworks from the boat. It's been a long afternoon, and I'm tired, but I can't deny that it's been nice to spend so much time with my family.

"This has been a fun day," Izzy says from beside me. "Thanks for taking us out."

I give her a nod. "You're welcome."

Her arm brushes mine, her skin still heated after hours under the sun. "I'm glad I'm here," she says softly.

*I'm glad you're here, too.* The words are on the tip of my tongue. But I swallow them back, cognizant that if I voice them, she might take it the wrong way.

When I don't respond, she goes on, "I didn't realize how much I was missing out on. The family stuff, you know?" She wets her lips with a swipe of her tongue. "LA isn't a bad place. In fact, I loved my life there for a very long time, but ... I don't know. I guess I've realized there are certain things that mean more."

"You don't have to defend yourself or your choices to me. It's okay to outgrow places and people. It doesn't make you a bad person."

Lowering her head, she toys with the hoodie she's got covering her lap like a blanket. "I know. But I don't want to let anyone down. My subscribers have always been there for me. They've watched me grow and they've cheered me on. I worry that if I decide that life isn't for me anymore, they won't understand."

I survey the sky, taking a moment to collect my thoughts. "Undoubtedly, there will be people who don't understand. But there will be others who love you for *you*. They'll follow you for whatever content you put out there. If you switch gears, others will discover you, too."

"You're right." She turns, her face lighting a bright red as a firework bursts above us.

Her expression is laced with a sadness I've noticed often since she arrived. An emotion she hides so well that a lot of people, including her sister, who's sitting at the back of the boat with my son wrapped around her, never get to see.

My chest aches with gratitude as I assess her. Because she trusts me enough to show me her true, honest self, to share that vulnerable side.

It's hard for a person who has no one to share those pieces of themself with.

I would know.

When the fireworks come to an end, Lili lets out a groan. "That's it? I want more!"

I stand, taking this as my cue to break the tension between Izzy and me. "Sorry, kid." I ruffle my granddaughter's hair as I pass her on the way to the line attached to the anchor. "That's all until next time."

She lets out a dramatic sigh behind me. "I hope they do more next year, then."

Beside her daughter, Layla shakes her head, trying to hide her amusement over the things that come out of Lili's mouth.

Once I've pulled the anchor, I start up the boat and head back to the dock. Reid and Via leave quickly, their laughter carrying behind them on the wind as they walk up the hill toward Brooks's driveway. They're wrapped up in one another, practically plastered together like they can't get close enough.

I was like that once, with my wife. And fuck, I miss it. I miss having a best friend, a lover. No one would fault me for moving on, least of all her, but honestly, it's not even her memory that keeps me at bay anymore. It's the worry that nothing and no one will fit right.

"See you later, Dad."

Layla's voice breaks me out of my thoughts. She pops up on her toes and pecks my cheek.

I pull her into a hug. "I'm glad you could join us today."

She pulls away, wearing a tiny smirk. "Us, huh?"

My gut sinks, but I keep my expression neutral and look over at Izzy. "She does live with me. We've sort of become a team."

Layla follows my line of sight to Izzy, who's picking up the boat, ensuring all our water bottles and food wrappers have been disposed of properly. "I can't believe she's working for you."

I shrug. "She needed a change."

"Yeah," she says softly, looking at her friend. "She did."

After one last hug from Lili, she and her mom head up the hill, too.

"And then it was just you and me, Captain," Izzy jokes as she shuffles to the side of the boat.

I hold out a hand to steady her as she steps out, and as we touch, a spark travels up my arm.

A breath of air escapes her, and she locks eyes with me, like maybe she felt it, too.

Once she's got both feet on the dock, I drop her hand, mentally shaking off the feeling of electricity. "It's been a long day, but a good one. For me, at least. Did you enjoy yourself?" I ask as I grasp the handle of the cooler bag and tug.

She doesn't fight me over it, signaling that she's got to be as tired as I am. "I did."

Despite the smile she gives me, her eyes swim with an emotion I can't name. Like she's got something on her mind. I don't press her on it, though, because I'm scared she'll bring up this connection between us.

I see the interest in her eyes when she looks at me. It matches the feelings I'm working so hard to extinguish.

The melancholic way she's holding herself in the passenger seat as I pull out of Brooks's driveway is like a knife to the heart.

"Do you want to stop and get slushies?"

A frown mars her gorgeous face. "Are they going to be open?"

"They're always open."

She brightens, a genuine smile lighting up her eyes. "Yes, please."

Ten minutes later, I pull into the station. While I lock the truck, she scurries inside. As she fills a cup with the blue raspberry flavor, she hums along with the song playing through the speakers, hips swaying to the beat.

I have to clench my teeth to keep from groaning.

I need to go out and find someone—a woman my age, or at least close to it—for a night of fun. Once I do, this feeling I have will go away. It *has* to.

If it doesn't?

I can't even contemplate that.

Without my prompting, she grabs another cup and fills it with the Coke flavor.

She turns to me when she's done, holding both cups and wearing a proud smile.

"Let's go, boss man."

I roll my eyes at the ridiculous nickname, even as my heart clenches. "You want anything else?"

With a thoughtful hum, she wanders down the candy aisle, flip-flops slapping against the dirty linoleum. She peruses the chocolate for only a moment before she snags two Crunch bars.

Holding them up, she says, "This was my favorite growing up, but it's hard to find."

I grab two more. "Get some extras, then."

"I don't need this much chocolate," she laughs, still looking beautiful despite a day on the lake and the garish yellow light flickering above us. "Pick something for yourself."

"I can get extra chocolate for you and still get something for myself." I crouch and pick a pack of Reese's to drive home my point.

She smiles at the orange package in my hand. "You *would* be a Reese's man."

Eyes narrowed, I purse my lips. "What's that supposed to mean?"

"Steady, reliable, always good." She gives me a soft, almost shy smile that looks so foreign on the face of this bold, confident woman. "I like Reese's." She swipes a pack for herself, juggling her three packs of chocolate and the two slushies with ease and speed walks to the register.

*I like Reese's.* That declaration plays over in my mind.

Because from her tone, it's pretty clear she wasn't just talking about the peanut butter and chocolate cup.

*I like Reese's* sounded a hell of a lot like *I like you.*

136

# fifteen

Izzy

"YOU DON'T HAVE any social media."

Derrick continues to browse his computer, steadfastly ignoring me.

"Did you hear me?"

He angles to one side and focuses on me, brow quirked. "It was a statement, not a question. I didn't think it required a response."

I spin in my office chair so I'm facing him fully. "You should have an Instagram profile for your business, at minimum. A place to showcase your work."

He blinks slowly. "So you keep telling me."

"No social media. No website. No sign out front. How do you get any work?"

He arches a dark brow, scratching at his jaw. He trimmed his beard this morning, so it's closer to stubble than I've ever seen it. "I told you, word of mouth. I don't need any of that other fancy shit."

I feel like slamming my head into my desk. "Regardless, you should have a place to showcase your work. No offense, but I wouldn't hire you if I couldn't see examples."

He taps his fingers against his mouth. "I have pictures on my phone."

Groaning, I hold my hands out and give them a shake, like I want to choke him. "Ugh! You are such a ... such a..."

He flashes a smile. "Such a what? Finish that thought, please."

His expression says *I dare you*, and I hate that my brain takes that and runs with it.

*What would he do if I said it? Would he put me over his knee and spank me?*

Unlikely, but a girl can dream.

"A *man*," I say, like the single syllable is a dirty word. "Please, for the sake of my sanity, let me work on a website and an Instagram page for you."

"No."

I'm not above begging, so I clasp my hands and stick out my bottom lip. "Please? I'll handle it all myself. You won't have to do a thing."

He picks up a pencil and taps the eraser side against his desk. "Aren't websites expensive?"

I shrug easily. "They can be, but I know people."

The people being *me*.

Frowning, he drops the pencil to his desk. "I don't want you to owe anyone any favors on my behalf."

*I wouldn't mind if he owed me a favor. I can think of some creative ways he could pay me back.*

"It's not a big deal, I promise. Please, say yes."

With a heavy sigh, he looks away. It only takes a few heart-beats before he focuses on me again, wearing a thoughtful frown. "Will it be easy for Jessica to handle once she's back?"

"Absolutely."

He rubs his lips together and closes his eyes for a moment. "Fine."

"Thank you!"

Under my desk, Wonton pops up and lets out a little yip to match my excitement.

Without a moment's hesitation, I get to work setting up the Instagram account, already thinking of which sites I want to return to for photos and videos.

I'm immersed in my work when Derrick stands up from his desk and stretches his arms above his head. I wish I could say I didn't turn to peek at his delectable abs, but I do. I can't help it. He goes for a run almost every morning, and he *has* to go to the gym to have the muscles he does, but I have no idea when he fits that in.

"Let's go get lunch," he announces, swiping his keys off the desk.

Wonton bolts out from under my desk and jumps up on his leg, tongue lolling and tail wagging.

"But I packed—"

He shakes his head. "If I don't get out of here for a little while, I'll go crazy."

"You know," I push my chair back, "you don't have to babysit me if you want to be out there working with your guys. I won't stop you."

"I'm not here for you," he bites out. "I have shit to catch up on."

I have to turn away so he won't see my smile. His cutting words should hurt, but it's impossible when he's only saying them because he's defensive. He was working on my sister's store the first couple of times I visited, so I saw firsthand how much he likes to be on site with his guys, working alongside them. Maybe he's not solely hanging around the office because of me, but I can't imagine I'm not at least a small part of the reason. He might not want to admit it, but he likes my company.

As he should. I'm a blast.

"Whatever you say, boss man."

I pick up my purse, then crouch and give Wonton a kiss on his head.

Derrick holds the door open for me, eyeing Wonton to make sure he doesn't follow us out, then locks up behind us.

My poor pup sits in front of the glass door, batting at it with his paw, his expressive little face so forlorn.

"I'll be back soon," I tell him, my heart aching.

As I turn and start for Derrick's truck, he's rounding the hood, shaking his head. "You and that dog."

"What about us?" I ask as I yank the passenger door open.

He pauses near the front of the truck, twirling his keychain around his finger. "It's cute, is all. He's like your kid."

"He is my kid."

A laugh sputters out of him, but he sobers at my flat expression. "Oh, you were serious. Do you..." He clears his throat. "Do you not want kids of the human variety?"

"One day I'd love to have them," I answer immediately, my chest warming at the idea. "But for now, he's my kid, and even then, he'll still be my first kid."

He shakes his head, the longish strands brushing his forehead, probably thinking about how crazy dog lovers are.

I'm buckling my seat belt when he climbs in the truck, and only a few minutes later, he parks on the road in front of the diner. I should have guessed. He's never said, but I have a sneaking suspicion that once Layla moved out, he became a regular.

He's hinted at how lonely he was once his house was empty. I can imagine that it not only made him eager to spend time around people but also made it more difficult to want to cook, since he'd only be cooking for himself.

As we step inside, the bell above the door chimes. He steers me toward a booth with a hand low on my waist.

The vinyl of the booth squeaks obnoxiously when my bare legs slide across. An older gentleman a few tables away gives a soft chuckle, though he attempts to hide it behind his coffee mug.

With a small shake of my head, I pick up the menu from the shelf on the side of the table. I've eaten here plenty, but I like to change things up, and there are several things left to try.

Rather than pick up his own menu, Derrick laces his fingers and rests his hands on the table.

The young, bouncy server appears, her ponytail swishing as she slides her notepad out of her pocket.

"Hi, guys. What can I get you? Your usual, Derrick?"

"Yeah, thanks."

"You got it." She continues holding her pen aloft rather than write it down. "And for you?"

"What's your usual?" I ask Derrick.

"Burger with fries and a Coke."

I purse my lips and blink once.

With a sigh, he looks up at the waitress. "A side salad instead of the fries, please."

Lip curling, she eyes him with skepticism. "Are you sure?"

"Yeah," he sighs. "This one is attempting to fix my diet." He points an accusing finger at me.

I shrug, unbothered. "Guilty."

"And what will you have?" she asks, her attention darting between us, her expression full of curiosity.

"The Caesar salad with a side of fries, please. And a water."

When she's gone, Derrick grins. "Fries, huh?"

"Fries go perfectly with Caesar salad. Besides, you got a burger with your salad. I'm not wholly against any foods in particular. It's all great. But if you only eat fried stuff that clogs your arteries, you're asking for trouble." I eye him with pursed lips. "You have to have the good with the good."

"The good with the good?"

Hands splayed on the table, I nod. "I personally don't like to think of any food as *bad*."

"I never thought about it that way," he says as the waitress sets our drinks in front of us. He takes a slow sip of Coke, then sets it down again. "I just figured that LA made you a total health nut or something."

"Maybe a little," I admit, looking away.

For the most part, I've worked past the issues I developed during the year and a half where I ate very little, and even less food with any real sustenance. I had surrounded myself with toxic people that convinced me that in order to "make it" I had to fit a certain mold.

But what is "making it" anyway? Shouldn't each person's definition be unique and based on their own goals?

In an effort to distract myself from wandering thoughts that will do me no good, I pull my notebook out and slap it on the table.

"Where's my pen?" I mutter to myself as I dive into my tote.

Derrick clears his throat, and when I look up, I find him holding one out to me.

I pluck it from his fingers and press the button on top with a *click*. "Thanks."

"I'm surprised you can find anything in that bag of yours. It's stuffed to the brim with—"

"My whole life?"

He lets out an amused huff. "Seems like it."

"I never know what I might need. This way, when I do know, there's a good chance I have it with me."

With an amused smile, he shakes his head.

Straightening in the booth, I get to work scribbling ideas for the website and Instagram page. The kinds of photos people would like and catchy captions. I even block out what kinds of posts might work best on certain days, but I won't know for sure until I start posting and can gauge performance.

Derrick watches me, his gaze unwavering, as I work. I don't let the scrutiny slow me down.

When our food is ready, I pack everything away and dig into my salad.

Throughout the meal, Derrick eyes my fries with longing. He does it so often that I pull the plate closer to my side of the table.

"Mine."

His lips curl in amusement. "I'm not going to steal your fries."

I bark out a laugh. "Are you sure? You looked like you were considering it."

His eyes darken, and he leans in closer to me, voice low, and says, "Trust me, Izzy. I don't act on every thought that crosses my mind."

My brain scrambles, and excitement skitters down my spine. Why ... why does it feel like he's talking about me?

*Is it possible Derrick wants me the way I want him?*

No. I can't imagine that's even remotely true. He might find me attractive, but there's no way it goes farther than that. He's too much of a stand-up guy to consider me anything more than his temporary roommate.

# sixteen

### Derrick

IT'S BEEN TOO long since I've been out with friends, so being here now is more than a little jarring. Bars have never really been my scene, but it's where the guys like to hang out.

Brooks claps me on the shoulder, his smile so wide and bright it's hard not to mimic it.

"Good to see out for a change."

"I figure it was about time." I take a slow sip of beer. "I don't get out much."

I've always been more of a homebody.

Patrick, at the other end of the table, lets out an obnoxiously loud laugh. "I'd be a homebody too if I had a hot piece of ass waiting for me there."

I bristle at the crass words. Not only is that an insult to Izzy, but to his own wife, too. Idiot. I've never really cared for

Patrick, but he works with Brooks, so his presence tonight isn't surprising.

"Watch your mouth," I mutter.

The asshole only laughs in response. "Oh, come on, man! You can't tell me you're not tapping that."

Red clouds my vision as I glare daggers at him. "She's the same age as my daughter."

He guffaws, his face red. Though I'm not sure whether it's because of his hysterical laughter or the absurd amount of alcohol he's consumed tonight. The guy was tipsy before I arrived. "What does that have to do with anything? She's legal, ain't she?"

Flinching, I ball my hands into fists. Men who say shit like that are exactly the kind of men the world should be wary of.

"Shut up, Patrick," Brooks barks, his tone harsh.

Patrick opens his mouth to spew God only knows what, but Brooks points at him with a scolding finger.

"I said no." My buddy settles into the seat across from me, head low and shaking. "Sorry about him."

"I'm not the one who has to work with him." I bring my beer to my lips.

My wife was killed by a drunk driver years ago, and since then, I've found that I don't enjoy drinking in the way I used to. It's not that I don't ever drink, but on the occasions when I do, I always find myself wondering why. Why would someone drink so much and think it's a smart idea to get behind the wheel? Why did the universe give one person the power to irrevocably change my family?

Brooks shrugs. "I only keep him on because of Tilly and the kids."

Tilly. Patrick's wife. She has MS and hasn't been able to

work in years. Not since her pain got so bad and she lost so much mobility.

"He's a piece of shit," I say anyway, keeping my voice low.

Brooks stuffs a handful of fries into his mouth, though it does little to hide his smile.

"That he is. I'm glad you came, though."

"Yeah," I say, surveying the plates full of appetizers littering the table. "I ... me, too."

I pick at the label on my bottle. Honestly, I'd rather be at home right now, lounging on the couch with Izzy and Wonton, watching *Gilmore Girls* and wearing a face mask. But I can't say that. I shouldn't even *think* it. Not that there's anything wrong with hanging on the couch with her. The issue is what that statement would imply. That I *like* her. Probably more than I should.

And that?

It's terrifying for many reasons.

---

I STAYED out longer than I planned—possibly in an effort to prove to myself that I *could* go out and have fun. But to be honest, not one ounce of joy was had.

Quietly, I unlock the front door and ease it open. When I step inside, I find Izzy curled up on the couch with Wonton in the crook of her legs.

The door squeaks as I close it behind me, the sound waking Wonton. His eyes shoot open and fill with terror when they lock on me.

*Oh, fuck.*

The little dog launches himself up onto the back of the

couch and then onto *me*. I catch him easily and hold him at arm's length while he growls and snaps and barks.

Izzy jolts awake and rolls off the couch. In the background, on the TV, Netflix asks if she's still watching.

"Jesus." Sitting now, she slaps a hand against her chest. "Way to scare a girl."

"I was going to sneak past so I wouldn't disturb you, but this one didn't let me."

Wonton, maybe realizing it's me now that he's heard the sound of my voice, has settled, so I tuck him under my arm and shut the door. Izzy still hasn't gotten up, so I move around to where she's on the floor and offer a hand. "Need some help?"

"I need a minute. My heart is racing."

I grimace. Dammit. I didn't mean to scare her. I assumed she'd already be in bed, so I didn't call or send a message to give her a heads-up, worrying that if I did, I'd wake her up. I guess that would've been a better alternative than this.

Finally, she takes my hand and lets me haul her up. "I could go for some water."

"Water, sure. I can get you some."

I guide her back onto the couch and set Wonton on her lap. Then I pad into the kitchen, fill a glass with about the amount of ice she likes, add water.

"Thanks," she says softly when I return and extend the glass to her. "Did you have a good night?"

With a sigh, I settle on the coffee table in front of her. I'm so close I could count the flecks of color in her eyes.

She cocks a brow and takes a small sip. "I take it the answer is no."

I shake my head. "I'm just ... out of practice, I guess."

"With socializing?" Her laughter has the water shaking

precariously in the glass. When she notices, she flashes me a sheepish smile.

"If you want to call it that. It's not that I never go out, but when I do, I find I don't enjoy it like I thought I would. I'd rather be at home. Unless—" I press my lips together, shutting myself up.

"Unless what?" She prompts, leaning forward to set the glass beside me. I have to tip my chin up to avoid staring straight down her tank top. "Oh." She presses a hand to her chest and straightens, her cheeks getting the softest shade of pink in the lowlight. "Unless you're picking up a woman."

"It's rare," I say a little too quickly.

She lifts a shoulder. "Everyone has needs. There's nothing wrong with a hookup."

I clench my fists, causing my fingers to rasp against my jeans. The idea of Izzy hooking up with anyone makes me want to scream, which is ridiculous. She's twenty-seven. Of course she has sex.

I stand up and put my hands on my hips before I do something stupid like grab her and toss her over my shoulder.

"I'm going to bed."

"Okay," she says, worrying her lip. "My adrenaline is still pumping after that scare. I think I'll stay up a little longer."

I nod with more force than necessary, probably looking like some ill-functioning bobblehead. "Good night."

"Night," she echoes.

With that, I head upstairs, shower, and get into bed.

Alone.

So very alone.

# seventeen

## Izzy

"WHEN ARE you coming back to California, honey? You've been gone for months."

It's on the tip of my tongue to correct my mom. To tell her that I have not, in fact, been gone for months, but then I realize she's right. I escaped LA in May, and already, we're nearing the middle of July.

"I..." I trail off, unable to find the words to explain to her that I don't think I'm *ever* coming back. Because I'm scared to make that commitment, and I'm not ready to defend my choices to her. So, instead, I say, "Wonton's leash is getting tangled up, and I'm about to head into Via's store. We'll talk again soon. Love you, bye."

I hang up before she can get another word in and let out a heavy breath, feeling like I want to crawl out of my skin.

Wonton spots Via inside and paws at the glass door.

When she hears him, she looks up and waves, which means I can't linger outside a moment longer to catch my breath after that phone call.

Inside the store, I let Wonton off his leash, and he runs straight for Via and circles her.

She crouches down in her paint-splattered overalls to scratch his head. "Hey, Wonton. Good morning to you, too."

I set my bag down on one of the tables and pick another plate to paint.

"Are you okay?" Via asks from behind me. "You're quiet."

"I was just on the phone with Mom." With a deep breath in, I set the plate on the table. Then I head over to the counter to pick my paints.

"Oh." She crosses her arms over her chest, her expression going distant. "How is she?"

"Good."

Via has a complicated relationship with our parents. She's the eldest daughter, and they placed a lot more pressure on her shoulders than mine. She was expected to be perfect, with a solid career in law and a husband and two and a half kids. When she divorced her husband and left law to move all the way across the country, our parents didn't take it well.

Despite how hard she tries, and how hard my parents do, too, they'll never have the relationship they all want. The divide is too great.

As the baby of the family, I was always awarded more freedom. They didn't really balk when I started my YouTube channel. Sure, they would've loved for me to be a doctor, or something of the sort, but my career took off quickly, so they kept their mouths shut about it for the most part.

Via pulls her phone out of her pocket, and a dopey smile

appears on her face. Must be Reid. I hope she never loses that look. She's so hopelessly in love.

"Reid's going to bring coffee by for me. Do you want anything?"

It's on the tip of my tongue to say no. I don't want her boyfriend to have to bring me something out of obligation. I'm the pathetic single little sister, after all. Though, ironically, I'm older than he is. But I really could use the pick-me-up, so I pluck up the courage to ask for an iced matcha.

"You got it," she says, her thumbs already tapping out a message.

There are a few other people in the store: A couple in the back painting on separate canvases. An elderly woman carefully adding details to a ceramic pitcher. And a mother with her two kids.

After Via slides her phone back into her pocket, she sits across from me at the same table I chose the last time I was here. Wonton settles beneath the table, resting his head on my feet.

"Oh," Via chirps, hopping up from the table a second later. "Your first plate."

I watch her scurry to the back, suddenly hit with a wave of sadness. It's been too long since I was here last. Despite being so close to my sister physically, I hardly see her. It's no fault of hers, or even mine. She's busy, and so am I.

Derrick probably thought I was out of my mind when I volunteered to work for him, but I needed a purpose, and he gave it to me.

I would've gone mad by now if I had nothing to do but take photos for social media accounts I'm currently avoiding.

I'm pulling my hair back and out of my face when Via returns with a visible pep in her step.

My sister is *glowing*. Her every movement is lighter than it was a few years ago. It's not just Reid; it's this *place*. Because she's finally found the place where she belongs. She's flourishing.

Not that long ago, I felt as though I was flourishing, too. Now I'm like a wilted flower—not quite worth throwing out of the bouquet yet, but it's obvious I'm suffering.

"Here you go." She gently hands over the plate.

I remove the honeycomb packing paper carefully, my throat tight. Suddenly, I'm sure the piece won't look at all how I wanted it to.

But when I pull the paper away, a breath whooshes out of me, and my heart flutters. It's perfect. The little flowers around the edge of the plate are beautiful. Sure, they're a little crooked, but that imperfection is what I was going for.

"Are you happy with it?" Via asks.

My smile is so big it hurts when I nod and wrap it back up. "It's perfect."

She nods to the blank plate on the table in front of me. "What are you going to do on this one?"

"I was thinking butterflies." I dip my brush into the paint and tilt my head, trying to envision the design.

"Oh, that'll be so cute."

The door chimes behind us, so, with a squeeze of my shoulder and a smile, Via leaves me to paint while she greets her new customer.

I take my time, working alone for the most part, sipping the drink Reid drops off and going over the colors multiple times to make sure they're vivid after being fired. When I'm finished, I put it on the cart in the center of the room for items that need firing.

Via's on the phone, answering customer questions when I

leave, so I wave, miming that we'll talk later, and guide Wonton out of the store.

My pup leads the way down the sidewalk with a pep in his step. I shouldn't be surprised, I guess. He slept the whole time I worked on my plate. While I'm in town, I make my way to the bookstore to see whether Ella has a new release I thought might find intriguing.

I scoop Wonton up before entering just in case the store's cat, Tremaine, is roaming about today.

Inside, Ella is reading a book behind the register. She promptly shuts the paperback and gives me a welcoming smile. "Hey, Izzy. What brings you in?"

I fish my phone out of my pocket and bring up the browser. "I was looking for this."

She bites her lip, squinting at the cover, brow furrowed like she's not sure she's seen this new release.

"It just came out."

"Oh," she says, popping up. "It might be in the back. There are a few boxes I haven't unpacked yet. Hold on." She holds up a finger for me to wait, then disappears into the back room, her hair swishing over her shoulder.

Adjusting my hold on Wonton, I walk deeper into the store, between the full shelves, breathing deep. I love how they're overflowing, with books stacked on the floor in some spots. I pause halfway down one aisle and scan the shelves to see if anything else jumps out at me. When I come across a cookbook solely dedicated to salads, I laugh out loud and snatch it up, certain it'll make Derrick laugh, too.

Is it odd that I find myself thinking of him in ways like this?

It makes sense, right? We've been living together and—

Closing my eyes, I blow out a breath. I have to stop overthinking things, especially when it comes to him. I'll drive myself insane if I don't.

For a moment, I consider putting the book back, but decide to hell with it and take it with me as I head back to the counter.

On my way, I stop at a section of coastal books—a collection that consists of nonfiction books about Maine and the ocean, and even a few romances set in the area. Unable to resist the New England summer vibe, I snag one of the romances.

"I found it!" Ella comes around the corner, holding the book proudly out in front of her, just as I'm approaching the counter. She scans it and holds out a hand for the other selections I've made. "A cookbook on salads?" She arches a brow, her lips quirking like she's trying her hardest not to laugh at me. "That's interesting. I didn't even know we had that."

With a grin, I tap my card on the machine.

She holds the small paper bag out to me. "Will I see you at book club?"

"Yeah, of course," I say with a wave as I head for the door.

"Cool. See you, Izzy!"

The warmth of the summer sun on my skin is rejuvenating when I step outside and set Wonton on the sidewalk. I'm rounding the corner when I catch sight of the ice cream shop. It's only open in the spring and summer, and right about now, it sounds like exactly what I need.

"Would you like some ice cream?" I ask Wonton.

I swear his tail wags faster in response.

Luckily, the ice cream shop isn't busy, so I tie Wonton up outside and pop in to order, making sure to keep an eye on him while I wait. I've been beyond paranoid since he escaped during the storm.

Once I've got a scoop of strawberry ice cream and a pup

cup, I head back out. I can't help but grin when Wonton greets me with an excited yip.

I set the cups on the table and untie him so I can set him in my lap. Then I scoot his cup closer, and he goes to town licking the vanilla ice cream, completely ignoring the bone in the middle. He likes to save that for last.

While he's occupied, I have a taste of my own. Some may consider strawberry a basic flavor, but nothing beats it, in my opinion. I swirl my tongue around the plastic spoon, making sure to get every drop before I dive in for another bite.

"I never thought I'd be envious of a spoon."

Jolting, I snap my head up, finding Derrick stopped a few feet away on the sidewalk. His cheeks slowly turn from their normal tan to red, like maybe he didn't mean to say that out loud, and my own cheeks warm as well.

"Hi." It's perhaps the dumbest response in the history of responses, but it's the only word rattling around in my brain at the moment. I'm too stunned to even come up with a witty quip about his comment.

He clears his throat and nods toward the chair across from me. "Mind if I join you?"

"Not at all. Do you want ice cream?"

I point with my spoon at the window into the shop. When I catch the spoon in my periphery and remember his comment, I blush all over again.

I'll never look at the utensil the same way again.

"Yeah, I should … I should do that." He runs his fingers through his hair. It's gotten long. I don't think he's cut it once in my time here, and I hate to admit it, but I've had dreams of pulling on his hair, riding his—

"Izzy?"

I want to melt into a puddle under the table like ice cream, never to be seen or heard from again. Just a sticky, forgotten mess on the sidewalk. "What did you say?"

"Do you want anything else while I'm in there? A drink?"

"No, I'm good." Somehow, the words come out with more confidence than I feel.

With a nod, Derrick steps around me and heads into the little shop.

I bite my lip and watch him at the counter, surreptitiously ogling him. A plain white Hanes T-shirt clings to his muscular chest, practically suffocating his biceps, and his gray cargo shorts hug his shapely ass in a way that has me thinking about things I most definitely shouldn't be. Not about my sister's boyfriend's dad. About my *friend's* dad. God, this is so fucked up.

I need to have sex, that much is obvious.

I've been relying way too heavily on my vibrator.

If I go out and have a little fun, then I'll be good. I'll stop thinking dirty thoughts about Derrick.

I try to convince myself. Really, I do. But who am I kidding? There's not a chance in hell that I'll stop. Not only is he hot, but he's kind and caring in that quiet, gruff way of his.

He drops a couple of bucks into the tip jar, and when he turns to head back out, I nearly break my neck turning away from the window and hoping to god he didn't catch me staring.

"Fuck," I curse under my breath when I find that my ice cream has melted. It's not a total loss—I wasn't ogling him for *that* long—but it's a bit soupy for my liking.

The wrought-iron chair across from me scrapes across the sidewalk, and Derrick settles his big body into it while somehow making the chair look comfortable.

As he gets situated, I assess that space between his neck and shoulder.

*What would it be like to press my face in that crook? What would he smell like?*

*Oh my God, I am certifiable.*

Despite my previous thoughts, I'm not interested in going out and hooking up for a night. I did plenty of that in my early twenties. So that means the minute I get back to Derrick's house, I'll be ordering new toys. Because I need something, anything, to take this edge off.

"What flavor did you get?" I ask by way of distracting myself from my sex-starved thoughts.

"Cosmic brownie."

"Like the Little Debbie kind? That's the brand, right? With the rainbow sprinkles?"

I'm rambling. About a brownie I haven't eaten since I was probably seven. But I can't help it. I babble when I'm nervous. It's not my best trait and often gets me in trouble, since I invariably spew out the very thought I'm trying to suppress.

Like the thought I keep having about how I very much want to feel the weight of Derrick's naked body on top of mine.

God, I bet he'd take such good care of me. He'd be sweet, but a little rough, attentive.

"That's the one," he answers. "You want a bite?"

I swear my heart stops. I force a harsh breath in and drop my attention to my ice cream. "No, I'm good," I say as I scoop up the soupy mess and shove it into my mouth. While keeping my eyes set on my bowl, I sort through the files in my brain for something safe to ask him, and when a topic finally comes to me, I clear my throat and dare a peek up at him. "What were you up to before you stumbled upon us?"

On my lap, Wonton has his nose stuffed all the way into his cup, and he's grunting as he tries to get ahold of the bone. I grab it with my left hand and hold one end of it steady so he can nibble.

"I had to run by the hardware store for a few things."

I frown and look at the ground by his feet. "You don't have any bags."

*What the hell, Izzy? Are you trying to make it sound like you think he came for you?*

"Loaded them in the truck already." He thumbs over his shoulder, gesturing to where his truck is parallel parked. "I saw you guys then. I wasn't sure if you saw me, so it felt rude not to come over."

"Plus, who can say no to ice cream?"

He cracks a grin. "That, too."

That look melts my heart, making it as gooey as the ice cream I'm finishing. It's way too easy being around him, talking to him. Even when I'm nervous and losing my shit over my own thoughts. And it's pure torture.

Why does the first man I'm seriously attracted to in years have to be *him*?

# eighteen

### Derrick

"THIS IS RIDICULOUS."

Izzy, with a DSLR camera hanging around her neck, fixes the collar of my shirt for the fifth time. The woman is insisting that I let her take photos of me for the website she's putting together.

I huff. "Nobody cares about what their contractor looks like."

Her hand stills but stays pressed against my shoulder. It's so small, her touch so delicate. If I put my hand over hers, it would no doubt swallow it whole.

"Putting a face with the brand is critical. A friendly picture helps tell your story, and your story matters. That alone can entice them to hire you over another company."

She takes a step back, the warmth of her hand disappearing.

"Whatever you say, boss."

Her lips fight a smile at the nickname. "Lean against the column there. Yeah, just like that. Hand in your pocket. Perfect."

It's cute, the way she directs me. Despite how little I want to do the photos, it's impossible to say no to Izzy. I would've gone just about anywhere she wanted for this photo shoot. Thankfully, she thinks taking them at home will not only show me off, but also several projects I've completed over the years. Like the covered deck out back where she has me posing now.

After she's taken a handful of photos, she steps up close, bringing her sweet vanilla and honey scent with her.

She takes the strap off her neck and holds the camera out so we can both see the display, then flicks through the photos.

"What do you think?"

I look down at her, wishing I could bury my face in her hair or count her freckles.

"I think you're extremely talented at everything you do."

Pink tinges her cheeks as she peers up at me through her lashes. "Thank you, but I promise I'm really not."

I'd beg to differ, but I keep my mouth shut on that matter. "Do you need more pictures, or is that enough?"

She twists her lips and flicks through the photos again. "I think we're good with what's here."

"Good." I nod. "Now go change."

Brow furrowed, she studies me, opening her mouth then closing it again before she finally stammers, "I ... why?"

"I'm taking you somewhere."

Her eyes narrow, skeptical. "Where?"

"The beach. There'll be a big bonfire there tonight. I thought you might like it."

It's not exactly my scene, but she has to be tired of hanging around the house.

"Okay." She bites her lip in a futile effort to hide her smile.

She hurries inside, with Wonton running after her. I'm slower to go in, and as I pour myself a glass of water, she scurries around upstairs, the boards creaking beneath her feet.

Twenty minutes later, she comes down in an off-white crochet dress that hugs every curve. I physically *ache* with the desire to put my hand on the soft divot of her waist.

She's braided pieces of hair, then pulled all of it back into a ponytail, with the exception of a few short pieces that curl on each side of her face.

"This isn't too much, is it?" She waves a hand up and down her body.

I clear my throat, forcing my heart back to its rightful place. "You look beautiful."

Her beaming smile makes the churning in my stomach more pronounced.

"Thank you." She grabs her bag and slings it over her shoulder. "Can we get slushies on the way?"

With a chuckle, I swipe my keys off the console. "Anything you want."

It's only when her cheeks pinken that I realize what my words could imply.

Wonton, not pleased about being left behind, hops up on the couch and pouts while he watches us through the window.

"Look at him." She nods at the house as she pulls her seat belt across her body. "This is why I take him everywhere. He's so good at guilt trips."

"Kids are good for that, too."

"Was it hard? Raising them by yourself?"

My heart stutters at the unexpected question. Without

responding, I back out of the driveway and head for the gas station.

By the time we pull into the parking lot, she's wringing her hands, and her shoulders are curled in. Like she's ashamed for asking the question. I can't blame her, since I've yet to speak since she brought it up.

"Yeah," I finally say. "It was difficult. And in ways I never could have imagined. Between parenting and working, I always felt stretched thin. And..." I lower my head. "Anyone that has to raise their kids on their own is a badass. It's not for the faint of heart. I'm lucky. My kids were relatively easy. But they were still children. When one or both was sick, that's when life was hardest. But hey..." I shrug, dropping my hands from the steering wheel to unbuckle my seat belt. "We made it, and I think they turned out all right."

"I'm not sure I could have done it," she admits, playing with a loose thread on her dress. "Just continue on after losing a spouse...."

"Trust me," I say softly, "you'd be surprised the things you can do when you're forced into the situation. I couldn't bring my wife back, but my kids needed a parent, so I had to step up for them. You do what you have to." I clap my hands and point to the store, ready to move on from the topic. "I'll grab those. You wait here."

I hurry inside and fill two Styrofoam cups, then rush to the counter and pull out my wallet. It's getting darker outside, and I want to get to the beach before sunset.

Greg chuckles, his smile amused. "Your girl really likes these things, huh?"

I tap my card to pay. "Yeah, she does," I reply, not bothering to correct him.

The moment I'm outside, before the station's heavy glass

door has even swung shut behind me, Izzy makes grabby hands where she's still sitting in the passenger seat.

I shake my head at her antics. I've created a monster. Once I'm in the driver's seat, I hand her one slushie and stick the other in the cupholder.

"God, I love these things," she says a few minutes later, the tip of her tongue stained blue.

"Really? I would've never guessed."

With a huff full of affection, she gives my shoulder a light punch.

Traffic is heavier than usual on the way, but it's to be expected, since it's tourist season. By the time I find a parking spot on the street a little over a block away, Izzy has finished her slushie, and she's buzzing from all the sugar.

"I can't believe you're taking me to a beach party." She hops out with more gusto than necessary and slings her bag over her shoulder. "This is going to be so fun."

I cross in front of the truck to meet her on the sidewalk and catch myself half a second before I instinctively stick out my hand for hers.

*What the fuck are you doing?*

It feels natural, to reach for her, and that is a major red flag.

I'm getting too close.

Too comfortable.

I'm silent on our walk over to the beach, but Izzy talks enough for the both of us, rambling about her progress on the website and what she thinks I could do to make things go smoothly when Jessica returns.

At the reminder that this thing with Izzy—living together, working together—is temporary, I find my shoulders curving upward.

I should be looking forward to the day she moves on.

Instead, the thought of being by myself again is more than a little depressing.

I'll get over it, though.

I have to.

I was fine before, so I'll be fine again.

Even if "fine" is a sad state of existence.

"Are you listening?"

"Huh?" I cock my head and peer down at her. Izzy isn't short. She's probably five-six or five-seven. Even so, she's small in comparison to me.

We're at the edge of the beach, millimeters from the sand. Music blasts, some catchy, sugary-sweet pop song that Lili probably loves.

Her smile falls. Only a fraction, but knowing I've disappointed her feels like a massive kick in the gut.

"Never mind," she says, her voice bright. She's generally a happy, bubbly person, but this brightness is pure fabrication. "It wasn't a big deal."

She grasps my arm, using it to hold her steady so she can take her shoes off.

And when she loops her finger through the back strap to carry them, I shake my head. "Give them here."

"I've got it," she says, opening her bag.

She won't look at me.

Dammit. My stomach sinks.

*What did she say?*

*What did I do?*

Maybe the better question is, what *didn't* I do?

Now, without her shoes, she surges ahead onto the beach.

I catch up to her easily, shoving my hands into my pockets. "The sun should be setting soon if you want to watch it."

"That's okay." Her tone is clipped and unfamiliar. "I'm going to grab a drink. You want anything?"

"I'm good, but I can get something for you. What do you want?"

She flashes me a sharp-toothed smile. "I'm capable of grabbing a drink myself. Wait here."

With a thick swallow, I dip my chin and stay put like a chastised dog.

I keep my eye on her, watching as she walks up to a small group of guys at the cooler. She points, and one of them grabs a beer from the ice, pops the cap, and passes it to her. She laughs at something he says, touching his forearm when she takes the beer.

I look away.

Red-hot jealousy pierces through me. A jealousy like I've never felt before. One filled with anger, and with sadness, because I want her laughing and touching me.

But that's ridiculous. This guy is clearly closer to her age. It makes sense for her to chat and flirt with him.

I'm too old for her. Despite my growing feelings, I have to remember that.

Liking her in any way that isn't platonic is *wrong*.

But I'm drawn to her. I can't fight the urge to watch her. I turn back to where she was, only to find her gone. The guy, too.

Panic surges through me as I turn one way, then the other, taking in every group near me. But I don't see her.

I'm being ridiculous, but I can't stop myself as I move down the beach in search of her. I scan the crowd, but with so many tourists here, it's hard to single out just one person.

This is my own fault. I should have listened to her. I was too in my head, and now it's bitten me in the ass.

Though maybe this is a good thing. Maybe she should go off with someone else. It'd be a good reminder that I can't have her.

Under normal circumstances, Izzy wouldn't ditch me. But I hurt her feelings. Unknowingly, of course, but I did. And now she wants to distance herself.

After ten minutes of searching, I still haven't found her. Despite how many times I tell myself to let her do her thing, I can't help but worry.

I make my way back over to the cooler where she went for a beer. Recognizing a few of the guys, I ask, "Do you remember a brunette? About this tall?" I hold a hand up to my chest at about the right height. "She was talking with one of your friends, but now I can't find her."

One points his finger. "Your daughter's over there, dude. Relax."

I flinch, and my stomach bottoms out. *Daughter.*

Even these guys know I'm way too old for her.

I follow his finger, though, and find her dancing with the guy she first spoke to. She moves her body sinuously to the music. A song about dancing with your hands tied. Her eyes are closed, and the guy's hand is on her waist, his eyes glossy with lust.

It's a punch to the chest—one I very much need.

"Thanks," I grumble.

I snatch a beer from the cooler and move away, but close enough to where I can still keep an eye on her.

I plop onto the sand and twist the cap off my beer, then take a long swig, sulking in my own misery.

Fuck, I'm pathetic, lusting after a woman almost half my age. A woman the same age as my *daughter.*

I've never been one to stew in self-loathing.

But in this moment, I've never hated myself more.

# nineteen

## Izzy

WHEN DERRICK BROUGHT up coming to the beach for a bonfire party, I was excited. I haven't been to one, and I was looking forward to hanging out with him outdoors rather than in the house for once. I never thought this was a date, even if I secretly wished it could be. So to be so upset when I realized he wasn't listening? Especially when I asked if he'd want to dance with me? It was foolish.

Even so, it hurt my feelings.

Now, Dylan's hands are warm on my waist, and my skin is kissed with sweat from the warm evening air and all the dancing I've done.

The sun set a while ago, but I wasn't watching. *Was Derrick?* He'd been excited about it, but rather than sit and watch with him, I ran away like a petulant child. I'm sure that only solidified how he thinks of me.

The sting of embarrassment over my behavior still clings to me, but I close my eyes and move with the music, doing my best to ignore it.

Dylan turns me in the direction that faces Derrick, and I find him in the same spot he's been in most of the evening. Sitting on the sand, nursing the same beer, eyes on me. His face goes hard when he catches me watching. Even from here, I can see the tick in his jaw.

*Good*, I think. *Be pissed. At least it means you care.*

When the song ends, I step away from Dylan. He reaches for my hip to pull me back in, but I take another step away and shake my head.

"I need some water."

"Come on, one more."

I laugh. "I'm thirsty."

"All right, but come find me." He flashes me a dimpled grin.

He's cute. Nice, too. But he doesn't make my heart skip a beat.

Not like the man brooding in the sand twelve or so feet away.

I stick my hand in the icy water and pull out a bottle. With a flick of my wrist, I twist the cap, then take a deep pull. The ocean breeze has the sweat on my skin feeling almost icy now that I'm not moving around.

With a sigh, I sink down into the sand, giving my feet a break and willing my heart to slow, and watch the waves lap against the shoreline. It really is so peaceful here.

A shadow looms over me, and without looking, I know who it is. I can feel the anger radiating from him.

"Let's go."

The growled command has me bristling. Who does he

think he is to make demands of me? It was *his* idea to come here.

My reaction to his selective hearing was immature, I can admit that, but only to myself. And I'm madder at myself than I am at him. I have to stop lusting after a man who's never going to be interested in me. Sure, sometimes I swear I catch him watching me, and sometimes he makes comments that can be interpreted as flirty. But at the end of the day, he'll never go there.

"I'm not ready to leave." I twist the cap back onto the bottle and set it in the sand beside me.

"We're going."

I look up at him, annoyance clawing at my insides. "No, you can go. I'm an adult. I can find my own way home." I lift my chin higher and glower. "Or maybe I'll stay out tonight."

His face, already white from the light reflecting off the full moon above us, goes ashen.

I shouldn't take satisfaction from that.

"I know you think I'm just a kid," I say, letting sand sift through my fingers. "But I'm twenty-seven. I'm a grown woman."

He looks away, jaw ticking. "I know that."

"Really? Because it doesn't seem like you do." Standing, I brush sand off the back of my dress. "Let's go, but *only* because I'm ready to leave."

I doubt Dylan will miss me anyway. There are plenty of other girls for him to hang out with.

I pick up my water bottle and shuffle to the nearest trash can, then head for the parking lot.

Derrick sulks behind me. I don't know what he's so pressed about, since he's getting what he wants. But he keeps his distance the whole way to the truck.

Annoyance flashes through me, directed at myself, not him. I need to get over this stupid crush. He's never going to reciprocate my feelings.

I'm being pathetic.

He unlocks the truck, and I reluctantly climb inside. Via's place is close enough that I could walk if I really didn't want to go home with him, or demand he drop me off on the way, but frankly, I don't want to risk finding her and Reid in a compromising position again.

We don't speak the entire drive, and when we get back to the house, I take Wonton out, then shut myself away in my room. After a quick shower, I climb into bed and let the tears fall.

It's painful, wanting a man who'll never want me back.

---

GOD MUST HATE ME.

It's the only logical reason. Because when I wake up, I find Derrick in the kitchen making breakfast.

No shirt.

Gray sweatpants.

The look is any woman's kryptonite.

He glances over his shoulder, catching me frozen in the doorway.

I still feel awkward. Does he?

"I thought I'd handle breakfast this morning," he says, his tone nonchalant. "Scrambled eggs and toast good with you?"

I nod, unable to get my mouth to form words, and shuffle to the coffeepot. Maybe caffeine will help.

Derrick slides a plate in front of me a few minutes later,

then sits beside me at the table. He's close enough that I can feel the heat of his arm even though we're not touching.

"I'm sorry about yesterday."

The unexpected apology barrels into me, making me rear back. "You are?"

Head hanging and forearms resting on the table, he sighs. "Honestly, I'm not exactly sure what upset you. I was lost in my thoughts, so I missed what you said. But that doesn't mean I didn't care to listen. Even so, I realize that hurt you, so I deserve the anger."

I wet my lips and inhale deeply, garnering my nerve. "I'm sorry, too. I shouldn't have gone off the way I did. I know we weren't on a date or anything"—I bark out a laugh like the very idea of it is preposterous, even though I secretly ache for exactly that—"but you brought me there, and I should've stuck by your side." I lower my focus to my table. "We didn't even watch the sunset."

*How could we, when I was being pouty and immature? My attitude surely reminded him of our age difference. Can I be forgiven because this crush has made me batshit crazy?*

He spears a piece of egg with his fork. "Can we agree we were both dipshits?"

His question pulls a small laugh from my chest. "Yeah, let's do that."

Since it's Sunday, we don't have to be at the office or on site, so I plan to work on the business's website and upload photos. I don't have to work from home, but I want to. I need something to keep my mind from wandering to things it shouldn't.

We finish breakfast, and when Derrick gathers up the plates, his fingers brush ever so lightly against mine.

It's an innocent, accidental touch, but one I feel everywhere.

I close my eyes, willing my racing heart to settle.

While Derrick loads the plates in the dishwasher, I'm frozen in my seat, having an internal meltdown.

Once he's shut the dishwasher door, he turns and leans his hip against the island. "Do you want to go out on the boat today?"

I'm tempted to say yes. Our time out on the water is always soothing. More than almost anything in my life, being out there with him feels right.

But I shake my head. "No, I need to get a few things done today."

His shoulders droop a fraction, but I pretend not to notice. Right now, I need some space. If I had anywhere else to stay, I'd be gone. At least for a bit. But I called the Inn last night, hoping a room had opened up, but they're still booked solid.

I could go back to LA, but the idea of being there is even worse than facing Derrick after last night's spat.

Determined to get my shit together, I slide out from the table and head upstairs to change. While I lace up my tennis shoes, Wonton does an excited little dance on his back feet.

"Do you want to go for a walk?" I ask in a singsong voice. "Come on, let's go." Tail wagging, he darts out of the room and down the stairs.

By the front door, I strap him into his harness and leash him up. "We're going for a walk," I call out to Derrick, though I don't wait for a response.

I get about a block from the house before I decide to turn around and grab a jacket.

"Just wait here," I tell Wonton in the entryway. I unclasp his leash but leave his harness on.

He wags his tail like he understands.

Upstairs, the pipes groan from Derrick's shower. Despite the updates he's made, this is still an older home with plenty of quirks.

I swipe my jacket off the closet door and turn, but the sound of the groaning pipes stops me. Because from here, it doesn't sound like old pipes.

No. It sounds like *moaning*.

Holding my breath, I tiptoe out of my room, my curiosity piqued, and to his door, which is open just a crack. I should go, pretend I didn't hear him, but fuck it if I can't help myself.

That's when I hear it.

This time when he moans, low and throaty, it's my name. *"Izzy."*

My breath catches. Those two syllables have never sounded so good.

Taking a step closer, I lean in so my ear is positioned in the gap between the door and its frame.

*He's touching himself while thinking of me.*

My heart takes off, thundering in my ears.

All this time I've been trying to convince myself that my silly crush is one sided, that he doesn't see me as anything other than a pseudo-roommate. Sure, I've caught him checking me out, but he's a man, and I...

*"Fuck, Izzy."*

Sweet Jesus.

The jacket slips from my grip and flutters to the ground.

I don't know what comes over me, but suddenly feeling bold, I push the door open wider. The smart thing to do would be to go downstairs, walk out of this house, and pretend this never happened.

*"That's a good girl."*

That simple sentence heats my core, and my panties grow damp.

With my lip pulled between my teeth, I bring my hand to the waistband of my shorts. It would be so easy to touch myself, tease my clit, slip my fingers—

*"Fuuuck."*

My core clenches at the sound, and all timidity leaves me.

I push the door open wider, then head straight for the open bathroom door, like I'm drawn to him by an invisible force. I stop at the threshold, and in the reflection of the mirror, I see his silhouette, shadowed by the steam.

My heart races. This is a terrible idea. There's a good chance he'll reject me. Yell. Hell, kick me out of his house.

My thoughts are swirling when his hand comes up on the glass, startling me. I jump, squeaking, giving myself away before I'm ready.

My heart drops to the floor at the same time the water cuts off.

"I-Izzy?"

Forcing air into my lungs, I step into the room and face the shower, propping myself up against the counter behind me.

He swipes a towel from where it hangs over the glass shower door. The fog is thick around him as he wraps it around his waist, hiding the part of himself that I'm aching to lay my eyes on.

The shower door slides open, and there he is, water clinging to his solid chest, dripping down his sculpted muscles and disappearing beneath the cotton.

I've seen Derrick without a shirt at least a dozen times, but it's different, knowing there's nothing but bare skin beneath that towel.

It would be so easy to tug it away. I'd drop to my knees,

176

wrap my hand around his cock and take the tip into my mouth.

I wet my lips, wishing I already had the taste of him there, and take him in from head to toe and back again.

When I meet his eye, finding a heat there that matches what's burning inside me, my core clenches.

Aching.

Desperate.

If he doesn't say something, I might die.

He puts me out of my misery. "What are you doing here?" Lust-dark eyes skim me, assess me the way I assessed him. "You left."

I flatten my hands on the countertop, then curl my fingers over the lip. "I came back for a jacket, and I … I heard you and…"

He raises a single dark brow in challenge, though I can't tell whether there's anger there, too, or desire. "And you thought what?"

Voice shaky, I say, "You said my name."

Water drips from his hair, down his forehead. God, he's gorgeous. He swallows, his Adam's apple bobbing. "I did."

The breath I didn't know I was holding whooshes from me. At least he doesn't deny it.

"I thought you didn't like me … like that." I force myself to meet his eye, a silent dare. Will he give me honesty, or will he lie, play it off?

"I like you *way* too much *like that*." He takes a step closer. That single move closes far too much space in this small room. I could count every one of his eyelashes if I wanted.

"Why haven't you done something about it?" I fire back, but my bravado loses all credibility when the words are nothing but breath.

He shakes his head, causing droplets from his wet hair to sprinkle around him. A drop lands on my cheek, and his warm thumb whisks it away a second after the sensation registers.

"I think the answer to that is pretty obvious."

I shake my head. "It's really not."

His attention drops to my lips, and I realize I'm licking them, like I'm anticipating the taste of him.

"You're too young for me," he says, zeroing in on my throat, where he can surely see evidence of my quickly beating pulse.

"I'm a consenting adult," I argue, making his lips twitch with an almost smile. "One who's wanted you for far longer than you've wanted me." I reach out and tentatively place my hand on his damp shoulder. I slide it up the back of his neck, gently tugging on his hair. "I want this. I want you."

With a curse, he angles in and presses his forehead to mine. His eyes are closed, breaths unsteady. "Don't say shit like that."

My heart lurches, and a shaky exhale stutters past my lips. "Why not?"

"Because I've only got so much self-control." His warm eyes meet mine, lusty and soulful all at the same time.

*Fuck self-control.*

With a breath in, I garner all my nerve and press my mouth to his. I stay like that, with my lips resting against him, not really kissing him. I'm giving him the choice. Letting him decide whether we go any further.

He groans low in his throat. The sound vibrates through him to me, and it takes everything I have not to push. Not to lick into his mouth. Not to drag my hands down his chest. But he has to meet me halfway, so I wait.

I feel it, the moment the wall he's been holding up crumbles. The sound he makes as he gives in is a cross between a cry and a moan. He cups my cheeks, his big hands hot and rough, and kisses me with a force that steals the breath from my lungs. I release his hair and slide my hands around his neck to his chest. His heart beats impossibly fast beneath my palm.

He kisses me like if he stops, I might disappear into thin air. It's intense, almost a little forceful, like he wants to sink into me until we become one. I've never been kissed like this—in a way that makes me feel wanted and treasured, desired and revered.

I grab the hem of my top and lift, tipping back so I can tug it over my head. Before it's even hit the ground, we're kissing again, like we can't get enough.

Every kiss I've ever had pales in comparison to the way Derrick consumes me.

Without breaking our connection, he grabs me by the waist and sets me on the counter. Then he moves those hands to my thighs and spreads my legs wider before stepping between them. Wrapping one arm around his neck, I arch back and rock my hips against him.

A towel.

That's all that separates me from his bare skin.

"Derrick," I breathe when he peppers gentle kisses down my neck.

When he hits a ticklish spot where my neck meets my collarbone, a shiver works its way through me, and goose bumps erupt on my skin. He presses open-mouthed kisses across my collarbone, then the swells of my breasts. My jog bra suddenly feels more constricting than ever. "Take it off," I beg. "I need it off. Too tight."

He obliges, deftly helping me slip out of it. The instant I'm

179

free, my breaths come easier, but at the fire in his eyes as he takes in my half-naked form, it's gone again.

He stares at my breasts, eyes dark with an obsession I've never seen before.

"C-Can I?" He looks up at me, catching his lip between his teeth. "Can I—"

Arching closer, desperate for his touch, I blurt out, "God, yes. Please."

Gently, he cups a breast in each palm, feeling their weight. I'm not flat-chested, but I'm not all that well-endowed, either. They're tear-drop shaped and far from perfect in my eyes. But in his? I see nothing but adoration for my body.

He swallows audibly and fixes his attention on my face. "You're perfect, Izzy. So fucking perfect. You know that?"

I nod, because right now, that's exactly how I feel.

He ducks his head, taking my left nipple into his mouth. He nips and flicks and sucks until it's a stiff peak, and when he lets go, I whimper. Blessedly, he's quickly paying the right the same attention.

When he finally takes my shorts off, he's going to find me *soaked*, and I don't care one bit.

I rest my hand on the knot of his towel and graze my fingernails over his bare stomach, relishing the way his muscles contract in response.

This time, I'm the one asking for permission to explore.

When he straightens and nods, I eagerly tug at the towel, and it drops, revealing him in all his naked glory. And glory it is.

His wide shoulders and tapered waist are like an arrow pointing straight to his cock.

He's already hard, or maybe still hard. I don't actually know whether he came in the shower. I wrap my hand around his length, and my stomach does a flip. Fuck, he's thick. Thick and long and perfect. My vagina is going to be *destroyed*, but in the best way.

He shivers at my touch and it's quite possibly the sexiest thing I've ever seen.

I lick my lips with anticipation and tighten my core muscles to quell the need pulsing there. "Have you thought about my hand on your cock?"

He closes his eyes, jaw clenching, and tips his head back. "Yes." He fists his hands at his sides, like he's working hard to restrain himself.

It only turns me on further.

I give him one stroke. "What about my mouth?"

His chest rises and falls with each heavy inhale and exhale, pulling my attention there. To the light dusting of chest hair. With my free hand, I trace my thumb over his right nipple and rake through the hair with my fingertips.

I bat my eyes up at him when he doesn't answer me. "You don't want me to put my mouth on your cock?"

His Adam's apple bobs, his dark irises burning. "You've got to stop talking about my dick."

A laugh escapes me, causing my chest to brush against his torso. My nipples pebble, somehow even harder than they already were. "Why?"

"Because every time the word cock leaves your mouth, I'm afraid I'm going to blow my load like a teenager."

I stick my lip out in a mock pout. "But it's my favorite word."

With his eyes narrowed on me, he grips my chin between his thumb and forefinger. "It can be your favorite word later."

He captures my mouth in a kiss before I can sass back.

I smile against his lips, pumping my hand up and down his length.

"Please," I breathe, my core clenching in anticipation.

"Please, what?" he mocks, licking his way down my neck and between my breasts. He drops to one knee, forcing me to release him.

At the sight of him kneeling on the floor before me, I whimper.

"Please, fuck me."

He tilts his head and smirks, the expression dark and wicked. "Are you sure you don't want me to lick this pussy first?" He rubs that aching spot between my legs, the one still covered with the tight material of my workout shorts. "For months, I've been dreaming about what this pussy tastes like."

I nod, whimpering again. There's no hiding my desperation. "Yes. Do that."

He chuckles, the sound a low rumble, and grabs my waistband. Then, in one quick move, he yanks them and my underwear down.

"Fuck." The word is a slow, low growl. "Look at you. So pretty and pink and soaking wet for *me*."

"Y-yes." I cup my breasts. "For you."

He presses two fingers against my pussy, spreading the lips. His eyes flick up to meet mine. "Put your feet on the counter."

I do as he says, spreading myself even more for him. It's not the most comfortable position, my back pressing into the mirror behind me, but with Derrick on his knees in front of me, I've never felt better.

His warm palms land on my thighs and spread them farther, and when he angles in, I swear he inhales my scent before he licks me. I gasp and squeeze my eyes shut at the sensation of his tongue on my most sensitive spot, my brain short circuiting. I've been dreaming about this—him—for what feels like forever, and it's finally happening.

When I look down, he's watching me, tongue flicking over my clit.

Hand trembling, I glide my fingers through his damp hair and tug at the strands. A tiny smile lifts the corners of his lips, though the expression is almost imperceptible with his face between my thighs.

"Derrick," I whimper, dropping my head back against the mirror. I rock my hips into his face and his hands tighten against my thighs, holding me down firmly. A silent command to let him do his thing.

It isn't long before an orgasm crashes through me. I cry out, my body shaking from the quivering high. He doesn't let up, though, not until the last of my orgasm has fled.

Only then does he stand. He keeps his left hand on my thigh while he strokes himself with his right, his focus drifting from my face to my breasts to my pussy and back again. As much as I want to reach out to him, I'm boneless. I will my hands to work, to touch him, to drag my fingers down his stomach, but I can't move.

His hand leaves my thigh, then he's grabbing me behind the neck instead. He pulls me to him, meeting me in the middle, and lavishes my mouth with bruising kisses that taste like me. Despite the intense orgasm he just gave me, my body craves more. It begs to be filled by him.

He pulls away, and with his forehead pressed to mine, he asks, "Are you sure about this? Once we do this—"

I silence him with a kiss. "I'm sure."

He looks up, uttering a "thank fuck."

Guiding his cock to my pussy, he pushes in a fraction of an inch and pulls back out. Then again. Teasing me.

The third time, he freezes, and his wide eyes meet mine. "Condom—I don't have condoms."

"I'm safe," I blurt out the words, desperate to keep him from stopping this.

"Me, too." The look of relief on his face would no doubt have me falling to my knees if I weren't seated on the counter, spread like a feast just for him. "I can … I'll pull out."

"You don't have to, if you don't want to. I have an implant."

"*Fuck*." He drops his head to my chest. "You're killing me."

"Please, don't die before you fuck me."

Chest shaking with amusement, he turns his head and presses a kiss to the underside of my jaw.

"Only you could make me laugh at a time like this." He rises to his full height, and looks down at me, taking me in, naked and vulnerable. "God, you're beautiful, Izzy."

*Izzy.*

I've never loved the sound of my name more.

With a hand on his length, he gives himself a couple of pumps, then lines up at my entrance. He eases in like before, but this time, he goes deeper. Back out. In again.

He takes my hips, pulling me closer and sliding in deeper at the same time. With a gasp, I sit up straighter so I can put my arms around his shoulders.

When he pushes in again, he fills me completely, consuming me.

"Derrick, oh God."

My body stretches to accommodate his size and I lean back again.

*Full. So fucking full.*

"Fuck," he curses, gripping my throat with one hand. "God, look at you. Look at the way your pussy takes my cock. Such a good girl."

With his other hand, he finds my clit and rubs circles with his thumb.

"Fuck, Izzy, you're so pretty." His eyes are glazed with lust and maybe something more as he takes me in.

He rocks his hips against mine, slow and steady. The deep, sure press of him has my eyes threatening to roll back. He fills me in a way I've never experienced before. It isn't even about his size. It's the way he knows exactly how to hold me, how to rock his hips so I get the best friction.

It's a reminder that Derrick is very much a grown man, one with way more experience than any of the guys I've been with.

"Derrick." His name is a plea. I reach for him, my fingers grazing his taut stomach. "Harder, please. I'm so close."

His eyes darken at my words, their normal golden brown going molten. "You wanna come all over my cock, pretty girl?"

"Y-yes," I stutter, nodding desperately.

He crashes his mouth to mine, stealing what little breath I have left.

He finds the speed and rhythm that has my body shaking, and when I go over that ledge screaming his name, he holds me through it.

His strokes slow as I come down from my orgasm, and he looks me over like he's memorizing every inch of me, every millisecond of this encounter. He clenches his jaw, looking away with a muttered "fuck."

Heart stumbling with fear, I cup his jaw and force his gaze back to me.

*Is he regretting this already? He hasn't even finished.*

"What?" I implore.

He swallows, and I swear the fear that's plaguing me flickers in his eyes. "I don't want this to end."

Relief sweeps through me, followed by surprise. Because he's talking about more than just *this*. He's talking about *us*.

Teeth gritted, he squeezes his eyes shut and pumps into me. Then, with a moan, he buries his face in the crook of my neck and comes. Palming the back of his head, I hold him, wishing I never had to let go.

We stay like that for a minute, maybe two. I'm not sure. Time feels weird. Like it's sped up and slowed down all at once. Probably because I'm struggling to wrap my head around what happened.

Derrick carefully pulls away from me. As he goes, he takes in every inch of my body, though it's not in a lustful way like before. Instead, it's as though he's checking me over to ensure that I'm okay. His attention lingers on my throat, like maybe, like me, he's thinking about what it felt like to have his hand there.

He's still inside me, still half hard. The urge to wiggle my hips, to bring that friction back, is strong, but I can't stay in this position much longer. Being fucked on the bathroom counter is hot and all, but it's not exactly comfortable.

Derrick pulls out of me slowly, and I whimper at the loss of him.

His eyes narrow in on that sensitive place between my thighs—aching from both the loss of him and what he just did to my body—then he's sliding a hand up my leg.

"What are you—"

His touch leaves me speechless. With two fingers, he gently pushes his semen back inside me.

The action is far hotter than I ever could have imagined, and I'm not sure I want to know what that says about me.

When his warm eyes meet mine, I search for any sign of regret there, but I find nothing.

Though the man can be so incredibly difficult to read.

His eyes still on mine, he slides the shower door open and reaches behind him to turn it on.

He waits for the water to warm, then he drags me inside with him.

"Just a shower," he says. "Nothing more."

It's a lie. We both know it.

He doesn't protest when I sink to my knees and take him into my mouth.

I don't protest when he lifts me and puts my back against the wall, then settles his cock deep inside me once more.

Now that I've had him, I don't know how I'll ever live without this.

# twenty

Derrick

I HAD SEX WITH IZZY.

I. Had. Sex. With. Izzy.

Sex with Izzy, I had.

Izzy and I had sex.

My brain takes the words and twists them, turns them, reorders them. Like eventually they'll form a different outcome. But they won't. I—*we*—crossed a line we can't come back from. Frankly, I don't want to.

It was an accident. At first, at least. The initial confrontation. There's no way the sex could be categorized that way. I didn't know she'd come back to the house, and God help me for needing some kind of relief. I was content to take it into my own hands, literally. I might see the way Izzy looks at me, but I never would've crossed that line. I just … couldn't. Not until she crossed it for me.

I think of the way she looked on the counter—naked, with swollen lips and her face red from my beard.

"What are you thinking about?"

The sound of her voice jerks me out of my thoughts and back to the present. Where she sits on the kitchen island, legs dangling, she pops a grape into her mouth, waiting with an amused curl of her lips. Her hair is damp from the shower, her cheeks still flushed. My T-shirt dwarfs her small frame, the white fabric falling delicately off one shoulder. I can't help myself when I step away from the stove and place a kiss there. That small intimacy feels even better than the sex. It's not like I'm a monk. I've had hookups over the years. But not *this*. Not with a woman I can cook for and kiss so casually and share my space with.

With a giggle, she glides her hand over my bare chest.

I go with total honesty. "I was thinking about you."

"You're not freaking out on me, are you?" She asks the question with a smile, but she can't hide the flash of fear in her eyes.

"No."

Shockingly, I'm not. Being with Izzy feels *right* in a way. Like she's been here forever, been *mine* forever.

She smiles and pops another grape into her mouth. It's a variety called cotton candy, and she insisted we buy them during our last grocery store run. I'm a skeptic, and even I have to admit they're good.

"Pay attention." She waves her hand to the skillet on the stovetop. "Don't burn my grilled cheese."

With a peck to her lips, I turn and do as I'm told. Then I'm plating our grilled cheese sandwiches, and she's carrying the bowl of grapes to the table. I pull out a chair and sit down, tugging her into my lap as I go. It's precarious having her there, rubbing her ass against me, but I want her close.

I lift one sandwich and hold it up to her.

Tilting her head down, she fights a smirk. "Are you going to feed me?"

"I'm trying to."

Her smirk only grows. "I'm capable of feeding myself. My hands are working. It's only my vagina that's a little sore."

I nip at her jaw. "You and that mouth."

"You like my mouth."

I do, I really do. And not for the reason she's thinking. I like her sass and her smarts and her sweetness. All of it.

When she finally takes a bite, her eyes widen in surprise. "That has to be the best grilled cheese I've ever had."

"I told you."

When we finally extracted ourselves from my bed after a slow and careful round three, I told her I'd make grilled cheese for dinner, to which she scoffed. According to her, it's boring. Basic.

She takes another bite. "What more could a girl ask for? Cheese and a post-orgasmic glow."

Chuckling, I take a bite of the sandwich. We might as well share them. "Glad I can provide."

She wraps an arm around me and rubs the back of my neck with her thumb, her gaze locked on mine. It's intense, but not in a way that makes me want to look away. If anything, I want to sink into the depths of her. Read her mind. Memorize every detail of her. Every bit and piece of Izzy James.

It's there, in the back of my mind, my conscience. It taunts me, reminding me of her age. I ignore it. I don't want anything to ruin this. I haven't felt this kind of blissful, borderline selfish happiness since I was a teenager.

We finish off the first grilled cheese, then the second. When it's gone, Izzy turns around and straddles my lap. And when she rocks her hips against me, I groan. I don't know how, but he's already coming to life again.

"Simmer down, boss man," she murmurs. "My vagina needs a break. I just want to look at you." She takes my cheeks in her hands, studying me with a serious quirk of her lips like I'm a specimen to inspect beneath a microscope.

Her touch is reverent, her fingertips drifting over the slope of my nose. Her lips move, but no sound comes out.

"What are you doing?"

She smiles softly but doesn't stop. "Counting your freckles. I find I have quite the obsession with them."

"Just my freckles?" I taunt.

"And your lips." She traces the curve of them. "Your shoulders." Her hands are a warm caress over my deltoids. "All of you." She leans in for a kiss.

I slide my fingers through her hair, deepening the kiss. Her taste is imprinted forever on my tongue.

"Let's go somewhere tonight."

She sits back, resting her elbows on the table behind her, one brow lifted. "Where?"

With a hand tucked up under her shirt, I ghost my fingers over the toned skin of her belly. "We could get dinner on the pier."

She wets her lips with a subtle swipe of her tongue. "Like … a date?"

Straightening, I tuck a piece of hair behind her ear, my fingers lingering longer than necessary on her soft cheek. "Do you want it to be a date?"

Head dropped back, she lets out a huff. She moves to get

off me, but I grab her hips and hold her in place. "Where do you think you're going? What's wrong?"

When she pins me with a glare, her eyes swim with hurt. "If you have to ask me if I want it to be a date, it's not a date, Derrick."

Normally, I love when she says my name, but for the first time, it sounds wrong on her tongue.

"I'm sorry. I'm an idiot. I'm not good at this. It's been..." I blow out a breath. "A long time. Forgive me, please?" I cup her cheeks in my hands, rubbing my thumbs over her smooth skin. I could kick myself for framing it the way I did. She's right, it's definitely not a date if I ask her that way. "Will you go on a date with me? A real one?"

She dips her chin in answer, eyes bright. "Yes."

---

I GET READY, then sneak out of the house to let her do the same. To make it feel more real, I'll come back when it's time to pick her up.

With the radio playing softly, I drive into town and park my truck on the street.

It's been so long since I've been on a real date.

It's laughable, honestly, because my last real date was with her sister. The irony isn't lost on me.

The flower shop is at the end of the street, the bouquets displayed outside creating a riot of color. There are a few tourists milling around on the sidewalk, looking over the options. Rather than stopping there, I head inside.

Gloria looks up from behind the counter, a fake smile plastered on her face, but when she recognizes me, it morphs into a real one.

"Hey, Gloria." The old wood floors groan beneath my feet as I approach her. She had me renovate the shop about ten years ago, but we agreed that the original hardwood floors needed to stay.

"You're a sight for sore eyes." She looks me up and down, eyes crinkling at the corners. They glimmer with amusement. "What brings you in?"

Gloria and I went to school together, though we weren't much more than acquaintances.

"I need some flowers."

"You've come to the right place." She comes around the front of the counter. "Who are they for?"

"My ... I have a date."

"Ooh." She shimmies her shoulders. "Tell me more."

Heart thumping, I go ahead and put it out there. No use hiding. Once we're seen out tonight, the whole town will know. "It's Izzy."

Her jaw drops open. She snaps it closed, only to open it again and sputter, "Your son's girlfriend's little sister?"

My shoulders rise to my ears. "Why'd you have to say it like that?"

"Dirty, dirty, dirty Derrick." She clucks her tongue, smiling again. "You dirty dog."

I scrub a hand over my face, the stubble on my cheeks rasping against my palm. "I know. Whatever you're thinking, I know. Believe me."

She squeezes my arm. "I kid." Then she's sashaying past me and plucking a spiky-looking blue flower from a bunch. She flits around the shop, putting together a bouquet while humming.

"Do you think I'm crazy?" I finally ask her.

She pauses what she's doing, turns, and assesses me. "For

dating? Derrick, if anyone deserves someone who treats them well, it's *you*."

I shove my hands in my pockets. "The age difference isn't weird?"

"Let me ask you this." She picks through a basket of wispy looking yellow flowers. "Do you like her *because* she's young, or do you just like *her*? There's a difference."

"I like her."

I like everything about Izzy.

How she laughs.

How full of life she is.

The way her eyes sparkle when she's excited.

How much she loves slushies.

The list is endless.

"Then you have your answer."

She puts a few white flowers into the bunch and hands it to me, and I'm instantly hit with the floral scent.

A smile takes over my face as I assess the details. "It's perfect."

If Izzy were a bouquet, she would most certainly be this one. It's a little wild and mismatched, but unique and captivating. Beautiful.

She beams at the praise. "Good. I'm glad."

Once I've paid, I continue down the street. I stop at the coffee shop to kill time and grab my usual, then swing by the restaurant. They don't normally take reservations, but since it's tourist season, and since I've done quite a bit of work for them over the years, they make an exception.

As I step outside again, I pull my phone from my pocket and check the time. I'll be a little early, but I can park down the street for a few minutes if I need to.

The closer I get to home, the faster my heart beats.

I'm on the precipice of something new, something that could change my life. But only if I can get out of my head and stop overthinking it.

# twenty-one

Izzy

THE DOORBELL RINGS DOWNSTAIRS, sending Wonton into a tizzy.

His bark is high-pitched as he darts out of the bedroom and down the stairs. Derrick left a while ago, claiming to have some things to do before our date.

I fasten the clasp on my necklace, give my reflection one last glance, and carefully make my way downstairs. It's been months since I've worn heels, and my traitorous feet seem to have forgotten how to function in them.

With one foot, I gently slide Wonton away from the door, paranoid he might run out when I open it.

When I turn the knob and pull, the sight I'm met with sends a fizzy, warm thrill through me. It's Derrick. He stands on the doormat, wearing a happy but shy smile and holding a bouquet of flowers.

"Hi." For a moment, it's the only word my brain can conjure. Then, somehow, a flood of words comes tumbling out. "Is your key not working?"

He shakes his head. "A real date, remember? That means I pick you up at the door."

I swear my heart dips, a joyful swoon.

"These are for you." He shoves the flowers toward me.

I take them, smiling at the thistle and blue hydrangea and some sort of wispy white flower, along with several others. They shouldn't go together, but somehow, they do. Like us.

"Let me put these in water, then we can go."

Derrick waits outside the door, and just inside, Wonton whimpers in confusion while I take care of the bouquet.

When I'm finished and have given Wonton a few scratches, I slip outside and into the shadow of his tall, wide frame.

Small and feminine, that's how I feel around him.

I want to put my hand on his chest, stand on my tiptoes, and kiss him. And with anyone else, I probably wouldn't hesitate. But Derrick makes me nervous. He turns me into a giddy teen girl again, like I'm going on my first date.

With a hand on the small of my back, he guides me to the truck and opens the door. He waits for me to strap the seat belt across my chest before he shuts it.

Once he's buckled in beside me, he starts the truck and turns the radio down when it comes on blaring.

"Are you hungry?" he asks, backing out of the driveway.

"Starving."

I haven't eaten since the grilled cheese we shared earlier and after the insane number of calories we burned, I'm feeling it.

He reaches over and laces his fingers with mine, making my heart jolt with excitement.

Everything between us changed today.

I think we've both always known that if we crossed the line, it would be more than sex.

We don't talk much on the drive to the pier. It's a beautiful, warm evening. The breeze smells like sun and salt, and the sky is already beginning to turn a warm shade of orange.

I reach for the door handle, but before I can push it open, Derrick squeezes my hand.

"No," he says, throwing his own door open. He rounds the hood of the truck, walking tall, confident. God, he's gorgeous.

He offers me a hand to help me out of the truck. I'm grateful for it when my heels wobble on the gravel lot.

"You okay?"

"I'm fine. Just a little out of practice." I pick up one heel-clad foot and wiggle it.

He closes the truck door and locks up before taking my hand and guiding me over to the paved walking path that leads to the pier.

When he angles in close, I swear he gives a small sniff.

"What?" I ask, tugging a piece of hair forward. I inhale deeply, worried that it smells. I don't know how it could since he's the one who washed it for me this morning. "Do I smell bad?"

"No." I swear his cheeks go the faintest shade of pink beneath his scruffy beard. "You smell really good, actually."

"Oh." Warmth floods me. "Thank you."

"You know," he pulls me to the side suddenly, "we should talk about something before we do this."

I press a thumb to the lines between his brows, wishing I could erase the concern I see there. "What?"

He inhales sharply, then presses his lips together like he

wants to hold whatever's on his mind inside but knows he needs to spill.

Jaw flexing, he lets go of my hand and runs his fingers through his hair. As he lets the longish, wavy strands fall over his forehead, my stomach rolls with uneasiness. We didn't come this far for him to get cold feet, did we?

"I want to do this," he starts, meeting my eye. "But this is a small town. Your sister ... my son and daughter ... they're going to know at the speed of light. Are you okay with that? If you want ... if you want to keep this ... me ... a secret, I'll understand."

Heart aching, I put my hand on his cheek. It's warm, and his stubble is rough against my palm. "You're not a secret to me. But..." I swallow back a wave of trepidation. "Do you want to keep *me* a secret?"

He wets his lips and slowly shakes his head. "No. I'm scared, Izzy. I really am. But no, I don't want you to be a secret."

"Good." I kiss the corner of his mouth, finding it almost easy to reach in my heels. "Now let's go. I'm starving."

With a smile, he takes my hand again. There's a lightness to his step now, like a weight he's been carrying is gone. It hurts a little, that he thinks I'd want to keep him as a dirty secret. But it's hard not to appreciate his thoughtfulness.

Tomorrow, I'll tell my sister.

Hopefully before someone else does.

We steal glances at each other as we slowly trek the pier. The scent of the salty sea air smells more like home every day.

It's funny, that I don't miss LA at all. Sure, I've always traveled, vlogging various cities and countries, so I'm used to being away. But I always missed home after a few days. Now, the idea of going back fills me with anxiety.

Derrick leads me to the nicer of the two restaurants on the pier and gives his name to the hostess. It's strange, because even though it's a nicer establishment, I'm almost positive Via mentioned that they don't take reservations.

With a friendly smile, she pulls two menus from the slot on the side of the podium. Then she motions for us to follow her through the full dining room.

This restaurant is a favorite with locals and tourists, but it's only open during the spring and summer months, so I haven't been here yet.

The interior is navy and white, with hints of a lighter blue, but the theme isn't in-your-face nautical. There are no fish or rafts or nets pinned to the walls. It's subtle, with blue-and-white-striped booths and freshly painted walls.

Behind the bar, the wall is made of glass, and a sliding glass door in the center is open to let the breeze inside. The hostess leads us around the sturdy lacquered bar and straight to a prime table by the water.

"Enjoy your dinner," she says before leaving us.

"How did you do this?" I survey the beautiful deck. It's magical, lit up with fairy lights and cast in the glow of the setting sun. The water laps against the posts, the sky a warm orange hue. "I didn't think they took reservations."

With a shy smile, he unrolls his silverware and puts the cloth napkin on his lap. "They don't. It was a favor for me."

"Ah." I nod, going for teasing, though my heart is bursting at his thoughtfulness. "Small town life."

He chuckles. "Sometimes it pays to know people."

"This is"—I inhale deeply, letting the evening air soothe me —"wow."

I've been to some of the most highly rated restaurants

around LA, Manhattan, and London, but nothing compares to this, and it's all because of the man across from me.

Beneath the table, I pinch the inside of my arm and only barely keep from flinching.

Nope, not dreaming.

When the waitress appears with a breadbasket and a pitcher of water, she fills our glasses and takes our drink order, then disappears, leaving us to look over the menu.

With my elbows on the menu I have open in front of me, I lace my fingers and angle forward. "I think we should talk about what exactly is going on between us. I'm not trying to put you on the spot, but considering how public this is"—I look around —"my sister and your kids are going to be asking questions, and I'd feel better if we talked about how we should answer them."

Sighing, he scrubs a hand over his face. "You're right."

"We're not keeping this secret, but is this … are we dating? Just having fun? They're going to want to know."

I'm already dreading the interrogation my sister is bound to put me through. Though, strangely, I'm equally excited. My sister is several years older than me, and she was with her ex-husband from a young age, so we never gushed over boys together. Now we finally have the opportunity.

"Maybe we just tell them we're seeing where things go."

It's not the declaration of love and utter devotion I'd prefer, but I'll take what I can get.

I don't *actually* want him confessing such things this soon, but a girl can dream.

I dip my chin and give him a genuine smile. "Sounds good to me."

For now.

It's for the best, really. He might be older than me, but

we're in similar stages of life at the moment. He needs to figure out whether he's ready for a relationship after losing his wife and being on his own for so long, and I need to figure out what I'm going to do with my life. If I want to continue vlogging or change direction.

Across the table, Derrick gives me a shy smile. "What's your favorite color?"

It's such a silly question when getting to know another person. Even so, I find myself smiling back. "Yellow. What's yours?"

"Blue."

"Favorite animal?" I ask him, realizing that I'm actually eager to know these simple details. Random questions like these can really help two people learn about one another.

He presses his lips together. "You're going to laugh."

That alone makes me giggle. "Oh, now I'm really intrigued."

Sighing, he smooths the front of his shirt. "I like squirrels. They're kind of batty and stupid, but cute at the same time. I've named the ones that hangout in the backyard. Sometimes I slip them a snack."

"Hold on." I lean forward, flooded with delight. "How did I not know this?"

"I'm usually up before you are. That's when I sit outside with the squirrels. Harriet is my favorite."

"What did you name the others?"

"There's Peep and Tank—he's the chubby one—and Kissy, and then there's George."

"George?" Sitting back, I laugh.

"Yeah, he sits in the tree and throws shit at me."

Our waitress approaches with the bottle of wine we ordered, so we sit back, giving her space to fill two wineglasses. It isn't until now that I realize how close we've drifted toward the center of the table, as if drawn like magnets with opposing poles. Once she's filled the glasses, she asks if we're ready to order, but honestly, we haven't even looked at the menus, so Derrick asks for a few more minutes.

I peruse the extensive seafood menu, all the while smiling over the idea of Derrick sitting outside with the squirrels each morning. I'll be setting my alarm tomorrow so I can spy on him.

When our waitress returns, we're ready, and the second she's gone, Derrick takes a sip of wine and says, "Your turn. What's your favorite animal?"

"It changes constantly." Fiddling with one of my rings, twisting it back and forth, I give the question real thought. "Right now, I'd say whales are my favorite."

His eyes soften, the brown irises warm like melted chocolate. "I'm going to make sure you see a whale, Izzy."

"Let's hope." I hold up my glass.

"It's been an unusual year," he says, scratching at his jaw. "They haven't been hanging around as much as they normally do."

"It's okay," I say. With a teasing smile, I drag my foot against the inside of his leg beneath the table. "At least now you can fuck me on your boat."

He chokes—on his own saliva, I'm assuming, since the water and wine are untouched at the moment.

"Izzy," he gasps, pressing his fist to his chest and sucking in air.

"What?" I bat my eyes innocently. "I think about it every time we're out there. Have you not thought about it at all?"

He looks away, out at the water. The sunset is a beautiful mix of pinks and oranges. "More times than I'd care to admit."

"Good," I say simply, sitting back and feeling rather smug now that I know he's felt just as tortured as I have these past few months.

Our dinner is delicious, and when we're finished, Derrick leads me out of the restaurant and back to the truck.

On the way home, he turns into the gas station.

As he parks in front of the store, I can't help the smile that takes over my face. "Slushies?"

He turns to me, the neon of the station's sign illuminating him in a blue-green hue. "They are your favorite."

I follow Derrick inside, feeling severely overdressed as my heels click-clack on the linoleum. We head straight back to the slushie machine, as usual, and Derrick fills the cups. He's better at it than I am. He has an uncanny ability to perfectly swirl the mixture, whereas when I do it, it comes out in blobs.

I pop the straw through the hole in the dome-shaped lid and take a sip. "Perfection." I hum.

Derrick follows me down the candy aisle, where I snag a bag of gummy bears and another of M&M's, then swipe a pack of Reese's for him.

The man who's always behind the counter gives us an amused smile as we approach. I dig in my purse for my wallet, but Derrick has his card out and tapped to the pad before I can pull it out.

Side by side, we take our spoils out to the truck, Derrick making sure to get the door for me.

Instead of going straight home, he drives around Parkerville while we sip our slushies.

As nice as the restaurant was, this is my favorite part of our date—fingers tangled, a cool breeze, quiet country music floating on the air, and the sights of this beautiful town.

By the time we get back to the house, I've learned even more about Derrick.

Like how he broke his left arm playing baseball with his friends when he was in high school. How, when he was a kid, he dreamed of being a pilot.

I love earning each new piece of him, then hoarding it inside me like a precious treasure.

Derrick walks me to the front door, says a quiet good night, and kisses my cheek. Then he turns his key in the lock, pushes the door open, and saunters back to his truck to wait for me to go inside.

From the doorway, I watch his every move, filled with a mix of affection and humor and tenderness. His desire to make this date feel like a normal one, like I'm not currently living with him, is adorable.

I pick up Wonton and spin him around, pressing kisses to his head. "Wonton," I gush. "I think I might be falling."

Falling in lust.

Falling in like.

Falling in love.

Upstairs, I head to the bathroom to wash up for the night. The house is quiet as I change into my pajamas, though it's possible I missed him.

For the first time in a long time, I feel like making a video. I have no intentions of posting it, but even so, I'm determined to do it. For me.

I set up my camera on the small desk in the corner, unconcerned about my lack of makeup or the messy knot of hair piled on top of my head. I adjust the mic, make sure everything is working, and then I talk.

Gush is more like it.

About Derrick.

About how he makes me feel.

My excitement to see where things might go.

At the end, I say, "If you're watching this, then that means I marry him. It also means he's your dad. I love you." Like I finish all of my videos, I add, "Until then."

With one hand over the lens, I shut off the camera, unable to wipe the stupidly giddy smile off my face. I might be getting ahead of myself—okay, I definitely am—but never before have I seen a future with a man. Not even the few I've dated long term.

With Derrick, I see every dream I've ever had.

Coffee in the mornings with the person I love.

Dancing in the kitchen.

Singing in the shower.

Making love slow and hushed, and fucking like we can't get enough of each other.

Kids and laughter and happiness.

It won't be so perfect, of course, but it'll be as close to it as any two people can come.

I climb into bed and lie on my side. Wonton tucks himself into the crook of my legs.

Sometime in the night, a big warm body joins mine and I let out a contented sigh when he tucks me against his chest.

# twenty-two

### Derrick

IT'S DOWNRIGHT EMBARRASSING the way my heart is racing in my chest.

"Are you okay?" Reid asks around a bite of pancake. My own plate of pancakes sits untouched in front of me.

"Yeah, you seem nervous," Layla adds. "And while it's nice for the three of us to be together, it feels like maybe you had an ulterior motive for inviting us."

Kids see through everything.

I clear my throat, trying to dislodge my heart, and when that doesn't work, I take a sip of coffee. "I need to tell you something."

"What?" Reid pushes his glasses up his nose and forks another piece of pancake.

At the same time, Layla straightens and says, "Are you seeing someone?"

Reid whips his head to the side, scrutinizing his sister. "What makes you think that?"

She shrugs, not taking her eyes off mine. The intensity there holds me prisoner as, around us, the diner buzzes with its usual chatter. "It's the only thing that makes sense," she says. "We don't get together like this often, and when we do, it's because something is going on. Dad hasn't had a serious relationship since Mom. Lili and I are finally out of the house. It's time."

Reid looks from her to me and back again, like he's watching a ping-pong match. "Wait"—he finally settles on me —"*are* you dating someone?"

"It's very new." I fiddle with my straw wrapper, rolling it into a ball. I'm not normally a nervous person, but when I am, I get fidgety. "Like yesterday new."

I want to make it clear that this hasn't been going on long. That I haven't been hiding a relationship from them.

Layla points at me, her eyes narrowing. "Is it the librarian? The one with blond hair? I was at the library once with Lili and overheard her telling the other librarian all about how hot my dad is. So gross." She gags.

"Uh … interesting, but no, it's not her."

"Okay, what about—"

"It's Izzy. Isn't it?" Reid asks, though it's barely a question. His words are confident, like he knows he's right.

Leave it to my son to figure me out. He's always been too smart for his own good.

Layla makes a choked sound, her jaw dropping. "Izzy?" She scoffs, her expression one of disbelief. "Dad. She's *my* age. She's my friend. My boss. Oh my God, is this my payback? Because I brought you here to tell you I was pregnant, hoping doing it in public would keep you from freaking out? You thought you'd do the same, so I'd be forced to keep quiet?"

"Layla." Shoulders drooping, I shake my head. "No, that's not what I'm doing. But yes, it's Izzy. I like her. I *really* like her. More than I've liked anyone since your mom passed."

"Dad." Tears pool in her eyes. Those watery depths feel like a stab to my gut. "Don't say shit like that. It makes me feel guilty for being angry." She swipes away the moisture, then turns to her brother. "What do you have to say about this? Izzy's your girlfriend's little sister."

With a shrug, Reid shoves another bite of pancake into his mouth. "I'm cool with it."

Layla scoffs, stealing his fork.

"Hey!" he cries a little too loud, snatching it back from her.

"You can't be okay with this. It's weird!"

I scrub a hand over my jaw, that old worry about our age difference creeping back in.

"I *am* okay with it," Reid argues, stabbing another bite of his breakfast. "Dad deserves to be happy. He hasn't dated anyone more than once or twice since Mom died. It's safe to say if he's ready to see someone seriously, then he really cares about her."

Layla frowns. The hurt in her eyes makes me consider taking it all back. But selfishly, I keep my mouth shut. The idea of not being with Izzy physically pains me.

"Layla." I clear my throat. "I understand that this will be hard for you, and I'm sorry for that. But I can't turn my back on something—on someone—who makes me happy."

Head bowed, she takes several deep breaths. "Dad, I … I can't give you my blessing if that's what you're asking for, but I won't throw a fit either. This is … weird for me." Looking up again, she glares at Reid. "And I don't see how it isn't weird for you, too."

"Hey." He throws his hands up in surrender. "If I've learned anything since meeting Via, it's that when it's right, it's right, and you don't question it."

Lips pressed together, Layla regards me for a quiet moment. "This is going to take some getting used to."

That's all I need. While hope takes root inside me, I give her a small, understanding smile. "I know."

Reid wipes his mouth with a napkin, pancakes thoroughly devoured, and tosses it onto his plate. "For the record, though, I'm not calling her Mommy."

Layla chokes, while I'm overcome by a real, deep belly laugh.

# twenty-three

DERRICK IS down the street at the diner, breaking the news to his kids. Meanwhile, my sister is waiting inside the coffee shop —no doubt watching me have an internal freakout on the sidewalk outside.

*Stop being a wimp!*

Why am I so scared? I can't imagine my sister lecturing me. I'm a grown woman, not a silly teenager with a crush.

With a succinct nod, I repeat that phrase and head for the door. It's time to do this.

Before I can reach for the door handle, my sister pushes it open from the inside. "What's wrong with you?" she asks, brow furrowed. "You're hopping around like your tampon is in wrong."

"Via," I laugh, the vise in my chest loosening.

Years ago, my straitlaced sister would never have made a comment like that. It makes my heart ache in a good way to watch her grow into herself.

"Get in here." She steps to one side. "I already ordered you a matcha."

I follow her to where our drinks sit at the counter, waving to Cindy behind the register, then to a table by the front window.

She tucks a strand of hair, the same dark brown shade as mine, behind her ear with nails painted a bright orange color. That's something else that's changed. Before she moved to Parkerville, she only wore muted pinks on her nails. Tones that complemented demure, professional clothing. Now, she gets to express herself.

"I hate that we've spent so little time together since you got here. Thank you for inviting me this morning."

I take a sip of my drink to give myself a moment to collect my thoughts, sure she'll be blindsided by what I have to say.

"Yeah, I thought we should catch up."

"So"—she smiles, giving my hand a pat—"what's going on with you? Are you heading back to LA soon?"

"Uh, no, actually." I rub my nose, stalling. "I like living with Derrick. He's going to let me film some before and after builds for my channel."

She perks up, holding her cup with both hands. "That's cool. Do you think it'll go over well with your audience? It's different from your normal content."

I wipe at the condensation already forming on my cup. "I hope so. It was getting a little monotonous. I thought I'd try something new."

"It's good you're enjoying it." Her lips kick up on one side. "And how is it living with Derrick?"

My face instantly gets hot. I can only imagine how red it is. I'm assaulted by memories of the way he fucked me on his bathroom counter. I don't think I'm ever going to stop thinking about that. I take a long drink of my ice-cold matcha, willing it to lower my body temperature.

"It's going well. That's actually what I wanted to talk to you about."

"Ooh!" She brightens, patting my hand where it rests on the table. "Are you thinking about buying a place here? If you plan on staying a lot, it would be nice for you to have your own space."

"Actually—"

"Oh, is that why you're filming the before and after thing? Is Derrick fixing up a place for you?"

"Via, I ... no, I'm not buying a house. At least not right now."

"Sorry." Her smile falls. "I got a bit carried away."

"It's okay." I rub my fingers over my mouth, working up the nerve to get the words out. "That's not what I wanted to tell you."

"Okay, tell me. I'm all ears." She mimes zipping her lips.

God, I'm embarrassed. Not because I'm ashamed of Derrick in any way, but because of the overall situation. Because of the likely awkwardness it'll create.

"I'm seeing Derrick. We've ... there's chemistry between us, and we've decided to give this a shot. See where it goes." I shrug, like it's no big deal, when in reality, it's everything.

When she's silent, her mouth parted in shock, I find my own running to fill that void. "I really like him, Via-Mia. More than I've ever liked a guy, and you *know* how big my crush on Tyler Vandell was my sophomore year."

Via shakes her head like she's freeing herself from her stupor. "You and Derrick?"

"Yes." I nod, tracing my index finger over a whorl in the wooden tabletop. "We don't want to keep this a secret. You guys mean too much to us to do that, so while this is extremely new, and may seem strange to you, we wanted to be up front about it."

She tilts her head, looking at me in the way only my older sister can—with understanding and a little bit of humor.

"I can't say I'm surprised. I figured you'd hook up with him at some point, but I thought that's all it would be."

My heart lurches. "Why would you think that?"

With a snort, she wraps her fingers around her cup. "The way you look at him makes it obvious, and I guess I can't blame you. He's a good-looking man."

"Oh, God." I cringe, hiding my face behind my hands. "How do I look at him?"

"With hearts in your eyes."

I flush with embarrassment, wishing I could sink beneath the table. Maybe even the floorboards themselves. "I can't help it. He's so hot. In a rugged, good with his hands, lumberjack kind of way."

Via dissolves into laughter, practically melting into the table when she crosses her arms and lays her head on them.

"I can't believe you're laughing right now," I cry. "I thought you were going to freak out and judge me and tell me he's too old for me."

Straightening, she sobers. "Izzy." She clutches my hand and gives it a squeeze. There are already specks of paint on her fingers like she woke up this morning and couldn't resist working on a piece. "It would be hypocritical of me to judge

214

you for being with an older man when I'm with a man who's eleven years younger than I am."

"I'm the same age as Layla," I say, voicing one of my biggest worries. "That's weird, right?"

She hums, thoughtful. "I'm not going to sugarcoat that part for you. She's your friend and she works for you, so it may be hard for her to come to terms with. But if you and I are having this conversation, then is it safe to assume that you've decided it's worth the risk?"

"Yes." With a sharp nod, I reach up to tuck a piece of hair behind my ear, but I lower it when I remember I put my hair in a ponytail today. "I have."

"It's okay to be scared, but focus on what the two of you are building. Don't stress about the other stuff. Everything works out in the end. Just look at Reid and me."

"You're okay with this?"

She gives a soft laugh. "Of course I am. You're an adult, so is he. All that matters to me is that you're happy."

"Thank you."

My heart lifts, floating like a buoy. I needed her love and support even more than I realized.

"Are you telling Mom and Dad?"

I grimace. "Not yet. You know how Mom is."

My relationship with our parents might be less strained than hers, but it doesn't mean our mom doesn't judge me as well. There's no way she'd ever approve of this.

She laughs. "Believe me, I know. I don't blame you for keeping it to yourself. Should we head down to the shop? Are you in the mood to paint?"

I sag against the back of my seat, thankful for her ability to lighten the moment and get life back on track. "Yeah, that would be great."

Outside, drink in hand, I link my arm with hers.

In this moment, I feel eons away from the girl who was canceled all those months ago. I still have plenty of healing to do and mountains of details to figure out, but I think I'm finally stepping into the person I was always meant to be.

# twenty-four

### Derrick

SPINNING, Izzy takes in the newly renovated restaurant space. She's been filming as we go, but a lot has changed at this jobsite since the last time she was here. It almost feels like she's seeing it with new eyes—like *I'm* seeing it through new eyes, her eyes.

The restaurant is located about an hour and a half from Parkerville, tucked into the corner of a small inland town.

"I love that you kept these original stones exposed." She taps them with the toe of her pink sneaker. "They're incredible. They have to be really old."

"This place was built in the 1700s."

"Wow." She looks around, lips parted in awe.

I might be in the business of building, but even I can admit things aren't made with the kind of craftsmanship they once were. Back then, things were meant to last. Now, everything we touch seems designed to only function until the next trend comes along.

I trail behind her as she enters the party space we've sectioned off.

"If this place were mine, I'd paint the walls navy. Or maybe a burgundy. Ooh, I might even do black." She spins in a circle, her hair flying behind her. "I'd want it to be moody, with a few large art pieces displayed as a nod to the 1700s."

I lean against the wall, watching her, my chest swelling. God, she's so damn beautiful and smart and talented.

"The owners mentioned needing help with design. Want me to tell them you're interested in helping and see how it goes?"

She stops in front of me. Her eyes are wide and shimmering with gratitude. "You'd do that?"

Head tilted, I frown. "Why wouldn't I?"

It'd be easy enough. I can't guarantee they'll take us up on the offer, but it's worth asking.

Izzy closes the distance between us, and when she loops her arms around my neck, it's like the rest of the world fades away.

Playing with the hair at the back of my neck, she murmurs, "Could you stop making it so easy?"

"What?" Confusion laces the word.

"To fall for you."

*Oh.*

"Oh."

Pulse fluttering in her throat, she backs away slowly, her gaze dropping like she's scared of what she might see reflected in my eyes. If she did look, I have no doubt she'd see fear and excitement. Because I'm falling for her, too. Surely, she knows that. I wouldn't have slept with her, told my kids about us, if I wasn't. I haven't had a real relationship since my wife passed. I wouldn't have jumped into this without being absolutely sure of how I felt about her.

I show her around the rest of the restaurant, all the while replaying her words. My feelings for Izzy are strong and it terrifies me, because she *is* young, and I worry that she'll decide I'm not who or what she wants. I'm not sure I can handle losing another person I care about, but here I am, risking it anyway.

"You want a slushie?" I ask when we get in my truck.

She adjusts the air vent, letting the AC hit her at full blast. "I feel like I should say no, but I can never turn them down."

There's a gas station at the end of the street, so thirty seconds later, we're pulling in.

"I'll grab them. Want to stay here so I can leave the truck running and the AC on?"

"Sure." She nods and gives me a small smile.

Before we stopped in, I didn't think about the lack of AC in the restaurant. I'm used to working in hot temperatures, but Izzy isn't, and the last thing I want is for her to get overheated.

The gas station is even smaller than the one we normally go to, but that makes it easier to find the slushie machine. Though as I step up to it, my shoulders deflate.

There's no blue raspberry.

Strawberry. Grape. Mountain Dew.

I'm not sure she'll like any of these, but I get one of each anyway. If she doesn't, we'll stop at our usual place on our way home.

Izzy has her feet kicked up on the dashboard when I push my way outside, carefully cradling the three cups. Despite the glare on the windshield, I can see her arched brow through the glass.

As I approach her window, she drops her feet and pushes the button to lower it. "Couldn't decide?" A tiny smile plays on her lips.

"They didn't have blue raspberry."

She scowls, though it's pure tease. "Those bitches." As she giggles at herself, she takes two of the cups from me.

I hop in on my side with the third cup in hand and pass her two of the straws. "Taste test?"

"I guess." She frowns down at the cups. "But I don't think anything can beat blue raspberry."

I hold the first cup out to her, and when she closes her lips around the straw, keeping her eyes on me, I'm instantly hard, thinking about her mouth wrapped around other things.

She jerks back at the first taste and practically gags. "Oh my God, that's *awful*. It tastes like medicine."

"It's grape," I mutter, frowning at the cup. "It can't be that bad." With a smirk, I take a sip, expecting to prove her wrong. But no. It's absolutely disgusting. "Fuck." I choke back a cough. "What kind of monster would drink this?"

"The kind without taste buds," she jokes, eyeing the cups in her hands. "Please, one of you be good."

She sticks the Mountain Dew slushie in the drink holder and tests the strawberry one first. "Not bad." She hands it to me for a taste.

I take a quick sip, watching her. "It's okay."

She tries the Mountain Dew one and instantly shakes her head. "You can have this one. Give me the strawberry back."

With a chuckle, I exchange cups. It doesn't matter whether I like it or not, as long as my girl is happy. Quickly, I hop out, hit with a blast of summer heat, and throw away the offending grape one. Then I head toward home.

When I turn off early, Izzy shifts in her seat. "Where are we going?"

I keep my focus trained on the road and say, "There's something I want to show you." It wasn't until the street sign came into view that I decided I wanted to share this with her. It's a place not even my kids know about.

"Let me guess, you're not going to give me a hint."

I bark out a laugh. "Nope. Not a chance." With a grin at her, I turn down the bumpy driveway that's more mud than gravel. As we roll slowly, nature closes in on us, the trees forming a canopy above. It takes a good five minutes before the land clears. When we pull out into an open area, I ease the truck to a stop and undo my seat belt.

The lake glimmers in the distance, sunshine reflecting off the surface, instantly soothing me like it does every time I see it.

"What is this place?" she asks, her eyes wide and filled with wonder.

Without answering her, I get out of the truck and go around to open her door. She takes my hand without hesitation, letting me guide her through the tall grass. I'll have to check her for ticks later. Can't say it'll be a hardship.

"Where are we?" she breathes at my side, her head on a swivel as she takes it all in.

I stop when we get to the edge of the lake. It's a decent size, but there are only a few other houses built around it.

"This is my land," I finally answer, letting go of her hand so I can pick up a flat stone. I toss it and watch it skip three times over the surface before it sinks. "I bought it years ago."

It went on the market about twelve years ago. Brooks mentioned it to me, knowing about my mostly secret dream of buying a piece of land and building my own home. I love my house, but I've wished for more space and for a home I could build from the ground up.

Despite having the perfect piece of property, my kids were young, and I was burning the candle at both ends, so I put it off.

And the longer I did that, the easier it became.

Last fall, Brooks convinced me it was time to start clearing the land, but that's as much as I've done.

"Your land?" Izzy repeats, the breeze stirring her hair around her shoulders. "What are you going to do with it?"

"The plan has always been to build my dream house."

"So"—she bends and picks up a rock for herself—"why haven't you?" She tosses the rock and instead of skipping, it sinks with a *plunk*. "Dammit."

"Try one like this." I grab a round, smooth rock. "And flick your wrist like this." I demonstrate and wait for her to mimic the movement. Then I put the rock in her open palm. "Go."

She mimics the movement, and the stone skips twice. Her smile is infectious when she turns back to me. "Don't think I haven't noticed you're avoiding my question."

With a sigh, I scrub a hand over my jaw. "I guess I haven't seen the point. It's only me. My house is fine for a bachelor. A place like this ... it deserves more than me."

She turns to face me completely, sticking her hands in the back pockets of her shorts. It pushes her breasts out so they strain against the fabric of her white, ribbed tank top.

I have to look away. Otherwise I may maul her right here, out in the open.

"I don't know why you think you don't deserve things like that. You're enough, you know?"

*You're enough.*

My heart stutters, along with my breath.

The words are simple, but they feel like a lifeline.

"This is a beautiful spot to build a house," she says, gently placing a hand on my forearm. "I hope you do it."

Without letting go, she surveys the area. The trees, the water, the cleared land.

Does she see what I see? A Tudor style lake house with a wall of windows along the back, creating the most spectacular views of the lake? A dock for my boat? A yard with a playground for kids and—

Kids.

I haven't thought about the possibility of more children since my wife died. I was too busy raising Layla and Reid and working to think about what I might want if I met the right person.

A part of me feels too old to have more kids. I've already raised two. Would the age difference be strange? And what about Lili? She'd be older than an uncle or an aunt. Would that be frowned upon? Or does that even matter? I love kids, and I love being a dad. Before Izzy came along, I was lonely. The house felt too empty, too quiet.

"I can't believe Layla and Reid haven't talked you into building the house already. This place is magical."

"Uh…" I rub at my nose, stalling. "They don't know."

Sucking in a breath, she cocks her head and assesses me. "They don't know?"

"No."

"Who does?"

"Only Brooks. He's the one who found the land for me. And … now, you."

Her dumbfounded expression has me looking at the ground, toeing the edge of my boot into the dirt.

"Derrick?"

"Hmm?" I hum, still focused on the ground beneath me.

"Look at me." It's the pleading in her tone that has me looking up. "Why haven't you told anyone else?"

I shove my hands into my pockets and find a coin I'd forgotten about in one. I rub my thumb and forefinger over the warm metal, grounding myself.

"It was easier to keep it a secret. That way, if I never moved forward with it, I wouldn't let anyone down."

Her feet crunch over the dead leaves littering the ground from winters gone by as she closes the small distance between us. She stands beside me now, looking out at the lake. "What do you think now?"

I envision myself pulling up the driveway to a finished house. A deck where I can sit and drink my morning coffee and converse with the squirrels. The lake to boat in. And maybe, if things go right, this woman at my side.

"I think it's time."

# twenty-five

## Izzy

I STRETCH, searching for warm skin, but all I find are cool sheets. We haven't slept in the same bed every night, but most nights, and I find that I sleep better with Derrick.

I sit up and squint at the clock on the bedside table. A little after two.

Wonton cracks an eye open, watching me with disdain for disturbing his beauty sleep.

With a groan, I slip out of bed and slide my feet into my slippers.

Wonton huffs with annoyance and shuffles up the bed to plop on the pillow I last saw Derrick sleeping on.

Down the hall, I peek into his room but find his bed undisturbed.

Interesting.

I carefully make my way down the stairs, and when I hit

the landing, I find the kitchen aglow. "Hey," I croak. "What are you up to?"

Derrick turns to me, his eyes heavy. "What time is it?" he asks, stifling a yawn.

"A little after two." I pour myself a glass of water, then join him at the table, eyeing the papers spread out in front of him. Sketches of floor plans and room designs. There's a schematic of a fireplace with stone and built-in shelves near his right elbow. The design is similar to what he has here. "Feeling inspired?"

He lowers his head and scans the mess of papers, then, noticing the graphite smeared on the side of his left hand, he rubs it against his shorts. "Yeah." A tired half smile graces his lips. "I am. I felt silly holding on to the land like that, but selling it never sat right with me. It'll take a while, years probably, to get it done, but it'll be worth it in the end."

My chest warms with affection. "I'm glad you're going for it. You're clearly happy there."

He shuffles the papers into a pile and slides them to the right side. "What are you doing up?"

"My bed was cold."

"I'm sorry." Frowning, he scoots his chair back and opens his arms. "C'mere, baby."

I don't have to be told twice. I climb into his lap and wrap my arms around his bare shoulders, going straight to work on massaging his stiff trap muscles.

His hands roam down my body, settling on my hips, his fingers spreading across my butt. He pulls me impossibly closer, and as he does, he lets out a groan at the friction.

God, I want him.

We haven't done anything since the day we absolutely lost ourselves in each other and had three rounds back-to-back.

I've been holding back, and I think he has, too.

That day was so explosive that it frightened me a little—feeling so much for a man I don't fully know yet.

But maybe that's the thing—do we *ever* fully know other people? Each and every one of us is constantly growing and changing.

"I want to take things slow." His words are a whispered brush of breath against my lips.

I rock my hips slowly. "This is slow."

He chuckles. "Not what I meant."

"I know." I press my face into the crook of his neck, inhaling his scent. Oak and citrus and maybe a touch of spice. "Are you afraid I'll get sick of you? Because that's impossible."

"No." He flexes his fingers against my ass. "I just … want to do this right."

I lean back, resting against the table to put a little space between our chests. It wasn't my intention to draw his focus to my chest, but I do have to smile when he lowers his gaze and all but salivates at the way my boobs practically spill out of my tank top. "I think it's a little late for that."

With a rough laugh, he nuzzles my nose with his. It's a sweet gesture. So pure and unexpected that it makes my heart dip, then lurch yet another stumbling step closer to that scary four-letter word.

"I suppose you're right," he sighs, pressing a kiss to my neck.

"Besides," I go on, raking my fingers into the back of his hair, "what *is* right? What works for some doesn't work for all. We all have to make our own definition of the word. Don't you think?"

"I think," he brushes a piece of my hair behind my ear, "that you are entirely too tempting."

Smiling, I kiss his lips softly, chastely. "Come to bed. It's late."

He scoots the chair back, arms firmly around me. Standing, he repositions his arms, supporting my ass, then he carries me upstairs. Rather than take me back to my bedroom, he lays me down on his bed—which I have to admit is much more comfortable. When he heads for the door rather than climb in beside me, I sit up and rest my elbows on the mattress.

"Where are you going?"

He looks at me like I'm the crazy one. "To get Wonton."

My heart warms, sending threads of sated heat through my extremities. It's the little things—like thinking of my dog and knowing I'd want him in here—that make it so easy to fall for him.

When he returns with a sleepy Wonton under his arm, he sets him gently at the foot of the bed and then picks me up again and pulls back the sheets.

As he pulls the covers up and tucks me in, I give him a sleepy grin. "Are you going to read me a bedtime story, too?"

He closes his eyes, letting out a low chuckle. "Izzy, Izzy, Izzy." Then he climbs into bed beside me and pulls me close. He presses a kiss to the top of my bare shoulder.

I open my mouth to … I don't know, make another quip or beg him to undress me, but before I can, he groans.

"Go to sleep, Izzy," he murmurs. "We have all the time in the world."

It's that last part that has me drifting off with a smile on my face.

---

"HEARD you're boinking the hot dad."

Those are the first words I hear when I walk into book club.

"Jeez, Glenda." I close the door behind me and slip my shoes off. "At least get me a little drunk before you start making comments like that."

She places a piece of cut cheese on a cracker and holds it aloft. "I don't believe in mincing words."

"Don't we all know it." Ella appears from the kitchen, greeting me with a glass of wine and a hug.

I take a gulp. "Bless you."

She laughs. "I figure you need it. There's no way we're discussing the book today. We *all* want to hear about Derrick."

"We never discuss the book," my sister adds helpfully from her usual spot on the couch. "And try to keep it respectful, ladies. I don't need all the dirty details about my sister's sex life."

"Or your future father-in-law slash potential brother-in-law's," Glenda adds with a pointed finger.

My stomach lurches. *Is it too late to leave?*

Via covers her face, head shaking. "Let's just not, please."

"Yes, please," I agree readily as I drop onto the cushion beside her. My glass of wine is already half gone. "This whole situation is unusual as it is."

It's no surprise, though, that all of these ladies already know.

It's why Derrick and I told Via and his kids as quickly as we could. Neither of us wanted them to hear it through the Parkerville gossip mill—a mill led by Glenda, no doubt.

"We can't help it," Tammy says, fixing a plate with a few slices of deli meat and cheeses. "We all love Derrick. He's a good man. We want to see him—"

"Get some young ass. If anyone needs it, he does." Glenda

tips her glass in my direction, making me long to crawl beneath the table and die.

Sighing, Tammy shakes her head. In the corner, Cassandra pinches her brow.

"*Happy*, I was trying to say we want to see him happy," Tammy corrects.

"And get some," Glenda adds.

Head hung, I drop it into my hands. I'm desperate to flee outside to my waiting rental car, but I have a feeling these women would tackle me before I made it to the door.

"Really," Ella says, sitting on my other side and giving my knee a pat, "we're happy for you both."

"How many abs does he have? I've heard eight, but I haven't ever been able to get a good enough look to count them myself."

I purse my lips and squint at Glenda. "Mmm. Yeah, eight."

"Oh, sweet Jesus. What I would give to have a man like that over me. God, I just want to feel the weight of a man again, abs or not." She closes her eyes, as if visualizing it. "Oh, yes, that's what I need." When she opens them again and finds us all staring, she says, "Close your mouths before you catch flies. I might be old, but my libido is alive and well. I had a voracious sex life in my day. Ever had a threesome? Highly recommend."

I fall into a fit of laughter, unable to stop until tears fall from my eyes. This might be the most embarrassing night of my life, but it's also the most entertaining. "Glenda, do you have a vibrator?"

"No. Never liked 'em. I prefer the real thing."

I wag a finger at her. "There are so many to choose from these days. I think I know just what to get you. Actually..." I bounce a little on the couch cushion. "Maybe I'll order a few so you can explore your options."

With a toothy grin, Glenda claps. "If you're buyin', then honey, I'll give you a review of each one."

Beside me, my sister squeaks and says, "When did our book reviews turn into sex toy reviews?"

Ella wipes her fingers on her jeans. "To be fair, we never actually review the books."

When we all dissolve into laughter, and the conversation thankfully moves away from Derrick and me, I can't help but once again think about how much I love it here and how ready I am to leave my life in LA behind for good.

# twenty-six

Izzy

ANOTHER DAY ON THE BOAT, another day lusting after a sweaty, half-dressed Derrick.

I could get used to this life.

"It could be my imagination," he says, his back to me and one hand steady on the wheel, "but I have a feeling I'm being objectified right now."

I take a sip of lemonade and lift my sunglasses up a few inches. "Thoroughly."

He looks over his shoulder at me with a smile, and even though his eyes are hidden behind his own sunglasses, I just know they're crinkled at the corners.

Eventually, he finds a place to stop and lowers the anchor. As we bob on the waves, my stomach lurches. The waters are quite a bit rougher than normal today.

Once he's got everything situated the way he wants, he

pulls a beer from the cooler and uncaps it. With a smirk, he tosses the bottle cap to me.

I catch it, and after a quick glance at it, I frown up at him. "What's this for?"

"I don't know." He takes a long swallow. "Maybe it can be a good luck charm."

Heart thumping a little at the idea, I tuck it into a pocket in my tote bag for safekeeping.

When I look back up, Derrick's watching me like I'm a snack, and he's ravenous.

For the last week, we've spent our evenings watching *Gilmore Girls* like usual. Then we retire to his bed, where we never go further than cuddling.

It's *killing* me.

So today, I donned my most scandalous bikini in hopes of breaking him. The red color complements the tan I've slowly acquired from long days outside and on the boat. The top pushes my breasts together, making them look fuller and firmer than they actually are. It's basically a boob job in the form of a slinky piece of fabric. The bottoms are extra cheeky. So cheeky, in fact, that I've been too shy to wear them until now.

But today, I pulled them on without hesitation. That's how desperate I am to get him to touch me again.

I pull the tube of sunscreen out of my bag and hold it out to Derrick. "Do you mind putting some of this on my back? I had a hard time with it today."

Eyes narrowed, he scrutinizes the tube before he plucks it from my hand. Setting his beer bottle down, he pops the plastic cap open and squirts a quarter-size amount into his palm.

I give him my back, pulling my hair over my shoulder.

The sunscreen is cool against my heated skin, sending a shiver through me as he works it in.

"I know what you're doing," he says, his warm breath caressing me, one hand slipping beneath the strap of my top.

I peek over my shoulder and shoot him a smirk. "Is it working?"

"What do you think?"

Anxious to know, I press back until my ass connects with his quickly growing erection, pulling a needy grunt from him.

"I've always wanted to have sex on a boat," I confess.

It's actually not something I ever thought about. Not until I discovered that he had a boat. Then it became consuming. The idea of being out in the open, the thrill of potentially being caught.

"Izzy." He digs his fingers into my hips and holds me steady while he backs up half a step.

I can't help but wiggle, desperate to be close again.

"Please," I all but beg, chin tucked over one shoulder and eyes fixed on his. "I appreciate what you're doing, but my fingers are getting tired, and my vibrator is going to kick the bucket if I keep using it the way I have been."

His irises darken as he zeroes in on my lips. "You've been touching yourself while thinking about me?"

"Derrick," I practically whimper. "You're all I think about."

That simple confession finally undoes him.

Grasping my chin, he yanks me back for a kiss. His left-hand splays across my stomach, pulling my back flush against his front, and oh yeah, he's fully hard now.

At least I'm not the only one who's been desperate for this.

"You like using these to tease me, don't you?" He plays with the string of my bikini tied beneath my breasts.

"Yes." I look around, searching for any sign of life nearby

and finding none. Except on the Fourth of July, the lake has been practically empty. "I picked this one out just for you."

"For me, huh?" He presses a kiss to the top of my shoulder.

My core tenses at the connection. "I put it on so you could take it off me."

His dark chuckle sends a shiver coursing through me. "Fuck, Izzy." He gently bites my earlobe. "I'm trying to be good here. Take my time. I want to do things right with you."

"It's a little late for that."

"I guess you're right."

"It was so good with us—"

He slips his fingers just under the front of my bottoms, making my breath hitch. He stops right there, just a centimeter beneath the fabric, but it's enough to have liquid pooling in my core.

"Can you blame me for wanting you again?" I breathe out. "For thinking about how good your cock feels? Every time I'm in the shower, I think about how you knelt down on the floor and ate my pussy."

"My dirty girl." He lowers his fingers another fraction, taunting me with the promise of his touch. "I should've known slow wouldn't work for you."

"No." I tilt my head to the side, and when he sucks carefully on the skin of my exposed neck, I moan involuntarily. There will probably be a hickey there tomorrow, but I can't bring myself to care. "I think I've wanted you since the first time I saw you. I was a fool to set my sister up with you. You're the sexiest man I've ever seen. That first day, if you'd told me to drop to my knees, I think I would have said *yes, sir.*"

"Izzy."

"You have no idea how hot you are." I reach behind me,

my fingers digging into his bare thigh. "You were oblivious to how much I wanted you."

He presses a gentle kiss beneath my ear. "Only because I never would've thought someone as beautiful and as young as you would want a grumpy bastard like me."

"You're not grumpy," I protest. "You're lonely." I turn my head, forcing him to meet my gaze. "You're not going to be lonely anymore. Not if I have anything to say about it."

Heat flashes in his eyes, then his mouth is on mine, devouring me.

How has no one snatched this man up? He's so real and genuine. All he wants is to be cared for?

Hands on my hips again, he turns me, then drops onto the bench and pulls me in so I'm straddling his lap.

I could spend every day of my life with this man and it still wouldn't be enough.

Breaking our kiss with a pop, he tugs on the strings on the left side of my bottoms. "You have *no* idea how much I hate and love these things."

I give him a devious smile. "Believe me. I know."

With a shake of his head, he stands. Before I can protest, he tugs the strings at my right hip and pulls the bottoms away from my skin.

"Eyes on me, pretty girl," he says as he sets the scrap of fabric on the bench beside me. "Watch me eat this perfect pussy." Kneeling at my feet, he spreads my thighs open wide. "Look at you." He rubs his fingers over my folds. "So pink and wet. Begging for me."

Core clenching, I try to squeeze my thighs together. I'm desperate for friction. "Stop teasing me."

He laughs, the sound a vibration against my core, and when his tongue finds my clit, I drop my head back, unable to hold it up as tingles race up my spine. He licks and sucks, driving me to the edge and then pulling back. The boat bobs on the water, but somehow he stays steady.

When his mouth leaves my pussy, I whimper at the loss. The sound is cut off, though, when he gently sinks his teeth into the inside of my thigh, eyes on mine.

What does he see when he looks at me? Is he as far gone as I am? Does he want me as badly as I want him?

"Turn around. Arms on the edge of the boat, knees on the bench."

My heart jumps in my chest. "I—"

"Do it."

I don't have to be told twice. As much as I love the sight of Derrick between my thighs, this is somehow even better. There's a single vessel in the distance, but it's far enough away that they're not a worry.

With one forearm braced against the fiberglass edge of the boat, I slip my free hand down and brush my fingers over my clit.

Almost immediately his mouth is gone, and I'm hit with nothing but warm late-summer air.

"Did I tell you that you could touch yourself?"

"No, but—"

He smacks my bare ass, startling me. "Then what made you think you could?"

"Fuck," I groan, dropping my head forward. "This side of you is so hot."

"You like it when I boss you around?" he asks, caressing the heated flesh he just marked with his palm.

"Only in bed," I quip, looking back at him.

Heat floods me at the sight. He's in my favorite position—on his knees.

"Or," I breathe out, "boat, I suppose."

He grasps my butt cheeks and spreads them, then rubs his thumb against that forbidden place.

Licking his lips, he homes in on my face. "I bet you'd even let me fuck this pretty ass if I wanted."

"I-I would." The words are shaky, not because I'm scared, but because I want anything and everything with him. "I've never done it before."

"Me either, and we're not doing it today, so don't get any ideas."

"But one day?" I find myself asking, wiggling my hips, once again searching for friction.

"Yeah, baby. One day. If you want to."

I open my mouth to respond, but before I can, he licks and sucks at my already sensitive flesh, pulling nothing but a desperate cry from me.

Without my permission, my hips roll against his face, and he groans in appreciation. I want to turn around and watch him more than anything, but I do as I was told and keep myself braced against the edge of the boat.

The watercraft I spotted when we started has crept closer and it's still on the move.

"Derrick"—his name is a strangled breath—"boat. There's a boat coming."

He pauses long enough to say, "Then you better come fast." Then he slides two fingers inside me and sucks on my clit.

At the pleasure that jolts through me, I nearly collapse on the bench. My heart races from both the pleasure and the anticipation of the approaching vessel.

As they get closer, so do I. When they're close enough that I can make out the man at the helm, Derrick tightens his hold on my butt cheeks, keeping me from diving down and hiding. Thank *god* he didn't remove my top.

The boater lifts his hand and waves as he slowly cruises by. "Nice day, isn't it?"

"Great. Just fantastic." I wave back, barely holding myself up, my breaths coming quick. It takes all my strength to keep my features under control. My orgasm is *right there*, and as exciting as the prospect is of getting caught, I don't actually want this stranger to see me come.

When he's past us, Derrick ramps up his efforts, his tongue working expertly against my pussy. Within seconds, my legs shake. There's no way I can hold out much longer.

The orgasm that crashes through me is so intense, my vision goes black as I cry out. He keeps one arm wrapped around my torso, serving as an anchor. When I come to, he's pressing kisses all over my shoulders and neck.

Cupping my cheek, he waits for my eyes to meet his. "You good?"

I nod, my body feeling like Jell-O.

The smile that tips his lips is dangerous and dark. "Good."

He stands and moves around for a minute, but I'm still too out of it to focus on what he's doing. Finally, he pulls me off the bench and onto the floor of the boat, where I discover he's spread out a blanket.

His warm body hovers over mine, his hands exploring every inch of me before he undoes the ties on my bikini top. His movements are careful, reverent, until he yanks the fabric away roughly and tosses it behind him.

A loud laugh escapes me. "That better not have gone overboard."

Rather than respond, he dips his head to take one stiff nipple into his mouth.

My body bows off the floor, practically pressing itself to his, like if I could sink inside him and live there forever, I would.

"You make me crazy," he whispers against my skin, kissing his way between my breasts. "I've never felt like this before."

I drink his words in and greedily store them away in my heart like a squirrel hoarding nuts for the winter. This man lived a whole life before he met me. I understand and respect that. I'd never want to change it. Even so, I'm selfishly elated at the knowledge that what we have is special for him, too.

"You're so beautiful." He rears back and steadies himself on his knees. With his thumbs under his waistband, he shoves his trunks down and frees his cock. Once he's kicked the material off, he wraps a hand around his base and gives it a firm stroke, then another. Then he guides his tip to my entrance and pushes inside just an inch, his eyes closing. "Fuck, you feel so good, Izzy. You have no idea. This pussy was made for me."

I whimper at the sensation, and when he pushes into me completely, I relish the way my back arches, the shiver that rolls up my spine.

God, it feels so good.

He stays there for a moment, not moving, probably processing how perfect it feels, just like I am.

Then he rolls his hips. He starts slow, using gentle, careful strokes.

It's incredible.

But I need more.

"Harder," I beg, clutching his biceps. "Fuck me like you mean it."

His fingers flex on my hips. "You want it rough, baby?"

"Yes. We can do slow later."

He chuckles at that, the sound rough, grating. "Who am I to deny my girl what she wants?"

Clasping my hands, he yanks them above my head and holds them there, against the rough outdoor carpet of the boat, and fucks me hard and fast, just the way I want. In moments, my second orgasm plows through me, rendering me speechless. If I thought I was boneless before, it has nothing on this sensation.

"Fuck, your pussy is squeezing my cock so tight. You're going to make me come."

"Do it," I beg, pressing my head back against the floor beneath me, lifting my hips, desperate to make him feel as incredible as I do.

I've been dying to see him fall apart again since our one and only sex marathon. Nothing compares to the beauty of seeing Derrick come, of knowing that I can bring him that much pleasure.

"Come inside me again," I plead, chest heaving. "Please."

His eyes go impossibly dark at my request, then he picks up the pace, his hips pumping faster. He lets go of my hands, then grasps my thighs and pushes my legs up. I whimper, not from pain, but from the wave of ecstasy that overtakes me. Nothing and no one compares to Derrick. Of that, I'm certain.

"Fuck. Izzy!" He shouts my name as he comes, burying his face in my neck and slapping his palms against the blanket on either side of my shoulders. His body is heavy, but I welcome the pressure of it, our skin slick with sweat, our breaths coming fast and loud. His strokes slow along with our breathing and soon stop altogether, but he doesn't pull out of me right away.

Still seated inside me, he finds my lips and kisses me deeply. I practically melt into the kiss.

Brushing my sweaty hair off my forehead, he meets my gaze and holds me prisoner there.

I feel it then. The shift.

It's seismic.

And from the way his eyes widen, I think he feels it, too.

I've fallen.

Fully.

Completely.

Only for this man.

I love Derrick Crawford. More than that, I'm *in* love with him. And I think he loves me, too. Though neither of us gives voice to those scary words.

*It's too soon*, my conscience whispers. *Wait.*

For now, I will, but I can't wait forever. This man deserves to know how deeply my feelings for him run.

Derrick rises up, and still—impressively—half hard, he tucks himself back into his swim trunks.

I brace my elbows on the floor on either side of me, readying myself to sit up, but he presses a hand to my stomach. "Wait."

"Why?" I cover my breasts with my hands, suddenly feeling shy out in the open and under the clear blue sky.

He plucks my hands away easily, holding them captive in his. "Let me see you."

When I nod, giving him permission to look his fill, he releases my hands and looms over me.

Heart still thumping, I lie on my back, completely naked and spread out for him, and let him drink me in.

After several breaths, he grasps my thighs and pushes them apart. A flush spreads up my body, the heat of it nearly consuming me, as he stares unabashedly at my center.

242

His seed leaks from me, warm and thick, but then his fingers are there like last time, pushing it back in.

"Fuck," he growls, low and rough. "I love knowing you're mine."

"Possessive much?" I quip, though the words fall flat when they come out breathy.

A low chuckle rumbles in his chest. "Only of you. Stay here."

He hauls himself to his feet and plucks my top from the floor of the boat halfway toward the front and my bottoms from the bench.

"I was going to put these back on you," he confesses, holding each piece by its strings. "But I think you have to be a rocket scientist to figure this out."

Easing up to sitting, I take them from him with shaky hands. Damn, my muscles are weak from the workout he put me through.

It takes me a few minutes to get the scraps of fabric back on, my fingers not thoroughly working yet. I don't think I've ever been so thoroughly fucked in my entire life.

"You know"—I pull my hair back into a ponytail to get the long strands off my neck—"from now on, every time we're on this boat, that's *all* I'm going to be thinking about."

He snags a water bottle out of the cooler and takes a long sip. Then he passes it to me. A satisfied smirk graces his lips. I love the confidence oozing from him.

"Is that so?"

"Mhm." I take a small sip, and when the cool liquid hits my throat, I guzzle the rest of the bottle. "It already has me thinking about other stuff we could do."

He plucks another water from the cooler. "Care to share your ideas?"

"For starters"—I tap my lips, like I'm working it out, even though the thought is on the tip of my tongue—"I want to blow you while you're driving the boat."

He bangs his knee into the cooler with a curse. "Jesus Christ, Izzy."

"You don't like the idea?" I tease, fighting the urge to laugh.

Hands on his hips, he looks up to the sky, probably praying to the heavens and asking for guidance when it comes to me.

Even though I'm exhausted and thoroughly fucked, just looking at him gets me hot and bothered. Lean and muscular, thick thighs, a light smattering of hair on his chest. Even the hints of gray in his hair and scruff turn me on.

Derrick Crawford is *lethal*, and he doesn't even know it.

"This boat is going to be desecrated when we're done with it, isn't it?"

"Oh, yeah." I nod vigorously. "You'll never be able to sell this thing."

He shakes his head, his eyes twinkling with delight. "I have no plans to. Do you want to stay out longer or head home?"

*Home.*

My chest expands at the single word.

I stretch my sore arms and let out a long exhale. "Let's go home."

With a nod, he gets to work pulling the anchor up. As much as I want to get down on my knees and take him in my mouth on the ride back to the dock, I don't. I'll have to keep him waiting and wondering for that one.

# twenty-seven

## Derrick

A KNOCK on the front door startles me awake. Wonton, who's been snoozing on my chest, jolts, then uses my stomach as a springboard to launch himself over the back of the couch to bark at the door.

"Fuck," I groan, rubbing at my chest. The dog might be small, but those little paws are like needles when he uses that much force.

There's another knock, and then, "Grandpa!"

Rolling to my side, I snatch my phone off the coffee table and check the time *and* the date.

*Was I supposed to watch Lilibet today?*

With a groan, I heave myself off the couch. I worked on site today while Izzy met with the owners of the restaurant to talk design ideas, and she hasn't come back yet.

"Dad?" Another knock.

I stagger to the door, and when I yank it open, I throw a hand up to block the sun. "Sorry," I rasp. "I fell asleep on the couch."

"Hey," Layla says, her smile almost shy. We haven't spoken much since I told her and Reid about Izzy. I've been trying to give her space, figuring she'll come to me when she's ready. "Can you watch Lili for a while? Greta asked if I could pick up a shift. I don't want to say no to extra money."

For years, Layla spent her summers working at Greta's Fish House, one of the restaurants on the pier. Except for the occasional shift when Greta needed help, she didn't last summer, since she was busy working for Izzy.

"Yeah, of course." I step back and pull the door open wider. "You know I'll always look after Lili."

"Yay!" My granddaughter plows past me into the house with a bag slung over her shoulder and a handheld gaming system dangling from her fingers.

"I tried to get Reid," Layla says, head lowered a fraction. "I didn't want to bother you."

My stomach drops at that. What the fuck?

"Layla," I say, grasping her arm. "You're not bothering me. I'm always happy to help."

She nods, though she doesn't meet my eye. "Thank you. I'll probably be late. She needs me until closing."

"It's not a problem. If Lili needs to stay the night, that's okay, too."

Lips twisting, she lets out a breath through her nose. "I don't know."

Not wanting to be pushy, I shrug, play it cool. "The offer's on the table. Just let me know."

"Okay." She inhales, her chest expanding, then finally looks up. "Thank you again, Dad."

"You're welcome. See you later," I say as she heads for her car. I stand there until she drives away, my chest aching a little. The thing I've learned about having kids? The minute they're born, it's like a piece of a parent's heart lives outside their body. And even when those children grow up and have children of their own, that feeling never goes away.

After I've locked the door, I go in search of Lili, finding her on the swing on the back porch, playing her game.

"Hey, kiddo." I ruffle her hair, then take a seat in one of the Adirondack chairs.

She looks at me over the top of her game. "Are you still feeding the squirrels?"

I clasp my hands and rest my forearms on my knees, leaning toward her. "Did you think I'd stop? They'd never let me."

As if I've summoned them, Peep and Tank hop out of the large tree on the right side of the yard and creep up to the back deck.

"You want to give them some snacks?"

"Yes!" Lili shuts off her game and leaps off the swing.

Once she's got a few hazelnuts and walnuts in hand—from the stash I keep on the porch, though sometimes I spoil them with chopped up pieces of apple or celery—she crouches and slowly approaches the squirrels. They're just as used to her as they are me. She sets the nuts in the grass and holds perfectly still. It only takes a moment before the squirrels scamper forward and snatch them. Then they take off for their tree.

Laughing, Lili turns to look at me. "My mom told me you have a girlfriend." She stands fully then, her hands on her hips in an accusatory way. She looks so much like Layla when she was a little girl, sass and all. Layla has never revealed who

247

Lili's dad is, but I have to guess there are pieces of him there, too. I just can't see them.

"She did, huh?"

"Yep." She nods vigorously. "Does that mean you won't have time for me anymore?"

Her question is like a swift kick to the gut.

"Lili"—I kneel on the ground so I'm at her eye-level—"I will *always* have time for you. Having a girlfriend doesn't change that."

The word *girlfriend* feels strange on my tongue. I haven't had a "girlfriend" since I was dating my wife. And this is the first time I've referred to Izzy as such. Truthfully the word doesn't even come close to quantifying the depths of my feelings.

"Mom says Izzy is your girlfriend. Is she right?" She frowns at me, but the look is one of confusion more than dismay. At least I hope it is.

"Yes." I leave it at that for a moment, giving her a moment to say more if she wants to. When she doesn't, I ask, "Does that bother you?"

I'd rather my granddaughter talk about her feelings than keep them bottled up inside.

"No." Her nose crinkles. "It's just confusing."

"Confusing how?"

"You're my grandpa, so you're like ... old." She whispers the word like it's dirty.

I suppress a laugh. Leave it to Lili to keep me humble.

"But she's not old, and if you get married, does that mean she's my grandma? I don't think I can call her Grandma."

Head dropped forward, I pinch my mouth shut, barely holding back my laughter this time. "You don't have to call her Grandma."

"Oh." She brightens, her shoulders straightening. "Good. That was stressing me out."

"Was that all that was bothering you?"

"Just about," she chirps. "I'm gonna play my game now." With that, she scurries up the stairs and back to the swing, where she launches herself with so much force it hits the railing behind it.

Shaking my head, I stand, trying to ignore the way my knees groan.

Fuck, the kid is right. I *am* old.

---

IZZY WALKS in the door just as I'm setting Lili's dinner plate in front of her.

"Hey, we have a visitor," I call out in a cheerful tone. There's no telling what might come out of Izzy's mouth, and there's a fifty-fifty chance it wouldn't be appropriate for my granddaughter.

"Oh, hey, Lili." She sets her bag on the floor and scoops up Wonton from where he jumps at her feet, eager for her affection. "I missed you, too, boy." She showers the little white dog with kisses.

After she's thoroughly smothered Wonton with love, she sets him on the tile again. "Burgers?" she asks, surveying the counter. "Thank God. I'm starving."

She practically skips to me, and when she's standing inches away, she pops up on her tiptoes, going in for a kiss. But before she can make contact, she drops back down onto flat feet and backs up, eyeing Lili.

Lili blinks, unfazed. "You can kiss him if you want. I know you're his girlfriend. But I'm not calling you Grandma."

Izzy bursts into laughter. The sound is so light, so happy, that I find myself grinning.

"Noted," she says, wiping tears from her eyes. "I appreciate it." She bumps my hip so she can get by to make up a plate of food. I kept it simple, grilling burgers and corn on the cob.

"How'd it go with the Harrisons?" I ask as I sidle up beside her.

Her smile is nearly blinding. "Great. They understand that I don't have a background in interior design, but I showed them my ideas, and they loved it. I told them that if they're willing to let me film the progress, I'll do it for free."

"And what did they say?"

While she swipes a glob of mayonnaise across her bun, I pull a can of Coke from the fridge. Then I join Lili at the table where my plate sits waiting for me.

"They agreed right away. Frankly, I would've done it for free regardless. I don't feel right charging for a service I have no experience with yet. But I'm thrilled that they'll let me film it. I miss filming content," she admits with a slump of her shoulders. "I'm itching to pick up a camera again."

I don't like the reminder of LA, of the life possibly still waiting for her there. She's been vocal about her dislike of the city and she's been clear that she doesn't want to go back, but we haven't talked about her plans beyond that. Does she want to live with me? Is it too soon for that? Would she get her own place? Would she settle in Parkerville or in one of the surrounding cities?

"I've watched some of your videos," Lili pipes in.

"Really?" Izzy asks, her brows lifting with the same level of surprise I feel at my granddaughter's admission. "What did you think?"

"The makeup ones are kind of boring, but I like the ones where you travel. Are you going anywhere soon?"

Izzy shakes her head as she joins us at the table. "No, I don't have any plans right now. I'm exploring other things."

"Like what?"

"I want to help people decorate their houses, or in the case your grandpa and I were just talking about, a restaurant, and I'll film the content for my channel."

Lili scrunches her face, further smearing a drop of ketchup at the corner of her mouth. "That's boring. Stick with traveling."

Izzy laughs. "I'd love to travel some, too, but right now, there are other things I want to pursue." She zeroes in on me, making it clear that I am those "other things."

"Maybe when I grow up, I'll travel and film it like you."

Izzy chews a bite of burger, and once she swallows, she nods and gives Lili a bright smile. "You totally could. You can do anything you want."

Lili's eyes widen, excitement curving her mouth. "Anything?"

"Yep, that's the beauty of the world. If you want something bad enough and you're willing to work for it, the options are endless."

Lili turns to me with a determined jut of her chin. "Grandpa, I want to join the circus."

Involuntarily, I inhale sharply. The move causes me to choke on the hunk of burger I'm chomping on.

"I think I'd like to work with tigers," she says as I cough. "And walk the tightrope."

Exactly what I need, my granddaughter dreaming of working with wild animals and walking across a tightrope.

But she's a kid, and dreams are what keep us going. Right?

With a nod, I ruffle her hair. "Sounds like a great idea."

She claps her hands, bouncing in her seat. "I can't wait to tell Mom I'm going to work with tigers."

Head dropped back, I let out a sigh. Layla will never let me watch my granddaughter again.

---

LIGHT STREAKS across the family room walls, signaling Layla's arrival.

Lili is fast asleep, with her head on my leg and her little body curled into a ball with Wonton tucked up against her. Moving slowly, I stand and take her into my arms. She stirs a little but falls right back to sleep.

The kid has always slept like a log.

Except when she was a baby.

She screamed nonstop most nights for that first year. My heart broke for Layla as she navigated life as a young single mom. Reid and I have helped her as much as we can, and we'll continue to do so. I never want my kids to feel like they don't have my support.

"I'll get the door," Izzy whispers, setting her book aside. She tiptoes over and eases it open. In the driveway, Layla is pushing her door open, but when she sees me bringing Lili out, she eases back into her seat.

"Princess, I have to put you in the car."

Lili murmurs gibberish against my chest, a phrase I'm pretty sure was along the lines of *I don't want to.*

Izzy opens the back door for me, and I buckle Lili up.

As Layla rolls down the window, she flashes me a grateful smile. "Thanks, Dad."

"No problem," I say, straightening and tapping the hood of the car lightly.

Behind me, Izzy clears her throat. "If you don't mind, I'd like to talk to you."

I turn to find that she's not looking at me, but Layla.

My daughter purses her lips, uncertain, but nods.

For a moment, I stand between them, hesitating.

Izzy, swallowing audibly, locks eyes with me. "I'll see you in a minute."

*I've been dismissed.*

Spying is beneath me, but it doesn't stop me from peeking through the blinds anyway.

Izzy is bent over the driver's door, speaking with my daughter.

It occurs to me then that, as worried as I've been about Layla pulling back from me, I haven't asked Izzy how this is affecting her relationship with my daughter. They're friends and her being with me could ruin that.

If I were a better man, I wouldn't have let it get this far. I never would have laid a hand on her, but I don't regret it. Izzy makes my heart race for the first time in a long time. It's like I was living in pastels—my life, my surroundings, were fine, but muted—and then she came along and painted my world in technicolor.

They talk for a good five minutes before Izzy starts back to the house and Layla reverses out of the driveway.

Quickly, I back away from the window, nearly tripping over my own feet as I go, rushing to make it to the couch before she catches me.

Izzy gives me a confused frown as she comes in.

Locking the door, she asks, "You were spying, weren't you?"

"No," I lie, my heart still racing.

"Liar." Her soft laughter carries on the air as she plops onto the couch beside me.

"How'd it go?"

She gives me a small smile. "I think it went okay. It's going to be awkward for a while, but I'm hopeful we can move past it."

My chest constricts. I hope for that, too.

"I'm sorry."

"Don't be." She stifles a yawn. "We'll get there. She just needs time."

I give her a gentle tug, pulling her onto my lap and guiding her to straddle me.

"If you wanted to get me on top of you, all you had to do was ask."

A chuckle escapes me. "I like this way more."

Wrapping her arms around my neck, she presses her forehead to mine. "I have a confession to make."

My first instinct is to panic. A confession? That could be a concern.

When she doesn't go on, I swallow back my nerves and ask, "What is it?"

"I'm falling hard for you." She pulls back, catching her lip between her teeth. "I hope that's okay."

I smooth my hands down her sides and settle them on her hips. "Only if it's okay that I'm right there with you?"

Rather than answer with words, she leans in and presses her lips to mine. And when I carry her up to my room, we say even more with our bodies.

# twenty-eight

Derrick

"THE LIGHTHOUSE?" Izzy asks when I stop the truck. "What are we doing here?"

As I unbuckle my seat belt, I turn the key in the ignition. "It's a rite of passage for locals to climb the lighthouse stairs."

"But I'm not technically a local." She peers up at me, fighting a smile, humor shimmering in her eyes.

"You're an honorary local," I say. Then, after a moment of hesitation, I add, "And you could be, if you wanted." The moment the words are out, my lungs seize. I'm frozen where I am, waiting to see what she might say.

"I'm going to talk to a realtor soon about selling my place in LA." She stretches her fingers out in front of her. "The idea of going back doesn't make me happy. Canceled or not."

My heart pinches at that word. "Are you still canceled?"

She shrugs. "I'm not sure, to be honest. I haven't posted in a long while. The last time I did, I got chewed out, so I haven't been eager to try again. People will move on eventually if they haven't already. It's inevitable." Picking at the hem of her skirt, she keeps her head lowered, her shoulders slumped, like despite her words, this all still weighs on her. "That's the funny thing about cancel culture. No one ever truly stays canceled."

I place my hand over hers on her thigh and squeeze, hoping to imbue her with a little of my affection. Izzy is a people pleaser, feeling like she's hated hasn't been easy for her.

"You should try to post again."

She twists her lips back and forth in thought. "Maybe I will."

"You shouldn't give up on what you love just because people are assholes."

"I don't plan on it." She tugs on the bottom of her skirt. "I've just needed time." Squinting up at the lighthouse, she says, "We better get started. It might take me an hour to get to the top."

"Don't be dramatic," I tease with a pat to her leg. "I'd carry you before it comes to that, and this one isn't all that tall."

I hop out, then jog around the front of the truck to get her door. She takes my hand, her sandaled feet slipping on the gravel when she touches the ground.

With my hands on her waist, I steady her, though I can't help but simultaneously pull her into my chest. "I've got you."

Fingers tracing the collar of my shirt, she looks up at me through her lashes. "Do you?"

It's an easy answer. "Always."

As I release her so I can shut the door and lock the truck, she scans the lot.

"Is it even open to the public? There's no one here."

I step up to her and grasp her chin. "They do tours sometimes, but I know a guy."

She laughs, smoothing her hands down her white top. "Why am I not surprised?"

Gripping her hand, I guide her toward the entrance. I pause only long enough to pull the key from my pocket and unlock the door. Then, once we're inside, I lock up again.

"Wow." She turns in a circle, taking in the small space downstairs and the spiral staircase that leads to the lantern room. "It's not as big as I thought it would be."

"This lighthouse is on the smaller side. But the view is worth the climb."

She spins around, her skirt fluttering around her legs. "If you say so."

Gripping the side of her orange skirt, I growl out, "I feel like you chose this specifically to drive me crazy."

With a wink, she gives her shoulders a sassy little shimmy. "Maybe." She spins around quickly, her hair flying behind her, then starts up the stairs. She only makes it up a few before she turns and looks down on me. "Make sure you stay behind for *your* special view."

I groan and bury my face in my hands. "Izzy."

"What?" She looks over her shoulder, wearing an innocent smile. "I meant my cute outfit. What did you think I was talking about?"

I hop up the bottom few steps and pinch her hip, earning a giggle.

When we reach the top, she goes straight for the wall of windows encircling the small room and peers out at the ocean beyond. "Oh, wow." Her gasp brings a smile to my face. "Look at that view."

"It's even better outside."

She turns around and rests her butt against the window ledge. Behind her, the waves roll, and a boat cruises slowly by, painting a gorgeous image. "I have a confession to make."

"And what's that?"

"I'm a *wee*"—she holds her thumb and index finger an inch apart—"bit afraid of heights."

"I'll hold on to you." I tug on her wrist, and she comes willingly, letting me pull her in until there's only a breath between us.

Tilting her head back, she blinks up at me with wide, trusting eyes. "Promise me?"

With a thumb, I graze her bottom lip. I want to kiss her. I *always* want to kiss her.

In all the years I've been alone, not a single person has tempted me the way Izzy James does.

"I promise."

She grasps my hand and laces her fingers with mine. "All right, let's do this."

I open the door and keep a tight hold on her as we step outside and grab the railing. The wind sends her hair whipping around her shoulders. She tries to tuck the long strands behind her ears, but to no avail.

"Hold on." I let go of her hand, then quickly step behind her so I can wrap one arm around her torso and use the other to hold her hair back. "Does that help?"

"Yes. This is … look at that view, Derrick."

"Do you want to move closer to the edge?"

"*No*." The word bursts out of her. "No," she says, a little calmer this time, settling her hand on top of mine over her stomach. "I'm good right here."

The beach is a distance away, but we have a bird's-eye view of the people dotted along the shore waiting for the sunset.

"Would you take a picture with me?" she asks. "Maybe just our hands?"

"Sure."

She sets us up so our hands are clasped and resting on the railing—though she's careful to keep the rest of her body well away from the edge—and snaps the photo, getting our hands and the view beyond.

"Would you care if I shared this?"

"Shared it?" I ask stupidly.

"On my social media."

I hesitate. Because even I—someone not well versed in the happenings of social media—know it's a serious declaration.

But that hesitation only lasts a heartbeat. Let the world know she's mine. "I don't mind."

She taps on her phone screen for a moment, leaning into me like she knows I'll keep her safe, and when she's done, she tucks her phone away, and we take in the scene once again.

"God, I love it here." Her voice is soft, reverent. "I think whatever drew my sister here was meant for me, too."

My chest fills with warmth at that admission. "It's a special place."

I grew up here, raised my kids here. While a lot of people dream of leaving the place they've always known, eager for adventure, I'm not one of them. There's nowhere else on Earth that will feel like this place does. The town, the people, are like a beating heart that keeps the blood moving through my veins.

She turns around carefully so that she's facing me, her entire body practically wrapped around me. When she places a palm on my chest, I can't help but wonder if she feels the way my heart stutters at her touch.

"You're special, too, you know?"

I grunt. "I don't know about that."

She smiles, her eyes tracing the shape of my lips. "To me you are."

I can't stop the smile that overtakes my face. Being Izzy's someone special is better than being anyone else's something.

She stands on her tiptoes and presses her mouth to mine. The kiss is soft. Sweet. It feels like a promise.

Turning back around, she clasps her arms around mine where it's looped around her and smiles into the setting sun. I gather her hair back again, securing it in my hand.

"Thank you for bringing me here."

I bring my lips to her neck, just behind her ear. "Even though you had to walk up the stairs?"

Her breathy laughter causes her body to shake against me. "Yeah, even though I had to walk up the stairs. This is incredible. Look at the pier. The town. It's amazing from up here."

It really is. You can see Main street from here, as well as the cliffs beyond the beach.

"I was thinking," she begins, her body suddenly tense and her voice wavering, "I could start looking for my own place since I've decided to stay here. I don't want to overstay my welcome with you."

Going as rigid as she is, I grit my teeth. The idea of her moving out doesn't sit well with me.

It takes me a moment to gather myself, and the longer I take, the stiffer she grows in my arms.

"Is that what you want?" I finally say, going for as neutral as I can muster, and give her hair a gentle tug to look back at me.

"I ... no ... Not long term. But this is new. I was only

supposed to stay with you for a few weeks, and now here we are, and I just … I don't want you to get sick of me."

"Izzy." Her name is a soft exhale. "I could *never* get sick of you." The idea is ludicrous. "You have no idea what you've done for me just by being you. By caring for me. Even if this wasn't happening between us, I wouldn't want you to go."

Her eyes fill with tears, and my heart tugs. Dammit. I could kick myself for making her emotional.

"You mean that?"

I swallow past the lump of emotion in my throat. "Whole-heartedly."

She turns around again, hands on my stomach this time. "It's crazy, and maybe some would say it's too soon, but I can't keep it bottled inside any longer. I love you, Derrick, and you deserve to know that. To hear it."

I'm so stunned by her declaration that I swear my heart stops. All words leave me, and I gawk at her, silent.

"Oh no," she blurts, a look of horror overtaking her features as she tries to step away from me. "It's okay. Pretend I didn't say anything. I—"

I kiss her. I'm pretty sure I'll die if I don't.

And when I cup her face, my hands practically swallow it whole. Sometimes I forget how small she is compared to me.

I nibble her bottom lip, a gentle request for her to open up. When she does, I sweep my tongue inside. Claiming. Owning. Devouring.

This woman is *mine*.

When we finally come up for air, our breaths linger in the small space between us. "I love you, too, Izzy."

She angles back and hits me with a smile that is so bright I'm nearly blinded. Love, *my* love, makes her that happy.

"You love me?"

"I do."

"You have no idea how good that is to hear." She clutches my shirt, the fabric bunching in her grip, and tugs me toward the door to the lantern room with desperation. "Come here."

"What?" I ask stupidly as she opens the door and tugs harder. "What's going on?"

Inside, she rips her top off, revealing a smooth white bra beneath. "I love you, and you love me, and if I don't get you naked right now, I'm going to combust. There aren't cameras in here, are there?" She spins in a circle, holding her top against her chest.

"No cameras," I confirm.

"Thank God." She lets the shirt fall and reaches for the hem of mine.

Stepping closer, I lift my arms to help. And when she can't reach, I take over and tug it off completely. She bites her lip, drinking me in. The lust in her eyes is a massive ego boost. Licking her lips, she puts her hands on my chest.

"Your heart is beating so fast." She sounds surprised by that.

"It is," I confirm, holding back a smirk.

"Mine, too," she whispers, drawing her thumb around my nipple. "You know, I've never told a man I loved him before."

"Fuck." I drop my head back. "That might be the sexiest thing you've ever said to me."

"You're special, Derrick. I don't think you see it, but you are."

My chest tightens. I want to tell her she's wrong. That she's the one who's special, but before I can, she drops to her knees. She makes easy work of my belt, then yanks my pants down my thighs.

Head dropped back, I bite out her name. "Izzy."

She rubs her hand over my cock where it strains against the fabric of my boxer-briefs.

"Shh," she hushes. "Just watch."

Slowly, with her eyes locked on mine, she slides my underwear down, freeing my cock. It bobs between us. Grabbing it at the base, she gives it a squeeze.

"I want you to fuck me hard and fast."

I open my mouth to protest, but she shushes me.

"And when we get home, we'll go slow. Got it?"

I nod, swallowing. "Whatever my girl wants."

Her lips curl up. "I like the sound of that."

"Getting what you want?"

"No. Being your girl." With that, she takes my cock into her mouth, using her hand to apply pressure at the base. Then she pulls back slightly and licks the tip.

"I love your cock," she whispers the confession. "So much."

*Jesus.*

That alone makes my knees so weak I have to lean against the wall to stay upright. This girl and the things she says. They threaten to undo me.

I thought I could handle anything until Hurricane Izzy came along. Now, I'm just along for the ride.

She licks and sucks me, teasing me until my balls are tight and tingles shoot up my spine.

"Izzy," I warn with a gruff exhale. "Get up."

She doesn't listen.

"Get up," I repeat, grasping her hair gently.

She still doesn't stop.

"Izzy, if you want me to fuck you, you're going to have to stop sucking my cock."

Finally, she pulls back with a pop, wiping at her mouth with her thumb, her eyes hooded and her chest heaving with heavy breaths.

"C'mere." I grip her elbows and guide her to her feet, noticing that her knees are a little red from the floor. Dammit, I feel like an asshole for not making her stop sooner. "Lean over here." I direct her to the window ledge.

"Mm," she hums, wiggling her butt. "Sex with a view. I like it."

Shoving her skirt up, I let out a growl. "Izzy?"

Peeking over her shoulder, she sinks her teeth into her lip. "Yes?" She bats her eyes.

My words are choked, but I force them out. "Where the fuck is your underwear?"

She smiles so bright I'm nearly blinded. "At home."

I give her ass a light smack. "Don't do that."

"Why not?" She gives a soft laugh that turns into a moan when my thumb circles her clit. "I was determined to get you to fuck me."

Shaking my head, I stroke my cock and bring it to her entrance. "You just want to be dripping with my cum all the way home." I thrust into her in one swift move, making her throw her head back and cry out. "You're my dirty girl, aren't you? You love to have my cum filling this sweet pussy, don't you?"

She slams a hand against the windowpane in an effort to keep herself steady. "Y-yes." The word stutters out of her. "Oh, God. Derrick." My name is a whimper.

Fuck, I long to hear it again. "Say my name, baby. Tell me how much you want me."

"Derrick," she breathes, head tipped back, neck elongated. "I love you."

"Fuck, baby." I grip her hips, fucking her hard and fast. I'm not going to last long, but that's okay. We have all night.

*We have the rest of our lives.*

She gasps, her hand on the glass splaying wider. "I'm so close."

"Rub your clit," I tell her. "I'm almost there, too."

She obeys, and her cries echo through the lighthouse. "Fuck! Derrick!"

The pulsating grip of her pussy sends me careening over the edge. I come, leaning over the back of her body as I fill her.

As I come back down to earth and blink into reality, I brush her hair off her neck and kiss the skin there, finding it damp with sweat. "I love you," I murmur, needing her to hear it. To feel it.

She's quiet for a moment and then, "Enough to carry me out of here? I'm not sure I can walk."

Chuckling, my heart feeling lighter than it has in years, I pull out of her and yank up my underwear and pants. "I can try."

"Mm." She gives a tired hum, pressing her forehead against the glass.

I tug her skirt back down and spin in search of her shirt. Once I've located it and helped her into it, I snag my own off the wooden floorboards. With our clothes righted, we take a moment to catch our breath and look out over the water one more time. Then we carefully take the stairs down to the exit.

"Is there some kind of club for that?" she asks when we're safely in the truck.

"Huh?" I ask, my mind still scrambled from the unbelievable orgasm, as I adjust the AC.

"Well"—she turns her head lazily my way—"there's the

mile high club for sex on a plane. Is there something similar for lighthouses?"

I chuckle, turning out of the parking lot. "I doubt it."

"There should be."

She smiles over me, and even though the sun is almost gone, it shines directly upon me. That's exactly what Izzy is— my own personal sun.

# twenty-nine

Izzy

"NO."

"Finneas," I whine, covering my face. "I'm sorry."

"You can't move to Maine. That's so far away." Lips turned down, he pouts at me onscreen. "I can't say I'm surprised, though. Not with the way you talk about the place, not to mention your hot roommate, but I don't want to lose you."

"You'll come visit me, won't you?"

He gives a fake dramatic sign. "I guess so. Maybe in a couple of months. Fall in New England will make for good content."

"That's true," I agree. "Fall in Parkerville is magical."

The leaves turn the most beautiful shades of red, yellow, and orange, and they litter the ground like sprinkles on a cake. The businesses decorate their windows for Halloween. Last year, Via painted the windows of her store with a mummy theme.

"You're really leaving LA, huh?"

I sigh. "It was time." Deep down, I always knew LA was temporary, and now that I'm approaching thirty, my goals have shifted. I'll never regret my time there, but I would if I forced myself to stay.

"If you need help packing, let me know."

I level him with a skeptical look. "Finneas."

"All right." He holds his hands up like I've caught him. "I'll get Jordan to do it," he says, referring to his boyfriend. "But that's only because he doesn't have to worry about ruining a manicure." He wags his fingers at the screen.

"Ooh, those are cute."

"Please tell me you're taking care of your nails out there."

"Sometimes. Currently, though, I'm past due for a manicure."

"Let me see."

With a sigh, I hold my hands up, cringing as I show him how badly the blue polish has grown out.

"Izzy." He says my name again in a scandalized fashion. "You need to fix those."

"I know." I tuck my hands under my thighs. "I haven't had time."

Not between helping Derrick with the business and working on the restaurant. I've been sourcing furniture and sending it to the Grants—the restaurant owners—for approval. Working on their place might be the most satisfying thing I've ever done. It's rewarding in a way I didn't expect.

"Make time," he scolds playfully, pointing at the counter. "Like today."

"I'll try."

"Oh." He claps his hands and straightens. "Have you checked your Instagram?"

I snort. "No." I uploaded the photo from the lighthouse a few days ago and dipped. I only posted for the followers who have stuck by me. Who genuinely care. It was my way of saying I might be staying away, but I am all right.

His mouth drops. "Izzy, check it right now."

The moment the app loads and I see the number of notifications, my jaw drops. I click over to my main page, and when it registers that my 2.4 million followers has jumped to 2.5 million, my heart takes off.

"What the fuck?" I mutter, scrolling down and clicking on my last photo.

**@laura_luvs_uuu: Omg! I can tell from his hand alone he's hot!**

**@willowcreek4eva: So happy to see you back!**

**@hannahmarie02: OMG the veins in his arm. I'm drooling. Girl, show us his face!**

**@easybreezy: You dipped and got a boyfriend! Good for you! We've missed you!**

And, perhaps the best comment of all, is from a verified account with more than fifty thousand likes on it alone.

**@LUX: Good to see you back. Don't let the haters win. Muah.**

My phone clatters to the floor, and dumbstruck, I blink at Finneas.

Laughing, he claps, and I swear he's bouncing in his seat. "Looks like my girl is no longer canceled."

"I…" My stomach twists in an unexpected way. "I thought it was going to be like the last time I posted."

"People have moved on," he says with a dismissive shrug. "Far worse stuff has happened since then."

I don't ask because I don't want to know. "I ... even Lux commented."

"I know." He reaches offscreen, then brings an iced coffee to his lips. "Lux must've felt horrible about the hate you got. A few days after your last post, when people were still being dicks, she made a post calling them out."

My throat tightens, making it hard to speak. "I didn't know."

After that incident, I locked myself out of my apps to help quell the temptation to look.

"Looks like you're back, girl. If you want to be, that is."

"I want to be," I say carefully, tucking a piece of hair behind my ear.

Finneas visibly cringes again at the state of my nails, pulling a laugh from me.

"I'm not sure how I want to go about it, though. My content is going to change, and people might hate that but—"

"But your devoted followers will stick around," he interrupts. "You'd be surprised by how many people follow your account because of *you* rather than what you're doing."

A wave of gratitude for this man swells inside me. "Thanks, Finneas."

"I'm really going to miss you."

My chest pangs with sadness. "Me, too, but we'll still see each other. Bestie vacations, right?"

"You bet. And Jordan and I will come in the fall."

"Please!"

"I better go," he says, tapping his fingers on his desk. "And you, little missy, need to get yourself to the nail salon."

I roll my eyes. "I will."

"Today. I'll be waiting for pictures."

"Fine," I groan. "I'll see if Via wants to go."

"And if she doesn't"—he wags a finger at me—"then you go anyway."

With a mock salute, I say, "You bet."

"Talk to you later." Finneas blows me a kiss, and then he's gone.

My heart aches just a little as I log out of the video chat browser. As happy as I am with my decision to move here permanently, I am sad to be leaving him. He's one of the good ones.

With a cleansing inhale, I snatch my phone from the floor. Then I shoot Via a text about getting our nails done. Since Reid is with Derrick and Layla—headed out to see the property and talk about Derrick's plans for it, as well as get their blessing to sell the house, since it's where they were raised—Via might actually be available.

**Via: Sure, I can go.**

**Me: Pick you up in twenty?**

**Via: Sounds good. I'll be ready.**

I shuck off my sweatpants and oversized tee and slip into a dress in record time, then I toss my hair up with a clip. After letting Wonton out to pee and smothering him in kisses for being the goodest boy, I drive over to Via's apartment.

She takes the steps at a relaxed pace, a crocheted bag slung over her shoulder and her jeans streaked with paint and what I think might be charcoal.

"Hi," she says as she slips into the passenger seat. "Please tell me we're going to get coffee first. I need caffeine. I was up all night."

I grin, waggling my eyebrows. "All night, huh?"

She swats my arm. "Not like that. Though"—she laughs, strapping the seat belt across her chest—"sometimes it is like that, but not in this case. I was up working on a project. I went to sleep at a reasonable time, but then inspiration struck, so I got up and went for it."

Frowning, I ask, "You get inspiration in your sleep?"

"I was dreaming," she explains as I back out of the alley that serves as her driveway, "and in the dream I was painting. It was so beautiful, Izzy. The pink was the most unique shade I've ever seen. And the blue was so vibrant. I knew it was just what the piece I've been working on needed."

I shake my head, astounded at the way her brain works. "You're incredible."

She bumps her elbow lightly against mine. "So are you. Now, what is this I heard about you posting a man on Instagram? It's Derrick, right? Mom called me about it, but I haven't been online to confirm."

I take my eyes off the road for a second to gape at my sister. "How would she know? She's not even on social media."

Via waves a dismissive hand. "One of her friends sent a screenshot to her."

"Ugh," I groan, tossing my head back as I stop at the light. "I should've known. Why didn't she ask me about it?"

"I think she was hoping I'd spill without her having to confront you. You *are* the favorite."

My heart sinks. "Via."

"What?" she asks, her tone much more upbeat than mine. "It's true, and I'm okay with it."

I press my lips together and leave it alone. There's no sense in denying it. Our parents' favoritism has always been blatant, and it's absolutely laughable. For years, Via was the one who did everything that was asked of her, while I always marched to the beat of my own drum.

"Anyway, I'm sure she'll call you at some point. Figured I'd give you a heads-up."

A shaky exhale gusts out of my lips. "She's going to kill me when I tell her I'm moving here."

"You're moving here?" Via blurts out, jolting in her seat so she's facing me, more surprised than I expected her to be.

"Yes. I don't want to be in LA anymore. I love it here."

In my periphery, Via nibbles her lip in a way that tells me she's carefully weighing her words. "You're not moving for Derrick, are you?"

"No," I answer firmly. "I'm not. Yes, being here permanently will make things easier for us, but truthfully, I made this decision before anything even happened with him. I just needed to come to terms with it. Even though I know it's the right choice, I'm still closing a chapter on my life."

"I understand that. I guess that means I should share my news, too."

"Ooh." I wiggle my shoulders and dart a glance at her. "What is it?"

"Reid and I are looking at houses. Just something small."

"Aw, Via." I reach over and squeeze her hand. "I'm so happy for you."

"Thank you." She pulls a ChapStick out of her purse. "I've been putting it off, which is silly with as much time as we spend together. Most nights, I either end up at his place, or he ends up at mine. It makes sense to live together."

"I wondered why you hadn't already moved in together, but I didn't want to push."

She snorts. "Because I'm stubborn. Chase and I moved too fast. I didn't have time to really settle into our relationship before we were married. With Reid, I want to make sure I take my time making big decisions."

A chuckle escapes me as I turn into the parking lot of the nail salon. "It's probably a good thing you forced him to take it slow. Otherwise, he'd have already talked you into walking down the aisle."

"You know"—she stretches her fingers out in front of her, a nervous tic we both possess—"I secretly thought he would have grown bored with me by now, but he loves me just as much, if not more, than he did in the beginning."

My heart squeezes as I take her in. "That boy is obsessed with you."

She laughs, her eyes filling with tears. "He really is. God, I didn't know love could be like this. So … free. With Chase I … it was okay in the beginning, but it was like nothing I did was good enough. Like *I* wasn't good enough. Reid has never made me feel that way."

"He can't help it." I undo my seat belt. "That boy is pure golden retriever. All he knows how to do is show you love."

Blinking rapidly, she fans her face. "We better get in there before I get any more emotional."

I can't help but think about my own feelings for Derrick. I've had plenty of boyfriends, but I've never felt the way I do with Derrick. I've never loved another person in this way. With him, I feel content to simply exist.

The salon is an adorable little place with pale pink walls and other pink accents throughout. It's fun and girly and so much cuter than the white, uber modern salon I frequented in LA.

We also don't need to book appointments months in advance. Once we've checked in, we head over to the wall of swatches and polishes.

"I don't know what color I'm in the mood for." I tap my finger against my lip.

"I'm going with orange," Via says, already scanning the swatch of appropriate shades.

Still unable to decide, I pull out my phone and shoot a text off to Derrick.

> Me: I'm getting my nails done with my sister. I don't know what color to get.

It only takes a minute for his response to come through.

> Derrick: Can I pick?

> Me: Sure. Which color would you prefer to see wrapped around your dick later?

Those three little dots signaling his reply appear almost immediately. Then disappear.

Finally, I get:

> Red.

My stomach flips at that simple response. Red it is.

I pick up the swatch and choose a bright cherry red.

"What's that little smirk about?" My sister asks as we sit side by side at the empty manicure stations. "You texted something dirty, didn't you?"

I shrug, playing innocent. "Maybe. Maybe not."

Her laugh is a breathy huff. "I can't believe you're with my boyfriend's *dad*."

"It really is wild." There's no denying how complicated the whole situation is. "But I'm happy."

"You deserve it," she says, unscrewing the lid from the bottle of pastel orange she chose and pulling the brush out to assess the color.

"So do you." If anyone does, it's her. My wish for my sister is that she can have every good thing she's ever wanted.

275

There's one thing, I know, that was and will be a struggle, but I have no doubt that one day she'll be a mom.

"Who would've thought we'd both fall in love with Parkerville, Maine and its men?" She breathes a laugh. "They should put that on a travel brochure. Come here if you want to find love."

An hour and a half later, our nails are done, and we head to the coffee shop, having forgotten all our talk about our mother and our men.

"I love that we can spend time together like this," Via says, swiping her coffee from the pickup counter.

"Me, too."

Our age difference means that, as kids, we rarely had things in common, and by the time that began to change, she was with Chase, and he took up all her time.

"Are you coming to book club tonight? You've missed the last couple of weeks, and they've all been desperate to know where you are."

When the barista sets my matcha on the counter, I give her a smile and step away. "That's because now they know I'm with Derrick and they want all the tea."

Via groans. "You know what Glenda did last week? She got out a measuring tape and made everyone guess how long his dick is."

"What?" Laughter bubbles out of me. "Only Glenda. She's a hoot."

"She's something, that's for sure." Via sips her coffee. "I refused to participate, especially after she said that my guess would probably be most accurate, since I'm with Reid and all. She was not happy with me. I thought she might take her shoe off and smack me with it."

Tears prick my eyes as I toss my head back and guffaw. "Oh, wow. I love that woman."

Via shakes her head. "She's entertaining. Don't tell her, but I think she's one of my favorite parts of Parkerville."

"I won't say a thing." I mime zipping my lips. "It would go straight to her head."

"What do you think about heading to the beach?"

I scan the sky outside the window. "Sounds good. The weather is perfect for it."

"Do you know what they're up to today?" she asks, holding the shop's door open for me.

Pressing my lips together, I nod. "I'm sure Reid will fill you in."

"Or"—she bumps her shoulder against mine—"you could just tell me."

I shake my head. "It's not my thing."

With a sigh, she nods. "All right, I'll leave it there, but only because I get it. I wouldn't spill Reid's secrets either."

"We're so down bad," I groan.

Laughing, she loops her arm through mine. "Those Crawford men are special."

My mind is consumed with images of Derrick. The way he totes Wonton around the house. His willingness to eat popcorn on the couch and wear facemasks with me. The feel of his hands on my skin. "They definitely are."

"But let's forget about them for a while. I want to collect seashells for a piece I'm working on."

I give her a sharp nod. "No more Crawford talk. Got it."

At the beach, we wander and scoop up shells, giggling like little girls. I'm not sure I've ever been more grateful for my sister than I am as I share this perfect day with her.

# *thirty*

## Izzy

AFTER SPENDING HOURS COLLECTING SEASHELLS, building sandcastles, and talking about anything and everything, we head for book club.

Choruses of hellos greet us when we step inside, since we're the last to arrive.

"Grab a plate and drink," Glenda hollers from her usual seat. "And Izzy, I do hope you'll spill some juicy details about your man. I heard you two went to the lighthouse."

My face flames at the images that pummel me. *Are my cheeks as red as I think they are?*

"Uh ... yeah ... Derrick wanted to show me the view."

"In my day, we went there to ... what do you kids call it these days? Hook up?"

Beside me, Via angles in close and whispers, "Did you have sex in the lighthouse?"

Stiffening, I purse my lips and inhale through my nose, avoiding her gaze. If I look at her, she'll see the answer written all over my face.

Unfortunately, keeping my mouth shut doesn't help. Slapping my arm lightly, she says, "Oh my God, you did."

"You had sex in a closet on Halloween with Reid," I blurt out, my voice way too loud. "What's wrong with sex in a lighthouse?"

The room full of women dissolves into laughter.

"Trust me," Cassandra says from her spot on the love seat. "Most of us have had sex in that lighthouse. It's like a rite of passage around here."

"Oh, God." I nearly drop my plate in an attempt to hide my face.

*Does that mean Derrick knew about it being a hookup spot?*

Looks like we're going to have a conversation about this later.

I fill my plate with snacks and pour myself a glass of wine. Is the one glass more like two? Perhaps. But I need it.

Settling on the couch beside my sister, with Ella and Anna on my other side, I take a deep breath to help center myself.

Maybe if I stuff my mouth through the entire meeting, I'll make it out of here relatively unscathed.

Or not. Because the moment my sister opens her mouth, the room erupts.

"My sister's moving here officially," Via says.

"Izzy!" Ella squeals. "Really?"

"Yeah." I shove a handful of nuts into my mouth. "I love it here. So why not?" I shrug like it's no big deal, all the while racking my brain for topics that may distract the group and take the pressure off me.

"Does that mean you're moving in for good with Daddy Crawford?" One of the ladies asks.

Glenda clucks her tongue before I can answer. "That's not Daddy. That's Grandpa Crawford."

A wave of mortification washes over me. If I could melt into the floor, I would.

Covering my face with my hands, I ask my sister, "Why did you bring me here?"

She laughs. "You're going to be a full-fledged Parkerville townsperson. You have to pay your dues."

"I hate you."

That only makes her laugh harder.

"Do you think you'll get married?" Lucy asks from across the room. "Might I recommend—"

"Lucy, dear," Glenda interrupts, waving a dismissive hand. "No one wants to get married at your family's mausoleum. It's a mausoleum. There are dead people."

"But ... it's pretty," Lucy defends.

"I think we're getting a bit ahead of ourselves here," I say, my heart rate spiking and sweat breaking out at my temples. Not that I haven't thought about the possibility of marrying Derrick, but our relationship is brand new. I want to enjoy where we are before I think about marriage. So to once again try to take the heat off myself, I blurt out, "Reid and Via are looking at houses."

Did I totally throw my sister under the bus so that I can stop drowning? Yes. Do I feel bad about it? Not in the slightest.

She smacks my leg. "Thanks a lot."

I smile at her. "You're welcome."

With the attention momentarily diverted from me, I take a moment to compose myself. Who knows what else will come out of Glenda's mouth before the evening is over.

Luckily for me, though, the group stays focused on Reid and Via's potential move for a while. They give recommendations for realtors and available properties. She'll want to kill me later, but it's worth it for the reprieve.

It might be strange, how little I enjoy being the center of attention when I've made so much of my life available to the masses. But it's different when there's a screen separating me from the people eager for information.

Things are winding down when the attention does turn back to me. It's my own fault. Because I've been sitting here lost in my thoughts, thinking about the past year and all the changes and how there's one more change I'd like to make.

"I think I'm going to cut my hair," I blurt out.

Silence descends on the room. "That's lovely, dear," Glenda says, words dripping with sarcasm. "Schedule a trim in the morning."

"No. Not a trim. I'm thinking like chopping it. Like here." I clip my hair between my fingers to show them what I'm thinking. "That's what? About eight inches? Ten?"

It would bring my hair up to almost my shoulders.

"That's a lot, dear," Glenda says, trying not to cringe. "Are you sure?"

"Yeah. I'm ready for the change. It'll be good for me."

"If you're sure, I have my scissors in my car," Anna says, leaning forward at the other end of the couch. "Sorry, that sounded weird. I do hair. I could do it now if you want."

"Really?"

"Of course. Let me get them." She hops up and heads for the door. "While I do that, will someone grab a stool from the kitchen and maybe a towel?"

Via slowly turns her head in my direction, eyes wide. "Are you sure about this?"

"It's just hair. If I hate it, oh well. It'll grow."

Twenty minutes later I'm a whole lot of hair lighter, and Lucy is passing me a hand mirror so I can check Anna's handiwork. The wavy strands are about an inch past my shoulders. Exactly where I wanted them.

"It's perfect, Anna. Thank you." I slide off the stool and take the dustpan and broom from Lucy before she can sweep up the mess. "I've got it."

When the floor is clean and the food is put away, we depart for the night with a chorus of goodbyes.

As nosy and meddling as these women can be, it's life-affirming, knowing they're in my corner. These women would do anything for one another, and they've brought me into the fold. These kinds of friendships are hard to come by, no matter where a person lives.

"What do you think Derrick is going to say about your hair?" Via asks me as I navigate toward her apartment.

"I'm not sure," I answer with the shrug of one shoulder. "I didn't think about what his opinion might be. I did it for myself."

With a hum, she squeezes my arm. "Good. Never do anything because of or for a man."

"Never," I agree as I pull down the alley.

Reid's older model Mustang is already there, parked behind Via's car.

"Thanks for today." She undoes her seat belt. "And thanks for your help with telling the whole town that we're looking for a house. I'm sure the gossip mill is already doing its thing."

A laugh works its way out of me as I take in the building. "They're already planning my wedding, so we're even."

Before she can even get out of the car, Reid, wearing a grin, is opening the door to Via's upstairs apartment.

"Go get your man," I tell her.

"I will." With a wink, she closes the car door and all but skips up the stairs to him, where he pulls her into his arms and angles in for a kiss.

They're so in love it would be sickening if I wasn't also head-over-heels for a man.

Via turns and waves as I back down the alley, and behind her, Reid lifts a hand while whispering in her ear. By the way she swats at his chest, I can guarantee his words were naughty.

They're so insufferably cute.

At the gas station near the house, I run inside for slushies. I could curse Derrick for introducing me to my newest addiction. Anymore, I crave these more than coffee or matcha.

"Where's your better half?" Greg teases when I set the cups down to pay.

"At home. Probably asleep on the couch."

With a chuckle, he rings up the slushies.

"You've been good for him," he says as he takes the cash I hold out, the statement shocking me. "Derrick's always been a great guy, but he was more closed off before you came along. Now, he smiles all the time. You make him happy."

The compliment makes my heart stumble a little. It means more to me than he'll ever know.

"Thank you." I tuck my change away, fighting a blush. "He makes me happy, too."

Slushies in hand, I climb into my car and head home. As I pull into the driveway, I can't help but think about how much I *don't* want to get my own place. It's crazy. We haven't been together long at all, but the idea of not going to bed curled around him or waking up at his side makes me feel a little ill.

On the way to the porch, I take in the street and the yard, marveling at the leaves already beginning to fall in beautiful shades of red and orange. Before I can reach the door, it opens, and Derrick appears in the glow of the porch light, Wonton under his arm.

The surge of love that flows through me is downright frightening. How is it possible to feel so much for another human being?

His smile morphs into an open-mouthed look of surprise. "Your hair. You cut it."

"I did." I shake my head, causing my hair to sway. "What do you think?"

With a step in my direction, he cups the back of my neck. Then he drags his fingers higher and laces them in my hair, scraping the strands into a ponytail.

"Still enough to grab," he says with a smirk. "I love it."

"Enough to grab, huh? What if I shaved it all off?"

With his forehead pressed to mine, he says, "It's your hair. You can do what you want with it. I'll love you no matter what, but I do love to run my hands through it." He strokes the strands. "It's always so soft."

"I use a special rinse. You gonna let me in now?"

"Right." He releases my hair and takes the Coke slushie from me. "You couldn't drive by the gas station without stopping, could you?"

"You would have stopped too if you'd been dealing with Glenda all evening."

His laughter rumbles through me when I pass him and step inside. He locks the door behind him, then sets Wonton on the floor. My furry little buddy immediately scurries over to me, jumping up and down on his hind legs for attention.

Squatting, I shower my best friend in pets and kisses. There's nothing like the genuine, pure love of an animal.

When he's settled, I stand and slide off my shoes. "How'd it go with Reid and Layla?"

Derrick stuffs his free hand into his pocket and rocks back. "Surprisingly well, I thought they might not want to see this house go. Instead, they seemed almost relieved to see me moving on."

I close the distance between us. "They just want you to be happy."

"I know." His warm hand slides around my waist. "I missed you."

I melt into him. The words are simple but so powerful. There's something to be said about finding one's person. About that special ache that hits when they aren't near. It's not as though I can't be away from him. In fact, I needed a day with my sister. But I feel better when he's around. It's like before him, I wasn't whole. And I didn't even realize it. Now, though, when we're apart, I notice the absence of that piece of me.

"I missed you, too."

"Should I put some popcorn in the microwave? We could watch a few episodes of *Gilmore Girls*."

I take a sip of my slushie, brightening. "And put on face masks?"

He sighs like it's a hardship, but he does a terrible job at hiding the way his lips turn up on one side. "I guess so."

"All right, get that going, and I'll wash my face and grab the mask."

After I come back down, my face already slathered up, Derrick places the bowl on the table and sits on the couch so I can apply the mask.

"It's cold." He flinches away.

"No, it's not. You're such a baby."

He harrumphs. "I promise you, it's cold."

I hold my hand an inch from his face, the green mask thick on my fingers. "I just put it on my face. I can promise you it wasn't cold. Even if it was, it's worth it. You can't tell me your pores don't look better."

The sigh he gives is nothing less than dramatic, but he lowers his shoulders and doesn't complain again as I finish applying the mask.

I wash my hands in the kitchen sink, and when I return, he's got the show cued up. We're on season five since we've worked to slow the rate we've been burning through episodes. Though I've been through the entire series several times, I still want to make it last. He doesn't know it, but we're watching *New Girl* next.

Derrick settles back on the couch, puts the popcorn bowl in his lap, and holds an arm out, motioning for me to join him.

I curl myself into his side and soak up the heat radiating from his bare torso.

Wonton, not one to be left out, and a voracious lover of popcorn, is quick to jump up and circle several times before plopping down behind my bent knees.

Unable to resist his cuteness, I hold a piece of popcorn out for him. His little pink tongue shoots out and takes it, making me giggle.

Chuckling, Derrick squeezes me against his side. "You spoil him."

I roll my eyes. "And you don't? I've seen you sneaking him cheese, so don't try to play innocent."

"Look at that face." He nods at Wonton, who sits with his tongue hanging out, eager for another piece. "How can I say no?"

"But I'm supposed to?"

"I see your point." He grabs a piece and holds it out to him. Then he points the remote at the TV and starts the show.

By the time the episode ends, I'm fighting sleep.

Derrick presses a kiss to the top of my head. "Let's go to bed."

"I'm fine. Let's watch one more episode." There was a chance I could convince him up until a yawn escaped me along with the last word.

With a shake of his head, he turns the TV off. "No, bedtime."

Groaning, I climb off the couch, then head for the kitchen, with Wonton hot on my heels, eager to be let out the back door.

Derrick dumps the remnants of the popcorn in the trash, then gives it a quick wash and sets it on the drying pad beside the sink.

"Hurry, Wonton," I call out when he spends a little too much time sniffing one particular spot.

He turns to look at me, his expression disgruntled, as if he's saying *I'll go when I'm good and ready.*

Once he finds a spot that he deems worthy, he does his business and runs back into the house.

As I lock the door, Derrick steps in close so his front is pressed to my back, then wraps his arms around me.

"You're going to help me, right?" he asks softly, resting his chin on top of my head.

"With what?" I relax into his hold, all tension escaping me when he's close like this.

"Building the house. Picking out floors and cabinets and paint. All of it. I want you to put your touch on it."

I close my eyes and imagine the paint colors I'd want, my dream kitchen, wallpaper, all the little details.

"Are you sure you want my help?" He's had that land for years, and for as permanent as our connection feels, it's still new. A whole house is a huge commitment.

"Yes." There's no hesitation. "It's going to be your house, too."

"Hmm. You think so?"

He smiles, the weight of his chin changing against the top of my head. "I know so, baby."

He takes my hand and drags me upstairs to his room—our room, I suppose, since I've taken over, my shirt strewn over the back of the chair, shoes shoved in the corner.

In the bathroom, he turns the water on and dampens a cloth. Then he carefully wipes my face free of the mask. I do the same to him, making sure there are no green remnants left behind.

Once we've brushed our teeth, standing side by side at the sink, we finally crawl into bed with Wonton.

"Get over here," he grouses, hooking an arm around me and pulling me over to meet him in the middle of the bed. "That's better."

It's always better when he's holding me.

# thirty-one

## Izzy

THE SUN WARMS my skin as the boat bobs lazily in the ocean. September is winding down, and soon, my chances of spotting a whale will be gone. By the end of October, they'll have migrated elsewhere. I know they're around—I've overheard tourists gushing over them—but apparently, they're determined to elude me.

"I just want to see one." I lean against the side of the boat, head cradled in my arms, with my knees on the seat. "Is that too much to ask for?"

Over my shoulder, Derrick grabs a bag of chips and opens it.

I narrow my eyes. "When did you sneak those on board?"

"Woman." He cradles the bag protectively against his chest as he sits on the bench with me. "Let me have my chips."

With a faux dramatic sigh, I drop my head again. "Fine. But only if you share."

He gladly holds the bag out to me. Derrick's diet has vastly improved since I've been around. I think he's even beginning to like a few green foods.

I take a handful, then turn back to the water, my eyes shielded from the sun with a pair of sunglasses.

Behind me, Derrick fiddles with the string on my green bikini top. "How many of these things do you own?"

"An embarrassing number."

"I don't think I've seen you wear the same one twice."

Humming, I munch on a chip. "I have a bad habit of buying swimsuits. And companies send them to me, too, when I'm traveling, so I have an entire drawer full of them."

"And you brought them all with you?"

"Not *all*, but enough."

"Clearly," he laughs. The sound is cut short, though, when his eyes catch on something in the distance. "Izzy, look."

I turn back to the water and scan the surface, but excitement quickly dwindles to disappointment. "I don't see anything."

"Just wait," he says, fidgeting on the seat behind me. I don't think I've ever seen Derrick this happy before, and I know it's entirely because he's glad for *me*. "Keep looking."

My heart races, a mixture of anticipation and apprehension.

Because if he really did see a whale, who's to say it'll surface again here? It could be miles away before it comes up again.

"Be patient," he whispers, like he can feel how tense I am.

I've been waiting all summer for this, and as the warm days dwindle, my hopes have gone with them. The boat rocks gently with the waves. I've gotten used to the motion. Love it, really. The soothing rhythm is good for my soul.

Derrick leans in, hand splayed over my back, causing goose bumps to rise on my skin. As I obediently watch the water, I can't help but wonder if my body will always respond to him this way, or if one day, it'll wear off.

I'm about to open my mouth to tell him this is hopeless, to whine about how the universe just doesn't want me to see a whale, when in the distance...

"Oh my God." I grab his arm, my grip tight, and pop up on my knees. "Is that one?"

"A humpback," he says with a kiss to my shoulder.

It's embarrassing how quickly tears stream down my face. Of all the amazing experiences I've had, this tops it all. Nothing feels as powerful as witnessing nature in this way.

"Why are you crying?" he asks, carefully prying my hand off his arm and lacing our fingers.

"Because it's so beautiful." Another comes up near where the first surfaced, the sight making my knees weak.

Derrick grasps my waist to keep me from tumbling off the cushion.

"Just look at them." Nature is truly astonishing in her beauty.

I spent *months* moping over being canceled, as if that truly matters. How could it when moments like this exist? How did I let myself care so much about what a bunch of strangers thought of me? I don't *know* them. Their opinions are moot.

The pod of humpbacks stays nearby. They're close enough to see from time to time but far enough away that I don't feel like I'm intruding.

For an hour, we watch, and not once does Derrick mention

leaving. Not once does he sigh or fidget or try to steal my attention. He knows I won't want to leave until they do.

"They're magnificent," I murmur. "Look at them."

I have to wipe a few more tears away. Seeing them in person is better than I dreamed it could be.

"They are," he says softly, but when I turn, he's looking at me.

Eventually, the pod moves on, and an ache forms in my chest. I don't stop watching until several minutes go by without another glimpse of them.

When I've resigned myself to the knowledge that they're gone, I tug my sweatshirt on. With the day waning, it's grown cool.

"Moments like that show us how truly small we are," I gush. "Nature is so vast, so infinite and we only experience a blip of it. Life's short and things like this? I guess they remind me of why we're truly here. The real joy in life is being content to simply exist."

"It never gets old." He pulls the anchor, his muscles straining. "Seeing them. It's incredibly humbling."

I pack up our snacks and towels and anything loose to keep it from blowing away as Derrick puts the anchor away and starts the engine. "Can I drive?"

He chuckles. "Not on your own, but come here." He tugs me in front of him at the wheel, showing me the controls and whispering each instruction in my ear in such a sensual way that it has me squirming against him. His cock grows hard, making me eager to drop to my knees and make my boat blow job a reality. But before I can, he stops me with a hand on my hip.

"Another time." He presses a kiss to my neck.

I guess I shouldn't be surprised that he can read me so well.

While he helps me guide the boat back to Brooks's place, he plays with my much shorter strands of hair. I'm loving the shorter cut, the bold difference, but I won't lie and say I didn't wake up the morning after and panic a little when I looked in the mirror.

"Would you be okay with breakfast for dinner tonight?" I ask as he cuts the motor at the dock. "I was thinking about making egg sandwiches."

Derrick gives me a narrowed eyed look as he hops off the boat and holds a hand out to take the cooler and my bag from me. "Are you going to put fucking avocado on it?"

Humming, I tilt my head, pretending to consider the question. "Probably."

"Then no."

I sigh like it's a massive hardship, then let him help me out of the boat. "I suppose I could leave it off yours."

"Good. I don't like that slimy shit." He shudders.

He scoops up the cooler while I get my bag, and we head up the hill. Once we've loaded our things in the truck, Derrick opens the passenger door for me, and I climb in and immediately go for my phone so I can scroll through the hundreds of photos and videos I took of the whales.

The garage door opens, causing Derrick to pause in front of the truck.

I expect to see Brooks coming out to say hello, but instead, it's his wife. She's got her phone to her ear and her face is etched in panic. I sit up straighter and try to read her lips as she rushes to Derrick.

The two of them turn and dart into the house, so, with my heart pounding, I hop out of the truck and take off after them.

I've never been in here before, but I don't stop to take it in as I follow Maura and Derrick into the kitchen. When I round the bar that separates the room from the living space, I stumble at the sight of Brooks sprawled on the ground, his face pale. Too pale.

"There's no pulse," Maura cries. "He's not breathing. He's not breathing. He's not—"

Derrick drops to the ground beside his best friend, lacing his fingers together, and begins chest compressions.

"Is Dad going to be okay?" I turn at the sound and find Amanda standing in the doorway with her arms around her brother. Both kids wear horror-stricken expressions. They shouldn't be seeing this. All it takes is one look at Brooks to know this isn't good.

Their mom, busy speaking to the emergency operator, doesn't hear Amanda's question.

"Let's go this way." I usher the kids away. I don't have a clue where I'm leading them, but anywhere has to be better than here.

Amanda sits on a couch in what appears to be a den, wrapping her arms around her legs and folding in on herself. Jackson sinks onto the floor in front of her.

"Dad's dead, isn't he?" he asks, his voice small and scared. It's a sucker punch to my chest.

"I-I don't know," I answer as honestly. "Paramedics should be on their way, though. Can you stay here?"

When Amanda nods, I rush back to the kitchen, where Derrick is still doing compressions and mouth-to-mouth.

Maura's sobs are the most heartbreaking sound I've ever heard.

I've never felt so helpless and utterly useless in my entire life.

At the sound of sirens, I grip Maura's arm to get her attention. "I'll go outside and get them."

The ambulance is turning into the driveway when I burst out of the garage. It only takes seconds for them to grab their supplies and follow me into the house. As they step into the kitchen, Derrick backs away from Brooks so they can take over.

The hopeless, scared look on Derrick's face nearly makes me drop to my knees.

"The kids," I say, wanting to get him out of here. "We should go check on the kids."

"The kids?" he asks, his face blank, as if he's entirely forgotten they exist.

"Yes, Amanda and Jackson. We should check on them. They shouldn't be alone right now, and Maura needs to be with Brooks."

I want to get Derrick out of this kitchen more than anything. I hope there's a chance Brooks can pull through whatever has happened, but my gut tells me he's already gone.

"Oh, God. The kids." His horror-filled eyes meet mine. A low "fuck" leaves him, and then he takes off around the corner.

I follow him to the den, where Amanda sits in the position I left her in and Jackson is staring dejectedly up at the ceiling from where he's lying on the floor.

My stomach aches for them.

"My dad's dead, isn't he?" Jackson asks without looking away from the ceiling. "It's okay"—he turns his head and zeroes in on Derrick—"you can be honest."

"I don't know, kid." Derrick sits on the floor beside him and Jackson scurries into his lap. "I truly don't know."

Amanda bites her lip, tears falling silently down her cheeks. Sitting beside her, I wrap my arms around her. I expect her to push me away. She barely knows me, after all. Instead, she practically collapses into my arms.

These poor kids.

Maura rushes into the room. "They won't let me go with him," she practically shouts. "Why the fuck won't they let me go with my husband?" She turns around in a circle, her hands flailing. "I need my keys. And my ID." She pats herself down. "I have to … I have to follow them."

Derrick gently lifts Jackson and ushers him to the couch on my other side, then turns and clasps Maura's shoulders to still her. "I'll drive you and the kids to the hospital. Take a breath."

She obeys, and as she inhales, her legs give out, and she collapses against him.

"Izzy, can you get my keys?"

I give both kids a gentle squeeze, then ease off the cushion and approach Derrick, who's still holding most of Maura's weight. I shove my hand in his pocket, feeling for the keys. Once I've extracted them, I instruct the kids to follow me.

I have a feeling Maura needs a moment.

The ambulance is gone, the chaos has stopped. Now the house is eerily quiet.

The kids get in the back seat, and Amanda wraps her arms around her little brother. He cries softly, looking out the window.

I hop in the driver's side and crank the engine. It's another minute, maybe two, before Maura and Derrick come out.

The desolate look on her face feels like a kick to my gut.

Derrick helps her into the back and makes sure all three are wearing seat belts before hopping in beside me.

"You'll have to tell me where to go. I'm not sure where the hospital is."

Derrick nods, his eyes sunken and dark.

With a deep breath in, I give his knee a squeeze. Then I put the truck in reverse, wishing I could hug him and tell him it'll all be okay. But we don't know that, and no one in this truck needs false promises.

Ten minutes later, I pull the truck up to the emergency room entrance.

"I'll park the truck. Go on."

Derrick blinks at me for a moment, hesitant, but eventually nods. He needs to be with them right now, and there's a good chance it'll take me a while to park this monstrosity of a truck in any way that won't get me a ticket or a good keying.

Once I've parked in a way I think won't cause trouble, I take a moment to catch my breath. It feels selfish, the need to do that when Maura's world, her kids' world is potentially blowing up, but I need a moment to recover from the whiplash of this evening so I can be available to them and to Derrick in any way they need.

Everything was going so well until it wasn't.

Ten more seconds.

That's all I give myself to wallow before I get out of the truck and head for the entrance.

It takes me a moment to get my bearings when I step inside. Once I do, I head left, following the signs that read *Emergency Room*.

When I get to the first corner, I find Derrick pacing back and forth in front of the help desk.

"Hey." I put a hand to his back, hoping not to startle him. "Do you know anything?"

He shakes his head, his shoulders sagging. "He's gone, Izzy. I just know it."

"I'm so sorry, Derrick. Let's have some hope, okay?"

It takes all my strength to usher Derrick over to a set of plastic chairs. He's so much larger than me and so out of it that he's little help, but somehow, I manage.

"We don't know anything yet," I remind him. "Try to remain positive."

But I, like him, feel like there's no hope.

When someone's that pale and lifeless? It can't be good.

Derrick drags his hand down his stubbled cheek, making a rasping sound. "He's ... fuck. He's such a good friend, you know? His kids are still ... kids. They need him. It doesn't feel right. I couldn't get him to breathe. I tried, but I just..." He looks away from me, his shoulders shaking.

I've never felt so helpless as I do now, sitting beside him as he breaks down, unable to take his pain away.

I put my hand on his arm, offering as much comfort as I can. I don't say anything, because what can be said at a time like this? I won't placate him or spout a bunch of empty words. Until we know what's going on, it's better if I stay quiet.

The emergency room is small and relatively quiet. Rather than comforting, though, the silence feels truly isolating. I'd almost prefer for there to be more people here instead of only the two of us.

Wiping his face, he says, "They said they were taking Maura and the kids back to a private room. I don't have experience with this, but I have a feeling it's where they give you bad news."

"Or maybe Brooks is stable and in a private room, and that's what they meant."

He shakes his head like he doesn't believe me. Frankly, *I* don't believe me.

"Derrick—"

He shoots to his feet and paces the short length of the room.

I send a text to my sister, letting her know what's going on and to tell Reid. She might not know Brooks, but I'm sure Reid does, and he'll know what this is doing to his dad. Maybe he can help Derrick in a way I can't.

Needing an excuse to get up, I wander to the water cooler in the corner of the room and fill one of the paper cups. After a long inhale and exhale, I take a sip, finding that my throat is surprisingly dry.

Derrick does another few laps around the room before collapsing in the chair he occupied previously.

He bends over and drops his head between his knees like he's lightheaded.

"Derrick?" I hurry over to his side. Rubbing the back of his neck, I ask, "Are you okay?"

"No."

I wish I could take away his pain, but to get an honest answer out of him like this is all I can ask for.

"Here, drink some water." I all but shove the paper cup at him.

Straightening, he looks at it like it's a strange animal he's concerned will bite him. But eventually, he accepts it and drains the cup in one gulp. I hurry to refill it and bring it back to him. This time, I crouch in front of him, trying to get a good look at his face since I'm concerned he might pass out.

He holds the cup delicately between his fingers, like he's scared if he holds on too tight, he'll crush it, and takes careful sips this time.

"Maybe we should go," he says quietly once the cup is empty again. "Maura ... She doesn't need us anymore."

My chest aches at the defeat in his tone. "We can go if you want, but if you want to stay, we'll do that."

He mulls it over for a silent moment, then finally says, "Stay, I guess. I need to know, and Maura ... She'll need a way home. I didn't think about that."

"Okay." With a light squeeze to his leg, I stand, then throw the cup into the trash can beside the water cooler.

It remains eerily quiet in the ER lobby, where we sit side by side, for ten minutes or so, before an older couple comes hurrying inside.

Derrick stands immediately, recognition on his face. "Do you know anything?" he asks.

"Maura called and said that Brooks collapsed," the man says, running a shaky hand through his white hair. "Told us to get here as fast as we could. Are the kids okay? Is Brooks okay?"

"I don't know," Derrick croaks. "Maura and the kids are back there."

Like he's conjured her, the doors to our left open, and Maura appears.

It's obvious from her swollen eyes and red face that she's been sobbing. She runs to the people I assume are her parents and breaks down. They hold her, murmuring words of comfort.

Seeing someone breakdown like that?

It's a humbling experience. My heart cracks in two for her. For her kids. For Derrick.

She hiccups, and tears flood her eyes again. "He's gone. He's really gone. It was ... They're saying it was an aneurysm. He'd been complaining of headaches—" She holds her own head, taking several breaths. "I didn't think it was anything serious or I would've made him go to the hospital. I..." She straightens and looks at her parents. "Is this my fault? I should've known something was wrong. Brooks never gets headaches and..." Trailing off, she sinks to the floor.

Her mother goes with her, tentatively lowering herself, her husband helping her down. Then she wraps her daughter up and rocks her from side to side.

I feel sick to my stomach, like I could vomit into the nearest trashcan. Lightheaded, I sit. The last thing any of these people needs is to have to deal with me because I've passed out.

"The kids are saying their goodbyes now. His parents should be here any minute. He wanted ... he always said that he'd want to donate his organs, so we don't have much time." She wipes at her wet face. "God, I can't believe I'm talking about his organs right now. My husband is dead, and I'm worrying about that."

Maura's mother stands with the help of her husband, then the two of them help their daughter to her feet, though she can't fully straighten.

It's like, suddenly, she's carrying the weight of the world.

"Do you want to see him, Derrick? You can come back if you want."

Derrick freezes, then very carefully shakes his head. "I'm sorry, but I can't. I just ... I'm sorry. I have to go." He takes off toward the exit.

I stand and give Maura's hand a squeeze. I don't want to say I'm sorry. It's not what she needs right now. Instead, I say, "We'll check in and see if you need anything, okay?"

Maura nods, and her parents give me sad, appreciative smiles.

Outside, I find Derrick pacing in front of the hospital, hands clasped behind his head.

When he turns to me, his face is streaked with tears.

I hate this—being completely and utterly useless. I don't know what to do or what to say. His best friend just died. There's no way to ease a sting like this.

"Do you need a minute?" I ask him. "Before we go?"

He shakes his head, wiping at his face. "No, I need to get out of here."

"Okay. Truck's this way."

He follows and doesn't protest when I get in the driver's side. He's in no state to get us home.

The silence in the cab remains the whole way home, only interrupted by a sniffle from him every now and then.

Once I've cut the engine in the driveway, we sit, both staring out the windshield.

Derrick turns to me slowly, eyes swollen and nose red. "He's gone." He snaps his fingers. "Just like that. He was going about his day like normal and now he's not here."

With my hands settled on the steering wheel, I stay quiet and let him talk.

"Life is really that fragile." He looks out the window when he says it. "Nothing is a guarantee."

Silence falls once again. I let it linger for a moment before saying, "We better head inside."

Nodding, Derrick reaches woodenly for the door handle.

He manages to get the front door unlocked without difficulty, and when he pushes it open, Wonton greets us, bouncing excitedly at our feet. Ignoring him, Derrick heads straight upstairs.

Wonton lowers to all four paws and cocks his head at me, as if to say, "What's his problem?"

"It's been a bad night," I tell him as I scoop him up. "Let's take you out to potty."

Wonton quickly does his business, and since it's past dinnertime for him, he scarfs down his food the instant I set his bowl on the floor. I doubt Derrick is going to eat anything now, and the thought of food leaves my own stomach roiling, so I grab two cans of ginger ale from the fridge and a sleeve of graham crackers and take them up with me.

I find Derrick sitting on his side of the bed. His shirt is gone, and he's in the process of taking his shoes off, but he seems to have frozen.

"I brought sodas and graham crackers." I set both on the dresser, then step closer to him. "Why don't you get a shower? It might make you feel better?"

He nods, his focus fixed on the floor, and shoves his hair back with long fingers.

"Do you want me to turn it on for you?"

Another nod.

I hesitate, surveying him, his hollow eyes, slumped shoulders, sagging cheeks, then head for the bathroom and get the water running. He's still in the same position when I step back into the bedroom, so I kneel before him and untie his shoes, then slip them off. Once I've set them to the side, I rest my hands on his knees and rise up a little, finally garnering his attention.

"Tell me what I can do to help you? Please." I'm not above begging. It hurts to see him like this, like a heavy weight crushing my chest. If I can help in any way, I'd do it in a heartbeat.

"I don't know," he says softly. "I just don't know."

Angling in, I kiss his cheek. "I'm going to check on Wonton. You get in the shower, okay?"

I hate leaving him there, but I need to make sure Wonton ate and let him out again in a few minutes.

"I'll check on you in a few," I tell him as I slip out of the bedroom.

Wonton's bowl is empty, and as I pick it up, he wags his tail proudly. I clean it in the sink, and just as I set it on the drying pad, my phone vibrates in my back pocket. At first, I consider ignoring the call. I'm too drained. But I pull it out to check the display anyway, and when I see that it's Via, I answer.

"Hey, how are you doing?" she asks.

"Okay, I guess." I swallow past the lump that's been lodged in my throat for hours. "It was scary, but I'm mostly worried about Derrick. He's really out of it."

"Reid said Brooks is probably his closest friend," she says, her tone soft. "It's understandable that he's struggling."

"You're right. I just wish I knew how to help him."

"Just be there for him," she says simply. "That's really all you can do."

"I will be."

Once we've said our goodbyes, I let Wonton out again, then head back upstairs. Derrick's still in the shower, and under normal circumstances, I'd join him, but I don't think that's the right thing to do, so I opt to shower in the guest bath.

I feel like a new person, albeit still tired, when I get out and pull on my pajamas. I open the bathroom door to find Wonton sleeping on the floor, belly up. He startles, giving me an offended look, either because I disturbed his beauty sleep or because I locked him out of the bathroom. I'm not sure which.

The master bathroom is quiet, but light emanates from under the door, so I turn the TV on and flip through the channels until I land on an episode of *Friends*. I figure that's tame enough to have for background noise.

I'm a tad worried he might not want me in here tonight, but I don't want to leave him alone. So I set Wonton on the bed, climb under the blankets, and listen to the quiet whir of his electric toothbrush.

Wonton eyes me from the foot of the bed, his head cocked in curiosity. He's probably confused, since this entire evening hasn't followed the routine we established months ago.

The toothbrush stops, the faucet runs, and then the light goes off.

The bathroom door eases open quietly.

"Hey." His eyes soften when he finds me in the bed.

"Feeling better?" I toss back the blankets on his side, making space.

With a groan, he lies on his back and covers his face with his hands. "Yes and no."

My heart cracks at the pain in those three words. "Do you want to talk about things?"

His body shakes with an exhale, like he's on the verge of crying again. "No, I don't."

"Okay."

The show plays in the background, a quiet soundtrack to the moment. Wonton stands, circles, digs at the comforter, then plops back down again. We ignore it all, instead rolling to face each other.

One emotion after another flickers across his face. Pain, love, worry, regret, fear. It all lingers there until settling into something more neutral.

Cupping my cheek, he rubs his thumb over my bottom lip.

"What do you want? What do you need?" I whisper as he applies pressure to my mouth.

"Just you," he answers.

"You already have me."

He swallows thickly, his eyes taking in every detail of my face.

Then he leans in and kisses me. Slow and sweet.

Then more urgent.

With a groan into my mouth, he moves over me, removes my clothes, traces my skin delicately. Memorizing.

When he sinks inside me, our movements are slow, reverent. He makes love to me like he's terrified he might lose me, and I hold on tight, scared of the same.

When it's over, he holds me, and I pray to the universe that he'll never let go.

# thirty-two

Izzy

I WAKE TO AN EMPTY BED. Even Wonton is gone.

Blinking, I give my eyes time to adjust to the sun-drenched room, letting last night's events come back to me.

I ease out of bed and shuffle to the bathroom, then change into a pair of jeans and a tee.

Downstairs, I find Wonton asleep on his cushion. Based on the way he lounges rather than popping up and dancing around me, I assume he's been fed and let out, but Derrick is nowhere to be seen.

I start the Keurig, desperate for some caffeine, then peek outside, stifling a yawn. I scan the porch, then the yard, but Derrick is nowhere to be found. The shed isn't open, and it's quiet, so he's not mowing.

Once my coffee is brewed, I add a splash of oat milk and

take a careful sip. I prefer matcha from the local shop, but this will do.

Peeking out the front window, I find his truck is gone.

It's possible he went to get breakfast and is coming back, but after yesterday, a strange foreboding plagues me. I don't think it's as simple as that. So I jog upstairs and swipe my phone off the nightstand, then fire off a text.

> Me: Hey, just wanted to check in since you're not home. Is everything okay?

I stare at the screen, waiting for a response, but when it goes dark before a text comes through, I tuck my phone in my pocket and head back downstairs to make some breakfast.

I'm worried about him. I'm worried *for* him. He lost his wife in a tragic way, and now a close friend. That has to be difficult to cope with. I haven't experienced a loss like that.

I busy myself around the house. Straightening things and cleaning, all the while worrying about him, and after a few hours, when I still haven't heard from him, that worry turns to fear.

Instead of going through Via, I call Reid myself.

"What's up?" he answers.

I pace the hall, my heart pounding out of my chest. "Have you talked to your dad today?"

"*No.*" He draws the word out into more than one syllable. "Why?"

I swallow the boulder in my throat. It was a lump yesterday, and it's just continued to grow. "He was gone when I woke up, and he hasn't responded to my texts. It's not like him."

"Maybe he went to help Maura," he suggests.

"Oh, that makes sense." My face flushes. I feel silly for not having thought of that myself. "Thank you."

After a quick goodbye, I end the call and collect my things so I can drive over to check on him.

The whole way there, I tell myself that's exactly it. He is with Maura. But my hope dissipates as I slow in front of the house. I don't even pull into the driveway, because Derrick's truck definitely isn't there.

"Where could he be?" I tap my fingers against the steering wheel.

He could have gone to his piece of land. Maybe for some quiet. But even if that's where he is, there's no way I could find my way back there alone.

Frustrated, I head into town in search of his truck.

I'm surprised—though I shouldn't be—when I find it parked outside his storefront. Once I've parked on the opposite side of the street, jog up to the door. I reach confidently for the handle, only to find that it's locked.

Clasping my hands on the sides of my face, I peep through the glass and find him at his desk, completely oblivious to me. I knock, making him jolt in his seat. When he turns to me, he looks exhausted, like he didn't sleep at all. Dammit. Now I feel guilty for falling asleep so easily.

He shuffles to the door, his shoulders slumped, and turns the lock. Then he stands aside to let me in.

"Did you need something?" he asks once the door closes behind me. His tone isn't mean, but it's off. Maybe a little disgruntled?

Holding my breath, I take him in. The dark circles under his eyes, the disheveled hair, the wrinkled shirt. "I was worried about you. You were gone when I got up and didn't reply to my texts."

"I'm busy, Izzy," he rasps, his focus fixed on a point behind me. "I can't respond to you every second of every day. I have work to do."

The words are a physical blow so severe I rear back.

"Excuse me?" I blurt, my heart lurching. "I didn't know you found me so annoying."

With a wince, he pinches his brow. "I didn't mean it like that."

"Are you sure about that?" I don't want to have a fight right now, not when I know he's grieving, but his words hurt.

He swallows audibly. "I'm not good company right now. I left because I needed space."

"Space is fine," I say, taking a step closer. "But at least let me know you're okay if you disappear like that again."

He nods, looking down at the ground.

"Do you need me to help while I'm here or—"

"I want you to go."

*Ouch.*

The verbal punches keep coming. But he's not himself right now. That knowledge is what keeps me from dissolving into a puddle of tears.

"Okay. I'll do that. I … You know I love you, right?"

He won't meet my eyes, but he gives me a single broken nod.

Hands shaking, I turn to the door. I don't want to leave, but I have to respect his wishes. So without looking back, I pull the door open and stalk to my car.

I text Via the moment I'm in the driver's seat, begging to crash on her couch tonight. I have no interest in punishing Derrick. As much as the brush-off hurts, I want to give him the space he's asked for. And I can't do that if I'm in his house.

Via responds, telling me it's no problem, so I head back to

Derrick's place to pack a bag and pick up Wonton. My stomach churns at the thought of Derrick being alone, but bearing the brunt of his devastation is something I can't handle. If he needs me, I'll happily come running.

I pile my things in the car, a little horrified by how much stuff I packed for what I desperately hope will only be one night. But I packed a few extra sets of clothes just in case, along with pajamas, skincare products, and makeup. Not to mention all of Wonton's things.

It's silly, but I linger at the house longer than I should. Foolishly hoping he'll show up and tell me he doesn't want me to go. Not even for a night. But he doesn't come, so finally, I head over to Via's, sniffling back tears the whole way.

She's working today, but she's left the apartment unlocked, so I haul my things inside.

"Izzy," I tell myself as I slog up the stairs with a third load of belongings, "you have got to stop overpacking. This is ridiculous."

Inside, I set Wonton's cushion down and almost feel lighter when the little ball of fluff immediately dives for it.

Leaving him, I go down to the store, thinking the best way to pass the time and stop my brain from spiraling is to hang with my sister and paint a few pieces of pottery. She has plenty of other artistic things for customers to do in her shop, but the pottery is the only thing that interests me currently.

The store is full of end-of-summer tourists. I usually stop by early in the day, when it's still quiet, so except for at her grand opening, I've never seen it this packed. Pride fills me as I take in the scene. My sister followed her dream and has turned her studio into a profitable business. She spent way too many years being unhappy. She deserves the world, and instead of waiting for someone to give it to her, she went out and got it herself.

Via spots me and waves from the back, where she's helping a small group of people at a table.

There's a counter along the front, lined with stools. I set my stuff in front of one, then peruse the ceramic pieces.

I'm debating between painting a planter and a bowl when Via comes over and squeezes my shoulder. "How are you feeling?"

Turning her way, I force a weak smile. "Okay, but sad for Maura and her kids and worried about Derrick."

"I can't believe you were there when it happened. Reid said he'll check in with his dad tonight. Make sure he's okay."

The ache in my chest flares. I want to be the one to check on him. "Good."

"Do whatever you want." She gestures around the space. "We'll order pizza or something after I close up. Is that okay?"

Grateful for the gentleness my big sister possesses, I nod.

In the end, I choose the planter. It's the larger of the two pieces and will take longer for me to work on, thus distracting me longer.

Though I'm not sure the activity is all that helpful, since I keep checking my phone, desperately hoping for some kind of communication from Derrick. I know it's selfish. I know he's going through a lot right now, but it hurts to know that he's not okay and I can't be there to help. It's a physical ache, being shut out like this, but we all handle grief in different ways, and there's nothing I can do to change it.

As the sun sets, the store empties out. Via busies herself with cleaning up while I continue to work on the planter. I'm being way too detail-oriented, but after a while, I got into a

UNTIL THEN

groove, and it's allowed me to quiet my thoughts. So I'll keep at it until she's ready to call it a night.

Forty-five minutes later, she says, "I wanted to let you finish, but I'm starving."

I use white paint to highlight one of the tiny flowers, then set the brush down. "That's okay. I'm being overly critical over here."

"Do you want to talk about things?" she asks, dropping onto the stool beside me.

Tears prick at the backs of my eyes as I rinse my brush out in the cup of water. "No. I can't make sense of my thoughts, let alone put them into words."

"Okay," she says, her tone soft. "You know if you change your mind, I'm always here to listen. Day or night."

"Even in the middle of the night?" I ask with half a laugh.

"Even then." She stands and snags the cup of brushes, helping me clean up, then sets the planter aside for touch-ups in the morning.

"I already ordered the pizza." She loops her arm through mine. "I thought we could walk down the street and get it."

With a heavy sigh, I lean my head on my sister's shoulder. "Only if we get wine, too."

Laughing, she pats my arm. "Wine is always a must."

---

"I CAN'T EAT ANOTHER BITE," I groan, throwing down the small piece of crust I've just bitten into.

"I'm stuffed, too." Via rubs her belly. "It was good, though."

"It really was." I lean my back against her couch, stretching my legs out in front of me on the air mattress. I didn't know

313

she had this, but apparently, when I showed up in town, she ordered it, worried that my staying with Derrick may not work out.

Matthew McConaughey is on screen, teaching Kate Hudson's character how to ride a motorcycle. I've watched *How to Lose a Guy in 10 Days* more times than I'd care to admit, but it never gets old. It's a peak 2000s rom-com.

"How much is it killing Reid not to be here?"

Via rolls her eyes. "We're capable of being apart."

"I know." I bite back a smile. "But how many times has he texted you?"

She eyes her phone where it sits on the air mattress beside her. "Um…"

"How many times?" I reach for her phone just as she does. As we grapple for it, it slips out of her hand and slides across the floor.

We scramble over one another, and when I have the upper hand, I hold her at bay and snatch it up.

"Victory!" I hold the phone aloft, then pop up and run across the room, typing in her password as I go.

When it unlocks, her text thread with Reid is already pulled up. "What the—ah!" I throw her phone onto the couch and slap my hands over my eyes. "I just saw your boyfriend's penis!"

Okay, so it was only the top curve of it. He had his sweatpants tugged down, showing off his stomach and his…

"I'm going to throw up." I lower my hands, gagging.

"That's what you get for being nosy." Via picks the device up off the cushion and cradles it protectively against her chest.

Whimpering, I scrub at my eyes like that can rid me of the vision. "I wasn't expecting a dick pic!"

"That's not even a dick pic," she says, studying the screen. "It's a … I don't know, but it's not that."

"Well, I certainly know the girth of it now. Is your vagina okay?"

She drops her head back, groaning at the ceiling. "Kill me now."

With an accusatory finger, I point at her phone. "I'm never going near that thing again. Lesson learned."

"He's sent me a bunch of texts. I haven't replied," she says softly, lowering the device to the table. "This is our time together."

"I know," I sigh, letting my shoulders relax. She's steadfastly ignored her phone all evening. Then I had to go and ruin it. But in my defense, I wasn't wrong. He's been texting up a storm. "It was my fault."

"Let's finish the movie." Grasping my wrist, she tugs me back over to the air mattress.

I go willingly. It takes all of two steps, really, in this tiny apartment.

When the movie is finished, we start another, but we drift off in the middle. When I wake the next morning, Via is passed out next to me and early morning light is flickering in the windows.

I check my phone, hoping to find a message or a missed call from Derrick. But if he went home last night, he certainly didn't reach out.

My heart sinks. I've never felt so helpless.

I'm at a loss for where to go from here. I don't want to force my presence on him if he needs space, but I also don't want him to feel abandoned or think I can't handle this. It's complicated all the way around.

I open our message thread and survey the long string of texts I sent. All are marked read, yet there isn't a single reply.

I'll send one more, and then I'll stop.

> Me: I'm thinking about you. I'm here if you need me. I love you.

For a moment, I hover a finger over the Send button, questioning whether I should delete it.

But in the end, I send it and turn my phone off so I won't be tempted to check my messages.

"Everything okay?" Via's sleep-graveled voice asks.

"It will be."

It has to be.

# thirty-three

### Derrick

SLEEPING on the couch in the back office of my shop to avoid Izzy may be one of the shittiest things I've ever done. But I just can't be around her right now. Not because she's done a single thing wrong, but because my head is a complete fucking mess.

Brooks is gone.

Like the snap of a finger. A flick of a switch. He's just ... not here anymore.

Along with thoughts of him, my mind has been plagued with memories of my wife's sudden passing. It's hitting me now, that I never fully dealt with that grief. I couldn't. I had two young children to take care of. I had to be strong and forge ahead. It's sobering to realize I've been living in fight-or-flight mode for such a long time.

If I'd gone home last night, Izzy would have wanted to talk, and right now, I crave the silence.

Because I'm so damn confused. So lost.

When I turn my phone on, I'm flooded with missed calls and texts from Izzy, Maura, Reid, and Layla, as well as a few of my buddies who have obviously learned about Brooks's death.

"Fuck," I groan, powering it down again.

That's a problem for future Derrick. Right now, I'm not capable of dealing with that chaos.

Tossing the phone to the end of the couch, I sit up with a groan.

Aging is a shitty thing. One night on a couch, and suddenly, I feel like I'm ninety.

I take my time standing, then stretch my arms above my head. Once my back has popped half a dozen times, I stifle a yawn and make my way to the front of the store. I need coffee. Food, too, if the rumbling of my stomach is anything to go by. I can't remember if I've eaten anything since that handful of chips I snacked on while Izzy and I watched the whales. Fuck. Was that only two days ago?

There's the barest hint of sunrise through the front windows, which means I probably only got three or four hours of sleep.

With a peek at my watch, I determine that the coffee shop is, blessedly, already open. So I head that way. Getting caffeine into my system is the only thing I want to think about right now.

The bell dings when I enter, the sound far too cheery.

"Hey, Derrick. You're out early," Cindy says, tightening the straps on her apron. "The usual?"

I used to be out this early often, but since Izzy showed up, I've found myself wanting to be around her every second of the day, which has changed my routine pretty thoroughly.

But what is a man my age doing with someone like her?

Look what happened to Brooks. How could I seriously think I could get my happily ever after with her? I'm more likely to leave her as a widow.

"Yeah." I shove my hands into my pockets, breathing through the discomfort in my chest that comes with my spiraling thoughts. "Maybe a fresh chocolate croissant, too."

"Sure. They'll be out of the oven in a couple of minutes."

Once I've paid, I pull out a stool and wait, watching the town outside the window wake up.

I should head home and talk to Izzy. It would be the smart thing to do. The right thing. Only I'm not sure I'm capable of it.

"Here you go, Derrick."

At the sound of Cindy's voice, I hop up and stride for the counter.

"Did you need matcha for Izzy?"

I flinch, and my chest constricts. Fuck.

Clearly, Cindy could see the reaction, because her face falls.

"No, not today." I force a smile.

"All right," she says, though her expression is wary. "See you next time."

Head down, I rush back to the shop and lock the door behind me, then head straight for the back. I don't use the space often, but along with the couch, there's a fridge back here, as well as a small counter and sink and a microwave. The amenities will make hiding out here relatively easy, I suppose.

Hiding out—like a fucking wimp. Why? Because I don't have the nerve to face the woman I love? To tell her how terrified I am to love her, only to leave her too soon? No one should have to suffer the pain I've had to endure, especially her. The anguish on Maura's face two days ago? Her soul-crippling cries? How could I possibly put Izzy through any of that?

I gulp my coffee, ignoring the way it scalds my tongue and throat, desperate for its comfort. But rather than steady me, it makes my heart rate take off. The damn organ beats out of control, and my chest goes tight. Shit. It feels like I'm having a heart attack.

Fuck.

Maybe I *am* having a heart attack?

The tightness in my chest turns to shooting pain that makes me clutch at my T-shirt.

No.

No.

*No.*

Digging through my pockets, I search for my phone before I remember that I tossed it onto the couch. I stagger across the room and scramble to dig it out from between the cushions.

*Why did I turn my phone off?*

Gasping for air, I drop to my knees and power it on.

What feels like a lifetime later, it comes to life. With shaky fingers, I type in my password to unlock it, then dial.

"Nine-one-one, what's your emergency?"

"I'm…" I struggle to get oxygen into my lungs. "I'm having a heart attack."

# thirty-four

### Izzy

VIA PASSES me a steaming cup of tea. "I can't promise it's any good, but I tried."

Laughing, I hold the mug between my palms and relish its comforting warmth. "It'll be fine, I'm sure."

Her phone rings, and a photo of her and Reid pops up. She sighs like she knows she should hit decline, but before she can, I grasp her arm and stop her.

"Cut lover boy some slack, Via-Mia. A whole day without you is probably a lifetime to a golden retriever."

With a roll of her eyes, she slides her finger over the screen and answers. "Hey, Izzy is still—what?"

All color drains from her face, instantly putting me on guard. My heart squeezes as fear flashes in her eyes.

"We'll be right there," she says, pulling the phone from her ear. When she focuses on me, the look on her face—the mixture of sadness, worry, and fear—has my stomach rolling.

Standing on shaky legs, I grab her arm. "What is it? What happened?"

"Derrick's in the hospital."

"What?" My heart stops, and tears instantly fall. "What do you mean he's in the hospital?"

I shouldn't have left him.

Dammit, I thought I was doing the right thing, giving him some space, but oh God, I shouldn't have left him. This is my fault.

"He may have had a heart attack. They're running tests now. Reid and Layla are there with him."

"Take me. You have to take me," I beg my sister.

I'm still in my pajamas—ratty sweatpants and a sweatshirt that hangs halfway down my thighs, but I don't care. I need to get to Derrick.

Via throws on a sweatshirt and grabs her keys and purse. "Let's go. Come on."

"Fuck, I'm parked behind you," I curse when we step outside.

Hands fluttering, I turn in a circle, my brain losing all function.

Her arms provide a steadiness around me. "It's okay. I'll grab your keys. We'll take your rental."

She lingers for a second, still holding me, maybe to make sure I don't topple over the second-story porch railing.

So I grasp the rough wooden rail and take a deep breath. "I'm fine," I lie, needing her to hurry up.

With a nod, she ducks back inside, and when she returns with my purse, she locks up her apartment, then turns but doesn't head for the stairs. "Izzy?"

"What?" I practically cry, flapping my arms. "We need to go!"

"You're not wearing shoes."

I look down at my socked feet, and the tears come faster. "Fuck."

Quickly, she unlocks the door, and I storm inside. Thankfully, my shoes are beside the door. I shove my feet in quickly, then turn my ass back around and head straight down the stairs.

The drive to the hospital is a silent one, the only sounds my occasional sniffles.

Via parks the car near the emergency entrance and trails me inside. Once we're through the sliding doors, she scrolls through the messages Reid has sent.

"Reid says they'll be out in a minute, and you can go back."

I nod woodenly, overcome with grief and disbelief. I stood in this very spot not even forty-eight hours ago. I don't think I've ever hated a single place as much as I hate this one. The floors are too white. Too shiny. The chairs are uncomfortable and stick to my legs. And the TV in the corner is obnoxious.

The double doors open, and Reid and Layla appear.

I dart toward them, smoothing my hands down my sweatpants.

They both look worried, which only intensifies my panic.

"I'll take you back," Layla says softly, offering me her hand.

"Where's Lili?" I ask, looking around for the energetic little girl.

"She's with my neighbor. She babysits for me sometimes."

Reid heads straight for Via and pulls her into a hug so tight I'm not sure he'll ever let her go. The sweet, simple exchange causes tears to flood my eyes. This is bad. I should have forced him to come home with me. I could've kept an eye on him. I could've...

The crack in my heart fissures. None of it matters now.

"Is he okay?" I ask Layla, fear gluing me to the spot. My stomach rolls, churning so violently that I fear the pizza I ate last night will end up on the floor. Why did I think pizza and wine were a good combination?

"We're waiting for results." She tugs on my hand, guiding me to those dreadful double doors, and I take comfort in the warmth she imbues me with.

"I don't want to lose him," I whisper the confession.

"I know." When she pauses halfway down the hall, she releases my hand and faces me head on. "I know I haven't been very supportive of your relationship with my dad. But it's obvious you love him, and he loves you. At the end of the day, that's what matters."

I sniffle back another round of tears threatening to fall. "Thank you." I pull her into a bone-crushing hug. "I hated the idea of ruining our friendship, but..."

"You don't need to explain. Go on in." She nods at the closed glass door covered by blinds. "Take your time. I'll be in the waiting room."

"Okay."

While she walks away, her steps echoing on the linoleum floor, I stand frozen outside the door, terrified of what I might find on the other side.

My heart races and my knees shake, but eventually, I take a deep breath and slide the door open.

Derrick lays in the bed, awake and alert. The sight of him is an instant relief. He looks far better than I anticipated.

"Hey," he says, almost shyly.

My bottom lip trembles in response.

Opening one of his arms, he says, "Come here, baby."

The tears win out as I hurry over to his side. I hug him as best I can, inhaling his familiar scent greedily, desperate to replace the smell of antiseptic.

"Are you okay?" I mumble into his neck. "A heart attack?"

He rubs my back, comforting me when it should be the other way around. "That's what I thought, but I don't know. They ran some tests, and it seems like they'd be a lot more concerned about me if that were the case."

"What happened?" I pull away and drop into the plastic chair near the bed.

He tugs at the neck of his hospital gown in annoyance. "I was at the office, and I had chest pains."

Clutching his hand, I rub gentle circles with my thumb. "I need more details than that."

With his other hand, he scratches at his heavily stubbled jaw. "I was thinking about you—about our age difference and how I don't want that to happen to me. How I don't want to leave you alone like that. And I spiraled, because my love for you is selfish. I know what the pain of losing a partner feels like, and I don't want that for you."

I reel back like he's slapped me, pulling my hand out of his. "Are you breaking up with me?" I scoff through my tears. "You've given me so much more than any other man ever has. You think you're too old for me? Newsflash, Derrick, you should've thought about that before you made me fall in love with you."

"I'm not breaking up with you," he murmurs. "Unless that's what you want. I just want you to understand where my head was at. Brooks's passing ... it's brought up a lot of emotions I thought I'd moved on from. I know my thought process was illogical. It doesn't matter how old a person is. Tragedy can strike at any age. I should know that better than anyone. But like I said, I wasn't thinking logically, and that's how I ended up here."

I press a hand to his jaw, relishing the sensation of his scruff. "Clearly."

The door slides open, and we both turn to the doctor who's stepping into the room.

I squeeze Derrick's arm. "I'll be outside."

"No." He grabs my hand and holds tight. "Stay. I want you to stay. I *need* you to stay."

The desperation in his voice has me softening, has the pain in my heart dulling to an ache. "All right. I won't go anywhere."

The doctor clears his throat as he approaches the bedside. "Mr. Crawford, your EKG came back normal, with no signs of a heart attack."

The relief that floods me almost makes me feel lightheaded.

"Echo and x-ray were good," he continues. "Your blood work is excellent. There's nothing of concern."

"I-I'm not," Derrick sputters. "It wasn't a heart attack?"

He shakes his head. "Your heart is fine. Given your rundown of the episode, I think it's safe to say you had a stress-induced panic attack. To someone unfamiliar with panic or anxiety attacks, it can feel very much like a heart attack."

Tears of relief spring to my eyes.

He's fine.

He's okay.

I can breathe now.

"We want to monitor you for another hour or so." He looks

at his watch. "If everything is still good then, we'll get you out of here. Be sure to follow up with your primary care provider in about a week."

"Thanks," Derrick says, his cheeks pink. "This is … a relief. Embarrassing, too, but I'm glad it's not serious." With a heavy exhale, he fiddles with the thick blanket over his legs.

The doctor nods. "No need to be embarrassed. This kind of thing happens more often than you'd think. Try to take it easy. We'll check on you again in about an hour."

With a nod, he exits the room, closing the door behind him.

"I had a panic attack," Derrick mutters with a self-depre-cating laugh.

I run my fingers through his hair, pushing it off his fore-head. "I'm glad that's likely all it was."

"Get in the bed with me," he says, tugging on my hand. "I want you closer."

"Derrick—" I protest, but he shakes his head forcefully.

"I need you here. With me."

My heart stutters. Who am I to deny the man what he wants?

He gingerly scoots over, making room for me beside him.

Once we're lying side by side, I rest my head on his chest, listening to the steady beating of his heart. I've always loved the sound of it, but it's even more precious now. I can only hope it beats this steady and strong for a very long time.

With a kiss to my temple, Derrick says, "The next time we're in the hospital, it's going to be because you're having my baby."

Eyes wide, I straighten and gape at him. "You want to have kids with me?"

He shrugs, pulling me close again. "I'm scared of starting

over, but I love being a parent, and it'd be a privilege to do it with you." He brushes his lips over my forehead. "What do you say?"

Laughing, I tap my fingers against his chest. "I think you better make me your wife first."

His mouth tips up in a grin, his eyes crinkling. "Done."

# thirty-five

### Derrick

THE FUNERAL HOME IS PACKED, but that's not surprising in a small town like Parkerville.

It's a strange feeling, wanting to be here to honor my friend while simultaneously wishing I was anywhere else.

Izzy and I take our seats, followed by Reid, Via, Layla, and Lili.

Maura asked me days ago if I would speak. I wanted to say no, but I won't let her down. She's been through so much.

Izzy settles a hand on my thigh, providing some much-needed comfort.

I saw my regular doctor yesterday, and we discussed my panic attack. He said if it becomes an ongoing issue, we'll talk about anxiety medication. It feels good to have options, but I'd be thrilled if it never happened again. It was terrifying, the fear that I might be dying.

When it's time for me to speak, I stand on shaky legs and make my way to the microphone.

I clear my throat, desperately wishing I had thought to bring water with me.

"Hello, everyone. If we haven't met, I'm Derrick. Brooks and I go way back." I clear my throat again. This is much harder than I thought it would be. Already, I sound like a rambling idiot. "When I tell you that Brooks has always been the best kind of person, I mean it. Not everyone is as kind or as thoughtful as he is." I flinch. *Was*. He *was* kind and thoughtful. "I'm not very good at this," I admit, tapping my fingers against the podium. "I guess I should've written down what I wanted to say, but I wanted to speak from the heart, so here we are."

I search for Izzy in the sea of people. I can make it through this if I focus on her.

"Brooks was always there for me, no matter what I needed. We could all learn a lesson in kindness and care from him. He went above and beyond for everyone he knew, because that's the kind of man he was. The love he had for his wife and kids was immeasurable." I swallow and lick my dry lips. "I'll never be able to repay him for all the things he did for me, but I hope he knows how much I appreciate it. To Maura, Amanda, and Jackson, know this: he may be gone, but his love will never leave you. It's all around you and always will be."

I stop there. If I don't, I'm bound to say something stupid, though if I did, I have no doubt that Brooks would be laughing his ass off, wherever he is.

With a nod to the gathered crowd, I return to my seat by Izzy, and shortly thereafter, the funeral wraps up and the immediate family heads to the burial site.

"You did good," Izzy says, descending the steps with a hand on my arm.

My gut clenches. "It was terrible."

She shakes her head. "I promise you it wasn't. You doubt yourself too much."

We were invited to go to the community center for food and dessert after the funeral, but I don't have it in me to spend more time surrounded by so many people. I feel guilty about skipping out, but Maura and the kids will have their family to support them, and if I've learned one thing this week, it's that I have to take care of myself. I don't need to have another panic attack so soon after the first.

Izzy and I say our goodbyes to Reid, Via, Layla, and Lilibet, and the moment we pull out of the parking lot and head toward home, my shoulders feel lighter.

"I was thinking"—Izzy lets her hair down and shakes her head gently—"would you mind filming with me? If you're up for it, I would like to introduce you to my followers."

As I process her question, I expect to feel a wave of anxiety. Since I stumbled into that kitchen and saw Brooks lying on the floor, every request, every new experience, has been fraught with anxiety, like the walls are closing in. But, strangely, I almost feel giddy. Because this gorgeous woman wants me to be a part of her online presence.

"I'll film with you."

Her beaming smile makes me even more certain that agreeing was the right thing for me.

At home, we change into casual clothes, then settle on the couch in front of her camera and annoying bright circle-shaped lights.

"Are these necessary?" I ask, shielding my eyes.

"Yes. Don't block your face." She fiddles with her camera

MICALEA SMELTZER

settings for a moment, then sits down beside me, holding Wonton. Her body, like usual, practically melts into mine.

"Hello, everyone," she begins with a wave. "It's been a while since the last time I sat down to film a chit-chat video with you. As you can see, I have a special guest."

She turns and gives me a wink.

My stomach lurches when I realize I'm literally in the spotlight. "Hi, I'm Derrick."

Until now, it hadn't dawned on me that if I was going to sit beside her for this video, I'd have to participate.

Her soft laughter brings me some much-needed comfort, along with the warmth of her hand when she slips it into mine.

"You're probably wondering where I've been. So here's the rundown: I moved to Maine a few months ago. It was supposed to be temporary, but I fell in love. With this place. The people. And this man." She looks at me, and I see it there, that love reflected in her eyes. "Things will be changing around here. I'll probably post fewer videos, and I'll be pivoting directions. I understand if not everyone will want to stick around. But my life is changing, and I want my content to reflect what's real. Because that's what it's always been about for me. I'm going to introduce content centered around renovation and home decorating and even some business decorating. I'm even considering going to college for design."

My breath catches. I had no idea she was thinking about going to school, but I can't stop the foolish smile that takes over my face at the idea. That's my girl. Going after what she wants.

"I want to thank you all for your love and support. Many of us have grown up together, and I hope we'll continue to move through life this way, one chapter at a time. I've always ended my videos with two simple words. I'm sure by now you

332

know them. *Until then*. Over the years, many people have asked about the meaning behind that phrase, and I've never answered, but I want to now."

She looks at me with a smile before facing the camera once more.

"For me, *until then* has always been about the future. Waiting for that something or someone that made me feel complete. The moment where I knew I'd found the place, the feeling I wanted to stay in. I've found my *until then* in Derrick. He's the beginning and the middle and the end for me."

I can't stop myself when I lean in and kiss her.

Her words … fuck. Knowing I'm her *until then* means more than even hearing *I love you*.

For a long moment, we just look at one another, like we're staring into our future. But finally, she faces the camera again.

"I'll see you guys next time."

She gets up and shuts the camera off, then the lights.

I follow, spinning her and taking her cheeks in my hands. Taking in her every feature. The long dark lashes. The slightly pink cheeks. The curve of her top lip. The slope of her nose.

"I'm your *until then*?" I rub my thumb against her cheek.

Her smile is soft, eyes glistening. "You're my everything."

# *epilogue*

## Derrick
### Spring

I KISS my wife beneath the gazebo I built for her, in the shadow of the house I'm constructing for us, too.

Today, I finally get to call Izzy my wife.

I let her go to a chorus of cheers and whistles.

A year ago, to the day, I walked into my house to find her crashing there. She's never left, and I certainly don't plan on letting her go.

Our romance happened quickly, but when it's right, what's the point in waiting?

I knew early on, long before I wanted to admit it to myself, that this is exactly where we would end up.

The lake glimmers behind us, the setting sun glinting off the surface.

Izzy, as if she's thinking the same thing I am, kicks off her heels and takes off toward it.

I follow, grinning at the collective gasp behind us. I catch up quickly and scoop her into my arms. The skirt of her dress is loose and flowy, allowing her to put her legs around my waist.

"Do you care if your dress gets wet?"

Arms looped around my neck, she shakes her head. "It's just a dress."

The water is only a couple of feet deep around the dock, but when I launch myself into it, I go under. I hold her up as best as I can, knowing she'd probably want to keep her hair dry and her makeup fresh, and when I emerge, I take her in. Her green eyes, her wide smile, the dress flowing behind her with the soft current.

She wraps her arms around my neck again. "Do they all think we're crazy?"

"Probably. But it doesn't matter."

With her pale pink nails, she scratches my scalp in a way that sends shivers down my spine. "Why is that?"

"Because"—I smile, memorizing every detail of this day, the way the sun shines on the diamonds embedded in her wedding band, the happiness in her eyes, the exact pattern of the lace on her dress—"nothing can take away from how happy I am now that you're my wife."

She bites her lip, fighting a smile, but the effort is futile. "You're my husband."

We stay in the water for a moment, soaking it all in, just the two of us, while our guests move to the reception tent.

When everyone is gone, we walk out of the water hand in hand.

"What next?" I ask her, spinning her into my chest.

"Whatever it is," she says, peering up at me, "we'll figure it out together."

"Until then?"

"Yeah." She stands on her tiptoes in the grass, arms winding around my shoulders. "Until then."

# *epilogue*

## #2
### Izzy

Derrick lies on his side on the floor, staring at our baby girl.

I swear I blinked, and she went from a newborn to a full-on baby.

Nine-month-old Eleanor babbles in her adorable baby speak, and Derrick smiles.

"Is that so, baby girl? And then what happened?"

She babbles some more, rolling onto her stomach and giving him a drool-filled smile, showing off her two teeth. He rubs his hand over her soft dark hair. There's not a lot of it, but it's growing in.

I thought I loved this man before, but witnessing him with our daughter is on a whole new level.

Eleanor giggles, reaching out with a chubby hand to grab his nose.

Derrick takes her hand and presses a kiss to her silky skin.

We spend most of our time in the nursery these days. It's become our favorite room in the house. When we found out I was pregnant, we immediately got to work planning all the details of the space. Every inch has been customized, some details his, some mine. He was still in here working on finishing touches when I went into labor.

"Ellie"—he taps her nose—"do you want a brother or sister?"

He looks over at me with a wink.

We didn't plan on having another child so soon, but I'm already eight weeks pregnant with baby number two.

I shouldn't be so surprised.

My husband is hot, and I have a difficult time staying away from him.

My life looks vastly different from what it was just a few years ago, but I wouldn't change a thing. I found what—and who—I'd always been searching for.

Luckily, most of my followers have stuck around despite the pivot in my content and life. It's incredible to know that so many of them like me for who I am and not just the videos I put out.

Lux even sent a gift when I announced my first pregnancy.

Life can work in mysterious ways at times. When I got canceled, I was sure my life was over, and I knew things would never be the same.

They certainly *aren't* the same, but that moment really was the beginning of everything.

# acknowledgments

So many of you have demanded this book and it's made me so happy that you fell in love with Derrick and Izzy like I did and wanted to see them get their happy ending. I knew probably middle ways through 11:11 that they would end up together, so yes, that hint I left about Izzy's husband in the epilogue of 11:11 was Derrick.

Emily, I feel like I always have to call out our friendship and how lucky I am to have you. Not a day goes by that I'm not grateful to have a best friend like you. Thank you for once again creating not one, but two, incredible covers for this book. I know it was a struggle but we got there in the end and both are *chef's kiss*.

Melanie Yu, I can't thank you enough for the time you took to sit down with me and go over the plot of this book. It was incredibly valuable to me to just be able to sit down and talk it out. Having you be a part of each of my books in some way has become integral for me.

Beth, you're probably cringing right now because I didn't have this ready in time for you to edit it and I definitely don't know the proper way to use commas. I'm so glad Melanie sent me your way and I value your edits and input so much. Thank you for making my books the best versions of themselves.

9 798330 454389